BEAST
THE ICE WITCH
CROWN

②

BEAST
THE ICE WITCH
CROWN

—— JOEL ROSS ——

HARPER
An Imprint of HarperCollins*Publishers*

ISBN 978-0-06-248462-8

Typography by Joel Tippie

18 19 20 21 22 CG/LSCH   10 9 8 7 6 5 4 3 2 1

First Edition

1

A BEE LANDED on a twig six inches from Ji's nose. He froze. The jagged leaves of the wasp pepper bush had already scratched his face and scraped his arms—he didn't need a bee sting, too.

He took a breath and crawled deeper into the prickly bush. The bee flew off, thank the moons, and he grabbed the cluster of juicy peppers.

"Got them," he called, squirming into the open.

"Finally," Sally said.

Ji pushed to his feet on the rocky hilltop that rose above the forest. "You could've helped."

"I get burs in my fur," she said.

"Yeah, well—" He squinted at her fuzzy hobgoblin coat and shaggy hobgoblin tail. "Good point."

1

"Unlike you," she said, taking a few peppers, "I can't shed my skin."

"I'm not half snake," he told her. "I'm half dragon."

"I'm half-starving." Sally popped a pepper into her mouth, chewed twice—and started crying. "Ow! Hot-hot-hot!"

Wasp peppers looked bland and boring on the outside, but inside they raged with fire: every bite felt like a sting.

"They're not so bad," Ji said, taking a bite and weeping.

Sally shuddered. "Not if you like chewing on broken glass."

"We have to steal real food soon," Ji said, when he could speak again.

"Roz won't let us." Tears soaked into Sally's furry cheeks. "And stealing is wrong."

"It's not so bad for Roz. Trolls can eat bark."

"And Chibo eats sunbeams," Sally said.

"I don't eat them!" her little brother, Chibo, called from where he was sprawled across a sun-dappled boulder. "I absorb them."

The Diadem Rite had transformed him into a half sprite. He usually kept his emerald wings folded inside his hunchback, but at the moment they were spread wide to catch the sun's rays for sustenance. He was skinny and bald, with bright green sprite eyes.

"The next stagecoach that comes through," Ji told Sally, "we'll raid for picnic baskets."

Sally took another bite of wasp pepper. When she stopped coughing, she said, "You know we have to wait for the Royal Library Coach."

"You can't eat books," Ji said, flapping his hand in front of his mouth to cool his tongue.

"Roz probably can." Sally wrinkled her nose. "Wait. I smell knights."

"How far away?"

She tilted her muzzle into the sky. "Delicious."

He blinked at her. "What?"

"What?" she said.

"You said 'delicious.'"

"I did not."

"Stop thinking about food! How far away are they?"

Her nostrils flared and her ears twitched. Not only did she have a hobgoblin's furriness and ferocity, she also had hobgoblins' superkeen senses of smell and hearing. "I can't tell."

"Go get a closer sniff."

She leaped onto the trunk of an elegant lacebark tree, then swarmed into the high branches overlooking the leafy expanse of Isalida Forest. Her tufted ears swiveled. She cocked her head, sniffed a few more times, and lowered herself to the ground.

"Maybe ten miles?" she said.

"You can smell people ten miles away?"

"Not usually," Sally said. "But they're riding horses."

"So it's the horses that smell delicious?"

"Oh, shut your ricehole. I never said 'delicious.'"

"Yeah, but now you said 'rice.' I'd polish a hundred boots for a half bowl of rice."

She flicked him with her tail. "The reason I can smell them is there's a lot of horses, and they were ridden hard."

A bubble of fear rose in Ji's chest. "Do you think the knights know where we are?"

"How could they know where we are?"

"They can't," Ji said, shifting nervously.

"There's no way." Sally gulped. "Is there?"

"Nah. They're—they're just riding in circles, hoping they stumble into us."

She cocked her head again and exhaled in relief. "You're actually right for once! They're heading away from us."

"Whew. Even ten miles is too close."

"Forget horses," Chibo called. "Sunlight is great, but I miss food."

For the past few weeks, they'd been surviving on pine nuts, unripe berries, and wild chilies—and one glorious feast of stolen steamed buns. Sure, they'd been downtrodden servants back when they lived at Primstone Manor, but at least they'd been well-fed downtrodden servants.

Ji was the youngest child in a family of servants. He'd worked as a boot boy for years, scrubbing filth from footwear. Sally was his best friend. She'd tended horses in the stables and dreamed about saving her brother, Chibo, who'd been sold to the tapestry weavers. Roz—his other best friend—was different. She hadn't been born a servant, but when her family fell on hard times her sister trained her to work as a governess.

A young noble named Brace also lived at Primstone. Brace was bullied by his cousins, Lady Posey and Lord Nichol. He'd been a timid, awkward, lonely kid, and Ji had befriended him—at least until their friendship was discovered. A servant and a noble weren't allowed to be friends.

Still, when Brace was invited to the Diadem Rite, the ritual that chose the heir to the Summer Realm, Ji and his friends were ordered to join him. They were told to help, not knowing that "help at the rite" meant "transform into beasts and die so Brace can wield magical power."

For some reason, nobody had mentioned that part.

The three friends rescued Chibo, but they didn't get to celebrate long. At the Diadem Rite, the Summer Queen summoned a water tree with killing branches, sharp enough to impale sacrifices and magical enough to drain their souls into the heir.

Ji and his friends—along with Nin, an ogre they'd met—were the sacrifices.

Brace was the heir.

No longer awkward, no longer lonely, and no longer a friend, *Prince* Brace believed that the Diadem Rite was the only way to save the Summer Realm. He believed it was the only way to save the human realm from the ogres and goblins and trolls. Ji didn't care about any of that. All he knew was that Prince Brace and the Summer Queen were trying to kill him—and his friends.

So he ruined the rite.

Instead of dying, he and his friends had been twisted into half beasts: Sally into a half hobgoblin, Chibo into a half sprite, and Ji into a half dragon—which meant faint scales on his skin, lizard feet with sharp claws, and the ability to shoot fire from his eyes if he touched gold or gemstones.

With the help of a scholarly mermaid named Ti-Lin-Su, they'd escaped Summer City and vowed to find the Ice Witch, the only person who could break the spell. (Well, the only person other than the Summer Queen, but she wanted to finish the Diadem Rite by impaling them on the branches of a new water tree and absorbing their souls.) The problem was, they didn't know where to start looking for the Ice Witch—other than in a library. Roz figured she could unearth some hints in old tomes, but the army had chased them into Isalida Forest, a dense woodland crisscrossed by carriage roads.

They'd been living there ever since, hiding from patrols, foraging for food, and waiting for the Royal Library Coach. Fortunately, Roz knew the route. Unfortunately, she didn't know the schedule. So the mobile library would roll through Isalida Forest eventually, but she didn't know exactly when.

"I'm so hungry I could *eat* a horse," Ji said.

"We're not eating horses," Sally growled. She loved horses, even the really tasty ones.

"I'm kidding," Ji lied, wiping hot-pepper tears from his eyes. "But the knights have food with them, right? So if we don't catch the library coach by tomorrow . . ."

"You want to steal from *knights*?" Sally asked. "No way."

"I could grab the food and fly away," Chibo offered.

"You couldn't grab an acorn at a squirrel feast," Ji told him, because Chibo's eyes didn't work so well. "And anyway, we can't let the knights know for sure that we're here. If they spot us, they'll search every inch of the woods."

Chibo stretched one wing. "Which means you can't steal from them, right?"

"I guess," Ji grumbled. "Though if we—"

"Do you hear that?" Sally peered down the hill. "Roz is knocking over a tree! She must've spotted the coach."

Ji's breath caught. "Where? Which way? Which road?"

"Down there." Sally pointed with one claw-tipped finger. "The trap near the stream."

"Piggyback time!" Ji told Chibo. "You remember the plan?"

"Of course I remember," Chibo said, his green wings flaring like gossamer curtains. "It's barely a plan—there's nothing to forget."

"Then put your wings away and climb on."

Chibo clambered onto Ji's back, his skinny arms around

7

Ji's neck. After two weeks of subsisting mostly on sunlight, he weighed less than a hummingbird's daydream.

"You coming, Sally?" Ji asked, even though he knew she wasn't.

She straightened the tattered shirt that fell to her knees. "I'm not a bandit."

"You're a fugitive and a hobgoblin," Ji told her. "And we need this stupid book to find the stupid witch to break the stupid spell."

"Maybe so," she said. "But I'm still not a stupid thief."

"You're not smart enough to be a stupid thief!"

"I'd rather be honest than smart."

"I'd rather be dishonest than hungry."

"You'd rather be dishonest than *honest!*" she said triumphantly.

He snorted a laugh, tightened his grip on Chibo's legs, and trotted downhill toward the carriage road that ran alongside the stream.

Leaves whisked past his face. He jogged through prickly shrubs that snagged his trousers but didn't scratch his scaly calves. When the slope steepened, he dug into the forest floor with his claws, while Chibo spread his wings, slowing their helter-skelter descent. Twigs snapped, leaves fluttered. Ji almost fell but managed to catch himself on a mossy tree trunk—with his face, because his hands were holding Chibo's calves.

He groaned for a while, then heard a *crack scrat-crrrt.*

"That's Roz," Chibo said into his ear. "Moving the tree into place."

"Okay," Ji panted, and continued downhill.

He stumbled from the woods onto a carriage road: two muddy ruts cutting between the trees. He stopped, listening to the forest. The stream splashed. The leaves whispered. He couldn't hear the *crrrt* of Roz dragging the tree anymore, but a faint squeak and rattle rose from lower on the hill.

"That actually sounds like a coach," he said, feeling a spark of hope.

"What else would a coach sound like?"

"I don't know. I never expected the plan to *work*!"

Chibo giggled and spread his wings. "I'll tell Roz we're on the way."

"Be careful."

"I am full of care!" Chibo piped, launching into the air from Ji's back.

He swooped a foot above the path. He couldn't see farther than an arm's length, so he felt his way with his wings: tendrils of green light that flicked around him like antennae.

Ji trotted after him. Their plan was simple. When the Royal Library Coach stopped at the tree Roz had pushed over, Ji would sneak inside and steal a book. Not just any book, though: the right book. Which was tough for someone who couldn't read.

Roz had spent hours teaching Ji to recognize the important words—"Articles," "Splendid," "History"—by scratching them into the forest floor with a twig. She couldn't steal the book herself because she wasn't as sneaky as Ji, and she didn't look as human. She was a foot or two taller than she'd been before the Diadem Rite had turned her into a half troll. Her skin had become granite flecked and a horn grew from her forehead. On the other hand, Ji still looked normal—at least his face and forearms did. So if the librarians caught him stealing, he'd pretend he was lost in the woods. Roz had promised him that if he said "I'm learning to read," the librarians would *give* him a book—and probably a snack, too.

Ji didn't believe that, of course. Roz always expected everyone to be as kind as she was. And anyway, librarians were spooky—they knew too much.

After jogging for a hundred yards, Ji spotted the cypress tree lying across the road, lacy branches brushing the ground. A stream burbled to his left, while the hillside rose steeply to his right.

A good place for a trap.

He scanned the woods until he spotted Roz standing beside a moss-covered boulder. She looked a little like another boulder, with her broad shoulders and stony skin—though most boulders didn't have horns, or gentle, clever eyes.

She lumbered through the trees, her beaded handbag

swinging by her side. "There's a carriage at the bottom of the hill," she rumbled. "With a team of six horses."

"Is it the Royal Library Coach?"

"Almost certainly. The coach is rather special. Twice the size of an average stagecoach and roughly seven thousand times as valuable."

"Because it's full of doolally books?" he asked.

Roz shot him a governess-y look. She was good at those: she'd learned them from her older sister, who'd been a governess at Primstone Manor and needed a glare that could scorch wood to keep the arrogant Lady Posey and Lord Nichol in line.

"Just remember, we need *Articles from a Splendid History*." Roz eyed him carefully. "It's the only book that will do."

"I know, I know," Ji said. "You told me a dozen times."

"I don't want you to get confused. Ti-Lin-Su wrote so many books." Roz smiled dreamily. "She's a poet, an essayist, and a historian. The most impressive author of the age."

"Do you think mermaids can write underwater? I bet they use squid ink."

Roz furrowed her brow. "I've no idea what they use, but they have a long tradition of literature and philosophy."

"You'd make a good mermaid," Ji told her. "Except if you lived underwater, we'd never have met. Mermaids don't need boot boys."

"I suppose not."

"Because they don't have feet," Ji explained.

The governess-y look returned. "In any case, *Articles from a Splendid History* is the only collection in which Ti-Lin-Su mentioned the myth of the Ice Witch."

"I'll find it." He looked toward the base of the hill. "If we get away with this, we'll be proper highwaymen."

"Speak for yourself," Roz told him. "I won't ever be a highwayman."

He groaned. "What're you, Sally? You don't want to steal, either?"

"As a matter of fact, I don't," Roz said. "Stealing is wrong and reprehensible, not to mention dangerous. However, I see no alternative."

"Then what're you talking about?"

"If we get away with this, I shall be a highway*woman*."

He laughed in relief. "So you're ready? You'll pelt the coach guards if I get in trouble?"

"I'm ready," she said.

"How's your throwing arm?" he asked.

Even before Roz had been transformed into a half troll, she could outthrow anyone Ji knew. And now she could toss thirty-pound rocks around like kumquats. She was strong enough to juggle boulders, and her skin was as hard as granite. But she'd never thrown anything *at* anyone before, and Ji worried that she'd lose her nerve.

"My arm is feeling quite well, thank you," she said.

"You're ready to pelt?"

"These are librarians, Ji. There is rarely a need to pelt librarians."

"It's a royal coach. There'll be guards and—" Ji shrugged. "The problem with you is that you're not very, y'know . . ."

Her eyes narrowed. "I'm not very what? Human?"

"You're not very *mean*," he said. "You're not mean enough, Roz! Just remember the backup plan. If they grab me, first try raining death down upon them like some kind of—"

"Savage troll?" she said. "Is that what you want?"

"That's exactly what I want! I need a troll with a lust for battle, not a love of poetry."

"I shan't let them capture you," Roz said.

"You better not."

"Neither will I!" Chibo fluted from above.

Ji looked toward the treetops. "Where are you, Chibo?"

"Here!"

"Where?"

"Here!"

"Where is 'here'?" Ji asked. "I can't see you."

"Really? Because I can see *you* perfectly with my perfect vision."

"Right, sorry." Ji scanned the trees. "Shake a branch!"

A clump of needles trembled at the top of a tall, skinny pine. When Ji squinted, he saw a slender shape against the cloudy sky. Chibo was standing on a branch that looked too narrow to hold anything heavier than a shoelace.

"What are you doing up there?" Ji asked.

"I'll swoop down at them if there's trouble."

"He's going to swoop at them," Ji told Roz, in disbelief. "That's his plan."

She lofted her eyebrow. "Perhaps you should trust him."

"Have you met him? He thinks a sneeze is how your brain shouts for help." Ji peered at Chibo. "You can't even see! You'll fly into a tree trunk."

"I will not," Chibo piped. "I've been practicing swooping."

"Oh, boy," Ji muttered.

Chibo flicked a wing toward the forest. "Now get in place before they see you!"

2

AN ANXIOUS KNOT formed in Ji's empty stomach. "Okay, here I go."

"They're only halfway up the hill," Roz told him. "You've plenty of time. Still, better safe than tardy."

"You mean 'better safe than sorry,'" Ji said, edgy from nerves. "You're starting to sound like Nin."

"I'll take that a compliment," Roz told him. "Nin is wise and brave and loyal."

"He's a buttonhead," Ji said, pleased that Roz still talked about Nin in the present tense.

"Nin is not a 'he'!" Roz rumbled, for the hundredth time. "Or a 'she.' Nin is a 'they'!"

Young ogres didn't decide if they'd be male or female until they reached adulthood, which meant they were called "cub" instead of "he" or "she." And things were even more confusing with Nin. The Diadem Rite had transformed a single ogre cub into an entire colony of ant lions. Hundreds of ant lions added up to one Nin . . . except that after dozens of ant lions had died in Summer City, the colony had fallen silent. *Nin* had fallen silent instead of chattering away in "mind-speak," which ant lions used in place of regular talking.

Ti-Lin-Su said that if a single ant-lion queen survived, Nin would recover. So far, that hadn't happened. So far, the clay urn where the ant lions lived had stayed quiet. And with every passing day, Ji's fear grew. What if they'd lost Nin forever?

"In that case," Ji said, "they are a whole colony of buttonheads."

"There's a slight chance . . ." Roz trailed off.

"What?"

"Well, *Articles from a Splendid History* is Ti-Lin-Su's most speculative work. She may have written a few words about ant lions."

"Like how to save Nin?"

"Perhaps. Her research is exhaustive."

"All books tire me out."

"Exhaus*tive*, Ji, not exhaus*ting*. Although it's true that the volumes probably weigh as much as you do. But only a few copies exist. That's why the coach takes one from library to library across the realm."

Ji scratched the scales on his wrist. "Do you really think you can figure out where the witch is?"

"I hope to find a clue."

"And if we find her, do you really think she'll help?"

"I . . ." Sadness rose in Roz's eyes. "I hope so. We cannot live like this."

"Yeah." Ji tugged his cloak around his shoulders. "Well, I'd better get in place."

"I'll tuck you in," Roz said, and they crunched downhill to the rutted road.

Ji peered toward the fallen cypress tree. "So if I'm the coach driver, I come around the bend, spot the tree, and rein in my horses right"—he stopped at a shallow trench between the two wheel ruts—"here."

"You're sure this is the place?" Roz asked, nervously tapping her handbag.

"Definitely. Yeah." They'd dug trenches on three hillside roads: three traps, because they weren't sure exactly which route the coach would take. Now Ji had to lie in this one and wait for the coach to stop directly above him. "Maybe."

If he was wrong, he'd get trampled by hooves and smooshed by wheels. At least half dragons healed fast. So even if he got a little smooshed, he'd survive.

Probably.

He crawled into the trench between the wheel ruts. When he lay on his back, the soil chilled him. He took a shaky breath and looked at the sky between the treetops.

Then Roz's granite-looking face blocked his view. "Are you ready?"

"If this coach doesn't have the book," he told her, "it better be carrying picnics."

"Chorizo and rice cakes," she rumbled. "That's all I ask."

"You eat bark!"

"Unhappily."

He wriggled to keep a rock from jabbing his side. "All I want is one bite of kimchi and I'll die happy."

"You're not allowed to die, Jiyong. Where would that leave me?"

"As a half troll highwaywoman bent on revenge?"

Roz's smile warmed him better than a campfire. "That sounds rather appealing. Very well, you may die."

"Hey!"

She brushed dirt off his cheek with a thick finger. "If the coach doesn't stop in the right place, don't risk it."

"If I don't risk it, we don't get the book," he said.

"That is true, but—"

"And if we don't get the book, we don't find the Ice Witch."

"And if we don't find the Ice Witch, we're stuck like this forever. Half-finished creatures with no home and no hope." She exhaled. "I cannot bear it, Ji. Not much longer."

"I know." He touched her forearm. "Getting twisted

into a monster isn't my cup of hibiscus tea either."

"Plus, Chibo's thinner than ever," Roz said.

"I'm more worried about Sally," Ji admitted.

"And me," Roz said, with a glint in her eyes.

Sometimes he thought she could read his mind. "Nah, you're fine. Anyway, if the stagecoach doesn't stop in the right place . . ."

"Risk it," she told him, her voice gruff.

He nodded. "Okay."

"We'll get the book." Roz swept a layer of concealing leaves over Ji. "We'll find the Ice Witch. And we'll break this spell before it's too late."

"Yeah," he said.

"Unless we're already stuck like this." Tears swam in her eyes. "We've no idea when the transformation becomes irreversible."

"We'll find a way."

Roz smiled and straightened up. "You always do."

Ji listened to Roz's heavy footsteps crunching into the woods and couldn't tell if he was happy that she believed in him—or terrified that she believed in him. Maybe both.

The leaves tickled his nose. The rock jabbed his side again. He listened for the coach but only heard birds squawking and trees rustling. Time snailed past. His stomach hurt and his scaly toes itched. A bug wandered across his forehead, reminding him of Nin. He fought to stay awake. Surviving on nuts and peppers left him tired all the time. His eyes closed and his mind drifted. . . .

A pool rippled on the ground inside a grand pavilion. The Summer Queen stood on a balcony. She lifted her arms. A water tree with glistening branches rose from the pool. The queen cast the Diadem Rite, the spell that crowned the next ruler of the realm. The spell that strengthened the new monarch by draining the souls of servants, twisting the servants into beasts before killing them. Brace wore the diadem and became the prince. The Prince of Summer. He vowed to protect his fellow humans and destroy the beasts—

The dream changed. A blizzard of colors swept across Ji's mind. Dozens of bald children worked at a tapestry loom that clattered and jingled. Louder and louder: clatter, jingle, jingle-clatter, clink-jingle.

Ji woke with a start—and gasped. Blackness roiled above him and tree trunks pounded down like monstrous pestles trying to grind him into paste. The air stank of wet leather and—

"Whoa!" a woman's voice cried. "Sa-sa-sa! Whoa, there!"

Horses! Those weren't tree trunks, they were horse legs. Horses were walking over Ji, their hooves punching the ground. Harnesses jingled and a coach creaked. The woman—who must've been the coach driver—called "whoa" and the horses stopped directly above Ji, nickering and stomping.

"Driver, have we arrived?" a reedy male voice demanded from inside the coach. "Unless I am greatly mistaken, we are nowhere near Greenmesa!"

"No, m'lord," the driver said. "When we rounded the last turn—"

"Enough excuses! Why in the name of the queen's left toe have we stopped?"

"I'm sorry, sir, but a tree—"

"Surely you don't deny that we are no longer making forward progress?"

"There's a fallen tree in the road, m'lord!'" the driver blurted.

"What an absurd place for a tree," the reedy voice told her.

"Tell the guards to move it, Father," a boy's voice broke in.

"You heard my son," the man barked. "Guards! Stop daydreaming and move that tree!"

Ji wrinkled his nose despite his fear of the horses heaving above him. The people inside the coach didn't sound like librarians to him. Not that he'd ever met librarians, but from what Roz had told him, they weren't called "m'lord" and were generally in *favor* of daydreaming.

A moment later, two pairs of leather boots smacked onto the road as guards jumped down from the running boards. The boots weren't fancy, but they looked well made—a good choice for coach guards, in Ji's professional opinion as a boot boy. For some reason, the sight of them reassured him. He found the tidy stitches pleasing and the heavy soles comforting.

Then he felt a flash of disgust. What was he thinking? *Sure, I'm a half-starving half dragon, half-hidden in a trench, but at least there are* boots?

One guard muttered something and the other gave a low chuckle. They walked past the horses, heading for the fallen cypress tree. Leaving the coach behind—leaving the coach unguarded.

Ji's plan was actually working!

Now he just needed to crawl beneath the terrifying horses to the rear of the coach, where—according to Roz—he'd find a door to the rolling library. He'd creep inside and look for the familiar words: "Ariticles," "Slendid," "Histiry," and "Ti-Lin-Su." He'd riffle through pages until he found the volume with "Ice Wich." Then he'd snaffle that book and Roz would solve a puzzle that nobody had managed to unravel in hundreds of years.

Easy.

And if he couldn't find the book, he'd knock on the door and beg the librarians for help. Except they didn't sound like librarians. Which meant there might be a need for the backup plan: attack.

3

WHEN JI ROLLED onto his hands and knees, the horses whinnied in alarm. Hooves stomped and tails lashed. Ji trembled and waited for the driver to settle the team. Then he crawled toward the coach.

Something jerked him backward.

He almost yelped in fear. He swung around, ready to fight, and saw that one of the horses was standing on his cloak. He cursed, took a breath, and tugged at the horse's leg. The horse didn't budge. Ji tugged harder—and the horse crooked her leg and smacked him in the cheek with her hoof.

This time, he cried out. Pain blinded him and the world spun. Or at least the undersides of the horses spun. Blood trickled to his chin, but he managed to pull his cloak free.

"Father?" the boy asked, from inside the coach. "Did you hear that?"

"All I hear is the sound of my lazy guards pretending to move that tree."

"I guess." The boy paused. "I don't want to go home so early."

"Nor do I," his father told him, "but we commandeered the Royal Library Coach because we had no choice."

Ji stifled a groan. Commandeered? That meant "legally stole," didn't it?

"There's no quicker way to return to Greenmesa," the man continued. "You read your mother's letter. All of our blue-bats are dying off? This is a tragedy for my orchards."

"Yes, father," the boy said morosely. "The harvest will fail without blue-bats."

"Perhaps your mother is wrong. Blue-bats do not die off for no reason."

The boy responded, but Ji wasn't listening. If they'd commandeered the coach, that meant they weren't librarians. And *that* meant Ji couldn't beg them for help if he needed it.

Well, at least it was the right coach. Ji wiped the tears from his eyes, then belly-crawled beneath the horses. He peeked upward and caught sight of the reins. He couldn't see the driver in her high seat, which meant she couldn't see him.

Exhaling in relief, he scooted toward the rear of the

coach—and a load of manure plopped to the ground three inches from his left ear. Oh, come *on*! He was just trying to find some dumb book—he didn't need to be bombarded with horse poop. He held his breath and squirmed onward. He ignored the pain in his cheek and tried to convince himself that nothing was splattering his neck except mud.

At the rear of the coach, Ji peeked from between the wheels. No guards in sight, no driver. He pulled himself to his feet behind the coach—and almost fell, dizzy from the blow to his face.

He steadied himself on a trunk lashed to the luggage rack. Fancy boxes and tasseled sacks were bound to the coach with a spiderweb of straps. And in a rear panel of the coach, a door had been painted to look like book-shelves. Ji reached for the bronze-colored "book," as Roz had told him. Sure enough, when he turned the book, a latch clicked and the door opened.

Ji froze at the sound, but nobody raised the alarm. With his nerves jangling, he climbed through the door into a dark, narrow space that smelled of lavender and glue.

A very dark space. Too dark to see.

"Great," Ji grumbled.

It was hard enough for him to recognize words when he could *see* them. This was impossible. So while the guards shifted the tree outside—while every second ticked closer to his discovery—he just stood there like a numbskull and waited for his eyes to adjust to the dark.

Slowly, the spines of books swam into sight around him.

Fat books, skinny books, leather-bound books, metal-bound books—and a hint of something else. A *something* that tugged at Ji's stomach. Not books. A pang like hunger, but not regular hunger. He frowned into the gloom . . . and heard the nobleman order his guards to hurry up.

Time to get moving.

Ji stuck his nose an inch from the nearest books, looking for "Arcitles," "Spendid," "Histiry," and "Tii-Lun-Si." He grabbed a narrow clothbound book with "Spleen" in the title, because that was pretty much the same as "Splendid." Then he remembered Roz's lectures about matching every single letter in a word, even though that struck Ji as being outrageously fussy.

His gaze snagged on titles with words from "Apes" to "Tinsel"—and a *clunk* sounded from outside. Just a horse stomping? Or the guards returning?

C'mon, Ji, he urged himself. *C'mon, c'mon. . . .*

He sat on a square leather stool and trailed his fingertips across dozens of books, from the highest shelves to the lowest. Letters squiggled and jumbled in the gloom. When the driver called and the coach jerked, Ji yelped. He was out of time. He grabbed the book that looked most like *Articles of a Splendid History* and scrambled through the door.

He tumbled to the ground behind the coach and

started to roll away, afraid of being crushed by the wheels. But the coach just stood there, the fancy luggage stacked high: hatboxes, travel trunks, sacks and bags bulging with goods. The guards were still dragging the tree, the driver was still facing in the other direction. Ji couldn't tell why the coach had jerked; maybe the horses had given a restless tug.

"Grab that branch!" one of the guards called. "Now pull!"

Ji was starting to slink away when he caught sight of a sack bulging with what looked like food. He'd spent enough time working in a kitchen to know. He darted to the luggage rack, untied the sack, and nearly fainted. *Avocados.* A sack full of avocados. Dozens of avocados. Shiny, lumpy, and green-black.

They were the most beautiful thing he'd ever seen.

He lowered the sack to the road—then caught a glimpse of tigerwood gleaming at the top of the luggage rack. A pretty little box was wedged between two trunks.

A jewelry box. Full of jewels. That's what he'd felt from inside from the library coach: a tug of dragonhunger in the pit of his stomach. What was in the box? Rubies or diamonds? Opals or amethysts or sapphires?

He didn't know. He didn't care. All he knew was, he needed them. Not for himself! Not because a bell chimed inside his half-dragon heart whenever he got close to jewels. After the Diadem Rite, he'd learned that dragons didn't hoard gemstones and precious metal because they liked sparkly things; they didn't collect valuables because they wanted to go on a shopping spree. No, a dragon's hoard served a purpose. Dragons converted treasure into fire, draining the power from gems to shoot flames from their eyes.

So Ji needed these gems to keep everyone safe. A dragon's fire-shooting power relied on treasure, and he couldn't protect his friends without power.

He climbed the rack and tugged at the tigerwood box. It didn't move. His palms itched and a thrill thrummed in his chest. He tugged harder, and the box shifted. Just a few more seconds . . .

"What is taking so long?" the nobleman demanded from inside the passenger compartment. "Are they waiting for the tree to move itself?"

"The path is clear, sir," the driver reported.

Oh, no. Ji yanked at the jewelry box, his pulse crashing in his ears, and—

"Thief!" the driver shouted. "Stealing the luggage—there's a thief!"

Footsteps pounded as the guards ran toward Ji. And this time, the presence of well-made boots didn't exactly comfort him.

"I'm learning to read!" Ji yelled, raising his hands.

In a single motion, the female guard drew and loaded her crossbow. The male guard raced toward the coach as the driver lifted her arm, her whip unfurling.

"I'm Lord Nichol of Primstone Manor!" Ji blurted, before realizing what he must look like. "'s *servant!* I'm his lordship's servant! I—"

When a rock hurtled from the woods and slammed into the crossbow guard's arm, Ji felt a flash of triumph. *Ha! Eat troll-rock, you skullbrain!*

Except the guard didn't flinch at the impact. Then another rock bounced off the male guard's hat, and Ji's relief died. Because stupid Roz was throwing stupid pine-cones.

"Rocks!" Ji screamed into the woods. "Throw ro—" He caught himself. "I mean, *someone* is throwing rocks!"

"Don't move!" the female guard shouted, while the male guard clambered onto the running board.

"What in the name of the Summer Queen's perfumed pillowcase is going on out there?" the nobleman bellowed.

The driver cracked her whip at Ji. "An ambush, sir!"

"Earn your wages!" the nobleman ordered. "Kill the bandits!"

Another pinecone bounced off the female guard's shoulder, and she fired her crossbow.

Ji's fear burned that moment into his mind like a paint-ing. He saw the scene from outside himself: an oversized coach, painted to look like a bookcase, waited in a forest, and a skinny kid in rags stood on the luggage rack, with blood sheeting his face and terror in his eyes. The driver's whip blurred, the male guard lunged, the female guard's crossbow bolt sped toward him.

Then a fuzzball launched itself from the woods and hit Ji like an ogre punching a piñata.

Pain burst in his arm. He was flung off the stage-coach and into the cover of the woods. He hit the dirt hard and smashed his head on a root. The world turned black and red. When his vision cleared, the fuzzball—Sally—was crouching over him, her eyes worried.

"Oh!" he said, his voice oddly cheery. "Hi!"

"There's a crossbow bolt in your arm," she growled, touching his shoulder gently.

"That's what *you* think," he said.

She loped toward the carriage road. "Stay here!"

"Maybe there's an *arm*," he called after her, "in my *crossbow bolt*."

The world wobbled and dimmed. His head throbbed and his legs refused to move. His gaze drifted in and out of focus.

He caught a glimpse of the driver screaming at the sight of Sally and whipping the horses into a gallop. He heard the Royal Library Coach creak toward a bend in the road. The humans shrieked when Roz burst from the woods. She crouched in the road for the book he'd dropped, then bellowed, "Stop them! Backup plan, backup plan!"

"I can't catch them!" Sally growled, chasing the retreating coach.

The emerald glow of sprite wings flashed between the trees. The horses veered from the light, the guards shouted, and Ji closed his eyes, his pulse pounding in his wounded arm.

His eyes opened three times before he fainted.

The first time, he saw Roz pounding alongside the coach while Chibo fluttered in front, slowing the horses. Sally appeared inside the library door, showing Roz book after book. Then Roz gave a trollish bellow and dove halfway through the door.

The second time Ji's eyes opened, the coach was a tiny dot halfway down the hill, and Roz's cloak and pink dress were fluttering in the wind, her slippered feet poking out through the door, and her head inside the library. The guards were shooting her legs with their crossbows, but the bolts shattered on her troll skin.

The third time, he stared longingly at the sack of avocados in the road.

4

THE WORLD SMELLED of pine needles and mud. Ji's head hurt and his arm throbbed. He opened one eye and peered into the darkness. Nighttime. Hours since the attack on the coach. None of the moons shone in the sky, none of the stars twinkled.

Snores sounded around him: Chibo's were surprisingly deep, while Sally's were purrs. Ji listened for a moment, then frowned. Where was Roz? He opened his other eye and lifted his head—which made his temples pound. He still couldn't see anything, but he heard Roz's deep, steady breathing.

The band of fear around his chest loosened. She was there. Thank the moons. He touched the bandage on his biceps. Pain throbbed from his elbow to his shoulder.

Apparently there'd been a crossbow bolt in his arm after all.

When he woke again, emerald light bathed the enclosed, tentlike space. After they'd roamed the thickets of the Isalida Forest for days, Sally had led them to a towering pine tree, as wide around as a house. The lowest branches swept the ground, and inside them an open space encircled the thick, knobby trunk. Once Roz had cleared the deadwood, Ji and Chibo carpeted the floor with moss, and they had the perfect hideout. Well, not *perfect*. They still hadn't had any food. Also, they'd been living in a tree. Plus, Ji didn't think he'd ever get the sap out of his hair, and Sally spent hours picking pine needles from her tail.

Dawn's light seeped between tree limbs above. Still half-asleep, Ji watched the glow of Chibo's wings and listened to an odd crunching sound.

From the other side of the trunk, Sally purred, "How can you eat those?"

"They're quite tasty," Roz's voice said.

Ji blinked himself fully awake and touched his cheek. The cut had already closed, thanks to his transformation into a half dragon. Ji figured that he recovered from injuries five times faster than before the Diadem Rite. A cut that would've taken a week to heal now only took a day or two.

"They're hard as rocks," Sally said.

"Troll teeth," Roz explained.

Ji pushed himself into a seated position. When he

moved his injured arm, the pain brought tears to his eyes.

"Are avocado pits even eatable?" Chibo asked.

"Edible," Roz said.

The green light shifted as Chibo moved. "Then are they *edible*?"

"They are if you ed them," Sally said.

Ji watched Roz pop a pit into her mouth, and he smiled to himself. At least they'd gotten away with the sack of avocados—but what about the book? He didn't see one anywhere. Instead, he saw the clay urn where Nin's antlion colony lived in the dirt beneath a half dozen leafy seedlings. He looked past the urn and saw Sally nibbling on an avocado and Chibo twirling in a circle, his wings extended.

"Did you see me swoop?" Chibo asked. "I told you I've been practicing!"

Sally's muzzle lifted in a smile. "You were fearsome, Chibo."

"I've never seen swoopier," Roz said.

"And Ji got the book," Chibo trilled.

Ji smiled to himself. So there *was* a book!

"Not exactly," Roz said, tapping something in her lap. "This is not *Articles from a Splendid History*. This is *Artichokes from Stem to Heart*."

Ji stopped smiling to himself. *The wrong book.*

"Oh," Chibo said, after a pause. "Well, at least we have food now. That's good."

"I prefer it to not having food," Roz agreed. "But even better, while I couldn't find anything to help locate the Ice Witch directly, I did read a curious passage about—"

"How did you read?" Chibo asked. "You were dangling from a coach!"

Roz rumbled a laugh. "Yes, but I was dangling from a coach for nearly ten minutes. And now I believe I know how to find someone who can find the Ice Witch."

"He could've gotten away!" Sally blurted, her hobgoblin tail lashing across the moss-strewn ground.

"Who could've gotten away?" Roz asked.

"Ji!" Sally's tufted ears flattened. "After he grabbed the wrong book, he stood there like a buttonhead, tugging on a box."

"Maybe it was full of kimchi," Chibo said.

"It was full of gems," Sally said. "At least, it looked like a jewelry box. And Ji stood there like a big, greedy lizard."

"Hey!" Ji said.

Sally turned to him, like she'd known he was awake. "Well, you did!"

"I could not have gotten away. The guards were too fast. They shot me with a crossbow."

"Because you were standing there trying to steal jewels."

His cheeks heated. "Maybe if you'd come in the first place, instead of whining about stealing things—"

"I don't know why I bothered saving your scaly bum."

"I didn't need saving."

"They shot you with a crossbow."

"That's what I just said!"

"Well—" Sally bared her teeth. "Well, *that* part is true! I thought we weren't supposed to let them see us."

Ji grabbed an avocado. "I didn't *let* them do anything."

"You did too. And now that nobleman will tell the knights where to find us."

"Fine. It's all my fault," Ji snapped. "We'd still be safe at Primstone if not for me; we'd still be human if not for me. And Nin"—he looked at the urn—"would still be alive."

"Enough!" Roz growled. "Nin's not dead! And I learned how to contact Lady Ti-Lin-Su."

"No way!" Chibo piped. "You did?"

"Yes. Apparently there's a method for speaking with mermaids across long distances."

"I bet it's 'blow into a conch shell.'" Sally made a face when Ji snorted. "What? Ti-Lin-Su is a mermaid. Mermaids like seashells. It makes sense."

"It's not blowing into a shell." Roz scratched her horn. "It's an ancient method that hasn't been used for centuries."

Chibo's green eyes sparkled. "Really? Wow."

"If it works, Lady Ti-Lin-Su will tell us where to find the Ice Witch."

Ji eyed Roz dubiously. "What's the method?"

"It's rather unusual." Roz cleared her throat. "That is, it's an uncommon or, erm, unexpected approach."

"What are you talking about?" Sally asked.

Roz fiddled with the strap of her beaded handbag. "It's a spell."

"*What?*"

Ji made a face. "We're not mages, Roz."

"I know that! But this is a simple spell that ordinary humans used to cast before we lost our magic."

"We're not ordinary humans, either."

"For once, that's a good thing. The reason nobody's used this spell for so long is that there's been no human magic. But we have magic now, from the Diadem Rite— and from our nonhuman halves."

"What does that matter?" Chibo asked.

"Humans never had much magic," Roz told him. "Only enough to give us a knack with pottery or applesauce, or, um—"

"The ability to soothe frightened sheep?" Ji suggested.

"Exactly! Little things like that. But hundreds of years ago, the first Summer Queen gathered all the human magic into herself, to stop the hordes from invading. Since then, we haven't had any at all, right?"

"But there's still magic in hobgoblins and dragons and trolls and sprites?" Chibo asked, his green eyes shining.

"Precisely!" Roz said.

"I don't know." Ji scratched his healing cheek. "You really think it'll work?"

"I don't see why not."

37

"Because we're not mages? Because we're hiding in the woods? Because we don't know what we're doing?"

"We *will* contact Lady Ti-Lin-Su," Roz told him, her jaw tight. "And she *will* tell us where to find the Ice Witch."

Ji saw the determination in Roz's face and sighed. "And she'll break this spell and make us human again?"

"She'll have to. We can't live like this. Hunted and hungry and—" She took a shaky breath. "And horrible."

Nobody spoke for a second. Ji prodded the pine needles on the floor with one of his thick, dragon-y fingernails. He knew how she felt. They all did. First they'd been turned into beasts, and now they were living like animals. They needed to be *themselves* again.

"Fine," he said. "So what do we need?"

"Running water," Roz told him. "The more complex the better."

"Complex?" Chibo asked. "How does water get complex?"

"By going through something like a waterwheel, perhaps? I've only seen the spell for humans, not for . . ."

"Beasts like us," Sally growled.

Sally kept grumbling, but Ji didn't hear, because he'd taken a bite of avocado—and he'd never tasted anything better. His head swam with the feel of the avocado on his tongue, and his mouth watered with the sheer deliciousness.

When he started listening again, Roz was still talking

about the ancient ritual: ". . . We envision the mermaid we wish to contact and send . . . bits of ourselves, it sounds like. Into the swirling waters."

"Bits of ourselves?" Sally asked. "Like hair and finger-nails?"

"Or fur balls, for you," Ji said.

"I'm not giving up my wings," Chibo said.

"I suppose we'll have to experiment," Roz said.

Even Chibo didn't like the sound of that. He wrinkled his nose while Sally groomed her tail. Ji ate two more avo-cados, dropping the peels into Nin's urn for the surviving ant lions to eat. If the Diadem Rite had turned Nin into a single huge ant lion, that would've been weird enough, but instead it had changed one ogre cub into hundreds of tiny ant lions. Dozens of the ant lions still built mounds in the dirt of the urn, but Nin's unbroken silence made Ji worry that the ogre cub was gone forever.

"How's Nin?" Sally asked Ji.

"I think there are more ant lions than before," he said, chewing his lower lip. "That's good, right?"

"If Nin hatches a queen, the colony will recover." Roz rested a trollish hand on the urn, careful of the ant lions crawling on the side. "That's what Ti-Lin-Su told us. The queen will strengthen the colony and Nin will return."

Ji laid his hand beside Roz's. "As doolally as ever."

"What's taking so long?" Chibo demanded. "Why doesn't Nin just hatch a queen already?"

"I'm not sure," Roz said. "Ti-Lin-Su didn't write much about ant lions."

After a short, unhappy silence, Ji looked at the light shining through the pine branches. "We'll leave at sunset to find water for this spell. I guess we'll try the stream."

"A stream isn't enough," Roz said. "The book said we need a complex confluence of currents."

"A what of who?" Chibo asked.

"I'm not entirely sure about that myself," Roz admitted. "Something like a canal, I suppose. Or many streams coming together."

"How about a waterfall?" Sally asked. "I heard one in the forest."

"That may work!" Roz looked at Ji. "Perhaps we should leave now."

"We can't travel in the daylight," Ji said. "We're too visible."

"Ugly, you mean," Sally said.

"Speak for yourself," Chibo told her. "I'm gorgeous."

"Between Sally's night vision and Chibo's wings, we're better off in the dark," Ji said. "We'll head for the waterfall at sundown. We'll cast this spell. Ti-Lin-Su will tell us where to find the Ice Witch. Then *bang*, the witch will cure us. Unless anyone has a better idea?"

"I have an idea." Sally bounded onto a branch overhead. "You can stop acting like a big jerk."

The leaves rustled, and she disappeared into the treetop.

"What's up with her?" Ji asked.

"She wants you to stop acting like a big jerk," Chibo explained.

"My plan actually worked for once! Well, my backup plan."

"Your jerky backup plan," Chibo said.

"We even got food."

"Jerky food," Chibo said.

"We didn't only get food, we also got *that*." Roz gestured toward a sturdy wicker basket on the ground. "Before the coach wheels came off—"

"Wait," Ji said. "What?"

"Don't worry," Roz assured him. "I took pains not to harm any of the books."

"I don't care about them! What happened with the wheels?"

"The coach sped along the hillside path," Roz said, "with me still in the doorway—"

"*Mostly* in the doorway," Chibo interrupted. "Your legs were outside."

Despite her granite-flecked skin, Roz seemed to blush. "It was quite improper."

"So you were dangling out of the Library Coach . . . ," Ji prompted.

"Yes, flipping through pages as fast as I possibly could. After I found the information, I dropped from the window and . . . scuppered the wheels."

"'Scuppered'?"

"Sally said she popped them off the coach like plucking petals from a flower," Chibo chimed. "And flung them into the woods."

"I'm afraid they'll spend a whole day walking from the forest," Roz said, "unable to raise the alarm."

"Wow." Ji grinned. "That's some high-quality scheming, Roz. With you scheming and me reading, we're basically identical!"

"Like artichokes and articles," she told him, and pointed again to the wicker basket. "In any case, that fell from the coach. And happily, it's full of linens. There's even a needle and thread."

"So what?"

"So you're good with a needle and thread."

"So are you!"

"I used to be passable at embroidery," she told him. "Before my fingers thickened. My dress is tattered and horrible."

"So is my arm," Ji said. "Crossbow, remember?"

"Sewing will take your mind off the pain while we wait for sunset."

"Fine," he grumbled, and started sewing.

Well, sewing and eating avocados.

Well, sewing and eating avocados and listening to Roz read a book, an old favorite that she'd stuffed into her handbag back in the city. Even after the transformation, Ji liked Roz's voice better than any music. And when she read tales of faraway places and ancient times, she seemed to wrap the stories around herself—around all of them.

A few pages into the story, Sally crept down from the treetop and straddled a low branch. And a minute later, they weren't cold and frightened, huddled in the skirts of a pine tree. Instead, they floated underwater, surrounded by colorful seaweed, watching mermaids sing and swim. They joined a merchant caravan, smuggled cabbages to the ogres in exchange for gold, and watched mages struggle to master human magic.

". . . and that is how the mages learned that magic always seeks Balance," Roz said, as Ji patched the sleeves of her cloak and dress. "If a spell heals one person, it will sicken someone else."

"Balance doesn't sound very nice," Chibo said.

"It can be cruel," Roz admitted. "There is a story of one young mage who'd mastered woodland magic. She drew power from the woods to share with her friends, but magic always seeks Balance."

"She lost her powers?" Sally asked.

"She lost her *self*. Saplings sprouted from her hair and hills rose from her collarbone. She transformed into a forest."

"A forest?" Chibo asked.

"That's right," Roz said. "And her name was Isalida."

Chibo's nearsighted eyes widened. "No way! She made this whole forest?"

"You mean she *is* this whole forest," Sally said.

43

"That's the legend," Roz told them. "That's the power of Balance."

"So what price are we going to pay for trying to contact Ti-Lin-Su?" Ji asked.

"Oh, it's just a minor spell," Roz said, a hint of worry in her voice. "I'm fairly certain that the worst possible outcome is contacting the wrong person."

Ji squinted at her. "Like who?"

"I'm not sure. The wrong mermaid? A dolphin, perhaps?"

"So we might ask some octopus to help us find the Ice Witch?"

Roz took a deep breath. "Apparently the spell relies on the complexity of the watercourse. The more complex the current, the more successful the spell."

"Apparently."

"I don't know, Ji! I'm not a mage!"

"That's weird. I thought you had woodland magic." Ji turned to the seedlings growing from the dirt in Nin's urn. "That's why you threw pinecones instead of rocks."

"I didn't want to hurt anyone," Roz said.

"Next time," Ji told the urn, "she'll rain down death with flower petals."

5

JI FINISHED MENDING Roz's cloak and dress and started fashioning a troll-sized backpack from the wicker basket. He was reinforcing the leather straps when Sally raised a paw to silence Chibo, who'd been singing to Nin's urn—a weird ditty that rhymed "beets" with "feets." Chibo hid his wings and Roz barely breathed. Ji even stopped sewing, as if soldiers might hear his needle piercing leather.

Finally, Sally said, "It's nothing," and everyone relaxed.

When the setting sun touched the hilltops, Ji filled the backpack with avocados, wasp peppers, and even a few linens, though he didn't know what kind of person traveled with napkins. Heck, what kind of person *used* napkins? Didn't they know what sleeves were for?

Then Sally prowled from the shelter of the pine tree. Roz moved the branches aside, and Ji took Chibo's skinny hand and followed. The mulch of the forest floor smelled like last week's tea. Night animals scurried through the underbrush and an owl hooted, marking its territory.

The air cooled moments before they reached a stream babbling in a rock-strewn gully. Sally headed uphill to a moons-touched grotto. An oval pool rippled at the base of lichen-stained boulders and a "waterfall"—not much taller than Roz—trickled between the rocks.

"It's smaller than it sounds," Sally whispered.

"It's perfect," Roz whispered.

"We're still not mages, though," Sally whispered.

"We're still not human, either," Ji whispered.

"Why are we whispering?" Chibo whispered.

"I don't know," Ji whispered. "But it's starting to freak me out."

"We must stand in a circle," Roz said in her normal voice, splashing into the pool. "In the water."

"C-cold," Chibo said when he followed.

The pool soaked through Ji's foot wraps and chilled his scaly ankles. "Ti-Lin-Su better know where to find the Ice Witch."

"She will if anyone does," Roz said. "Now hold hands. Um—" She shifted her grip on Nin's urn. "Ji, touch an ant lion and my hand at the same time."

Ji rested his hand on hers, in the dirt in the urn. "Now what?"

"Can you all see the reflection of the moons in the water between us?"

"I can't," Chibo said. "I mean, not really."

"Perhaps we should wait and use the sun," Roz said.

"I see a little glow," Chibo said.

"That's good enough," Roz told him. "Now look at the reflection and imagine Ti-Lin-Su's face."

"That's easy," Ji said, as ant lions walked across his fingers. "Her white hair matches the moonlight."

"I never saw her face," Chibo said. "Not clearly."

"Do the best you can," Roz said.

"I'm holding hands with ant lions," Ji told Chibo. "Believe me, you're doing better than they are. Now what?"

"Keep picturing her face," Roz said.

Ji looked at the wobbly moons reflected in the rippling pool. He imagined that one splash of water was eyes and the glow was hair. He could almost see a mermaid face in the ripples . . . but not quite.

"It's not working," he said. "Nothing's happening."

"Give it time!" Roz rumbled. "And try to put yourself into it."

"How?"

"We could spit," Sally suggested.

"Please don't," Roz told her.

The reflection of the moons blurred in the pool. Ji remembered watching Ti-Lin-Su swim through her water garden; he remembered seeing her burst from the surface, water sheeting her face. He remembered her silvery laugh echoing like the babble of a hillside stream. His memories unspooled, but nothing happened. He was just standing in a chilly pool in the dark woods with mud oozing between his toes.

"My fingers are cramping," he said.

"I can't remember her face," Chibo said.

"Maybe this current isn't complex enough," Sally said.

"Lady Ti-Lin-Su touched your wings, didn't she?" Roz asked Chibo. "In her water garden in the city?"

"She told me they're a tremendous gift," he said proudly. "Oh! Oh, do you think I should use them? I mean, I sort of remember what it felt like when she touched them."

Chibo's wings swooped from his hunchback, and the instant they dipped into the pool, Ji felt himself pour into the water, like he'd dived into a swimming hole. The current tugged at his heart and dragonscales thickened from his shoulders to his elbows. His vision of Ti-Lin-Su swept into the water as the reflection of the moons became the blurry face of a woman. First a wide mouth appeared, then a square chin and short hair. Not like Ji remembered, but still a face! The magic was working—the spell was working!

"Can you see that?" he said, whispering in awe.

"My goodness," Roz rumbled.

"Ask her," Sally breathed. "Ask her about the Ice Witch."

"Yeah, and"—Chibo's wings started glowing—"and how to help Nin."

The face came into sharper focus. A glint of gold

sparkled on the moons-lit forehead, and a chill rose from Ji's feet to his heart.

"Stop!" he shouted. "Stop, it's the queen!"

"Ahhh," the Summer Queen's reflection said with watery satisfaction. "Now thou art revealed to my magical touch. . . ."

Ji stumbled out of the pool. "Get away from the water!"

With a single beat of his wings, Chibo threw himself backward. Sally leaped into the air and grabbed a tree limb, while Roz stomped from the pool onto the bank.

The reflection faded, and nobody spoke. Ji pressed his palm to his pounding heart, staring at the pool, waiting for the queen's face to reappear. But the water remained water, dark and still.

"Apparently," Roz said, "this current is not complex enough."

"Th-that's the least of our problems!" Ji sputtered. "She found us! The queen knows where we are."

"She'll send knights," said Sally.

"She'll send mages," said Ji.

"She'll send Brace," said Sally. "He's not a scared kid at Primstone Manor anymore, getting bullied by Lord Nichol and Lady Posey. He does magic now—and he knows how to fight."

"My feet are freezing," said Chibo.

"Okay," Ji said. "Maybe *that* is the least of our problems."

Roz set Nin's urn on the ground. "And the greatest of our problems is this: We must contact Ti-Lin-Su if we're to break the spell. She's the only one who can tell us where to find the Ice Witch."

"The Ice Witch can't return us to normal if the queen catches us first," Ji told her.

"Capture is not as terrible a fate as a life consigned to"—Roz lifted one trollish, four-fingered hand—"to this. Being trapped forever as a twisted beast."

Ji glowered at the pool, hating the queen for making Roz hate her half-troll self.

"Um, Roz?" Sally said, her voice soft. "Your horn changed."

"What?" Roz touched her horn. "What happened?"

"It's more curved and . . ."

Roz choked back a sob. "Longer."

"I felt new scales grow on my arms," Ji said.

"Chibo's eyes got bigger," Sally said. "And I feel different too."

Ji peered at her in the moonlight. "You're a little shorter," he said, and didn't mention that her hands looked more like paws than before.

"It's the price of magic," Roz said, her voice unsteady. "Even for a failed spell, we paid with part of our humanity."

"Yeah, well . . ." Ji swallowed. "The Ice Witch can still turn us back to normal."

"What kind of horrible spell steals your *self*?" Sally snarled.

"I can't imagine this happens to normal humans," Roz said. "It's only because we're—"

"*Ab*normal *non*humans?" Sally interrupted.

"—already changing," Roz finished.

"Doesn't matter," Ji said. "Let's go."

"Go where?" Chibo asked.

"Away from the knights and the queen," Ji said. "Toward a river. We need to find a better current."

"You want to try that again?" Sally asked.

"Talking to Ti-Lin-Su is the only way to fix this," he said. "Although, next time, let's wait till we're *sure* the water's right."

Sally started to answer, then caught sight of her hands. Hard pads covered her palms and blunt claws curved from her fingertips. She closed her eyes for a few seconds. After taking a shaky breath, she grunted and led them away, through thickets and over fallen trees. Roz touched her horn and sniffled in the darkness, while Ji tried not to think about the thick scales on his neck. They scrambled along gullies until they reached a hillside surrounded by birch trees. Four moons shone through the leaves, brightening the night.

"Four moons." Roz wiped tears from her face. "At least that's good luck."

"It's about time," Sally said.

Chibo tilted his head back. "Looks like two big moons to me."

"Can you hear any soldiers?" Ji asked Sally.

"Not a murmur. And do you see those hills?" She nodded past the trees. "The forest ends on the other side of them."

"Oh, good," Roz said.

"Er," Sally said. "Just past the ravine."

"Oh, bad," Chibo said.

"What ravine?" Ji asked.

Sally pointed almost straight downhill. "Take five steps and you'll fall in."

Ji squinted until his eyes picked out a rocky slope dropping into the gloom. Still, at least they'd reached the edge of the forest.

"We'll keep moving till dawn," he said. "Then we'll find a place to camp. We'll travel at night until we reach a river—"

"Is a river enough?" Sally asked Roz.

"Perhaps not as good as the canals and waterwheels of the city."

"Look at us, Roz," Ji said, spreading his arms. "We wouldn't last three seconds in the city."

"You would," she said in a sharper tone than usual. "Cover your arms and legs, and you'd pass for human."

His cheeks flushed. Now *Roz* was mad at him?

"We could find a mill in a village," Chibo suggested.

"What if we summon the Summer Queen again?" Ji asked. "We need to be sure the water's right."

"What if we transform into beasts completely?" Roz demanded. "That's worse than anything the queen could do—"

From deeper in the forest, an inhuman howl tore through the woods. Goosebumps rose on Ji's arms and his throat clenched. The howl wavered, deepened, then rose again, higher and sharper, like a razor slicing through flesh.

"Wh-what?" Chibo stammered as the howl continued. "What—"

"—is *that*?" Ji finished.

When the howl faded, Roz pressed her palm to her chest. "A kumiho."

"Those are myths," Ji said.

"What are they?" Chibo asked.

"They're not real," Ji said.

"In the stories . . ." Roz hugged herself. "In the stories, the Summer Queen commands them, like the terra-cotta warriors."

Ji gulped. The terra-cotta warriors were clay statues with jaguar helmets and tomahawks who the queen could bring to life as mindless, merciless soldiers.

"She summons them to hunt her enemies," Roz finished.

"She's still weak, though," Ji said, his voice tight with fear. "That's what Nin said. That she'd be weak for months after casting a Diadem Rite. Plus, there's no such thing as kumiho."

"What aren't they, then?" Chibo asked.

"Fox-demons," Roz told him. "With poisonous rattle-snakes for tails."

Chibo whimpered. "Oh, badness."

"Maybe Brace summoned them," Ji said. "I mean, if they were real. Which they're not. Let's go down the ravine, slow and careful—"

Another howl cut through the night. Roz fell silent, and frost touched Ji's soul. Then two more kumiho joined in the yipping: a chorus of eerie, unnatural hunger echoed beneath the moons.

"Forget 'slow and careful,'" Ji said. "Let's do this fast and reckless."

THE NEXT TEN minutes stretched into a nightmare. The moons leered from above, the trees clawed and scratched. The hillside tumbled away, and every time the kumiho howled, a dagger of fear plunged through Ji's heart.

Also, his arm still ached.

When they reached the bottom of the ravine, the hills blocked the moons-light and oozing muck chilled Ji's lizard feet.

"Could you glow a tad brighter?" Roz asked Chibo. She plucked a leaf off her horn.

Green light brushed a sad trickle of water on the ground. Sally crouched on a fallen log while Chibo clung to Ji's shirt, trembling from cold and fear. Roz hugged Nin's urn in her arms, her dress torn again. At least the remaining avocados were safe in her new backpack.

Ji opened his mouth to speak, and all three kumiho screamed. They didn't howl, they *yowled*: long, wavering shrieks.

"They haven't done *that* before," Chibo whimpered.

Sally scowled into the darkness. "They must've caught our scent."

"How close are they?" Ji asked.

"Closer than they were."

Ji rubbed his face. "Okay, enough running. Time to fly, Chibo."

"R-really?"

"Can you see the hilltop on this side of the ravine?"

"Not even almost." Chibo's inhumanly large green eyes peered upward. "It's up there?"

"More or less," Ji said. "Sally, go with him. Roz and I will catch up."

"No," Sally growled. "We're staying together."

"If they catch us—"

"We're staying together."

"Chibo can't get away by himself!"

"I can fly," Chibo said. "They can't catch me."

"You have to land eventually." Ji turned to Sally. "Roz and I will slow them down."

"Roz?" Sally's muzzle curled. "You're making *Roz* fight fox-demons?"

A shiver touched Ji's heart at the thought of putting Roz

in danger, but he said, "She's tough."

"So is Chibo," Sally said, her eyes fierce. "We're staying together."

"Fine," Ji muttered. "If things go wrong, it'll be your fault for once."

Climbing the other side of the ravine took twice as long. Four moons swept across the cruel sky while branches slapped Ji's face and roots snagged his feet.

Finally, he reached the top—and stared in surprise.

Dozens of smaller hills spread below him. A few were terraced with rice paddies, and the flooded fields reflected the three moons high in the sky and the fourth closer to the horizon. A chorus of frogs croaked in the darkness, and a water buffalo lowed in the mist. A road snaked through the fields, past a handful of homes and barns. Well, past the smoldering *remains* of homes and barns. Tendrils of smoke still rose from the charred wreckage.

Roz set Nin's urn down, and Chibo's wings slumped.

"She burned them," Ji said, a sick feeling in his stomach. "The Summer Queen burned the farms so we wouldn't find any food—or help."

"How'd she know we would come this way?" Sally asked.

"She must've told her knights to burn all the villages around the forest."

"I guess they were full of rice," Chibo said.

Roz frowned. "I hope they weren't full of *people*."

"They wouldn't have helped anyway," Sally growled. "They would've screamed if they'd seen us."

"I am beginning to dislike Her Majesty," Roz said, raising the hood of her cloak to hide her curved horn.

"Beginning?" Ji asked. "She turned us into beasts—"

"Like you care," Sally muttered.

"—and tried to stab us with water-branches," Ji continued. "She sent an army to capture us and then she thought, 'What else can I throw at them? How about a fox-demon with a poison snake tail?'"

"A kumiho doesn't have *a* snake tail," Roz told him.

"But you said—"

"A kumiho has *nine* snake tails."

Ji groaned and Sally swore. Then Chibo noted, "They've been quiet for a while. Maybe we lost them."

"Or maybe they stop howling before they strike," Ji said.

"Do they do that?" Chibo asked Roz.

"I don't know." She squinted toward the rice paddies. "I'm trying to remember what I've read about them."

"Remember fast," Ji said, starting downhill toward the burned farms.

"There's a poem about fox pearls," Roz said, hefting the urn and following.

"They wear pearls?" Chibo asked.

"The poem describes four glowing white orbs that give a kumiho strength."

Ji kicked a weed. "We're being stalked by pearl-powered demons?"

"Well, it might be a metaphor."

Chibo shifted his wings for light while they crashed through brambles; then Sally waded into a flooded field to get the kumiho off their scent.

"Can we use rice paddies to talk to Ti-Lin-Su?" Chibo asked. "This is a lot of water."

"There's hardly any current, though," Roz said. "And I don't want to make the same mistake again."

The cold stung Ji's feet. Before heading in deeper, he told Chibo to climb onto his shoulders. Roz carried Nin's urn on her hooded head, using her horn for balance, while Sally's waterlogged tail drooped pathetically. When the flooded fields finally ended, they followed a trail between two smoldering buildings—and a beast snorted from ten feet away.

A kumiho!

Fear burst like fireworks in Ji's chest. He gripped Chibo's skinny calves tightly, while Sally bared her fangs, and a massive head swiveled into sight. Blunt horns jutted, baleful eyes peered, and the water buffalo lowed.

Not a kumiho!

Ji almost laughed in relief, and Roz murmured, "Oh, thank goodness."

"Did you get left behind, boy?" Sally asked the water buffalo.

"Don't get too close," Ji told her.

"He's tame, you chuckle-knuckle," Sally said.

Ji eyed the beast. "He's like two thousand pounds. He's

stronger than Roz. Water buffalo are worse than horses."

"They're harmless," Sally said. "Though my moms once saw one fight off three alligators who were threatening her calf."

"He thinks I *am* an alligator," Ji mumbled. "Is that a rope around his neck?"

"Yeah, he's caught on something."

"Good," Ji said. "That means he can't eat us."

"Oooh, you poor baby," Sally crooned to the monster, "are you stuck here all alone? Let me get this off you." She reached toward the great, horned head and removed the rope. "There! Now you can graze."

"You furry types stick together," Ji muttered.

"What was that?" Sally asked.

"Nothing," Ji said.

She patted the water buffalo on the nose, then headed downhill again. Three moons shone overhead when they finally reached the main road, while the fourth touched the top of a pointy hill.

"Four pearls," Roz said, looking toward the lowest moon. "Four white pearls."

"You think the kumiho's strength comes from the moons?" Ji asked.

"I—I'm not sure."

"Shht!" Sally listened for a moment, then shook her head. "I thought I heard something."

"B-but you didn't?" Chibo asked.

She shrugged and kept moving. The silence stretched taut, frightening Ji more than howls and yowls. Only a sliver of the fourth moon still peeked from behind the hilltop by the time they waded through a last rice paddy.

"I'm f-freezing," Sally stammered as they climbed from the water.

Ji's teeth chattered in agreement.

"Not me!" Chibo declared. "Because sprites don't get cold."

"Or b-because you've b-been on my shoulders the whole time," Ji said.

Chibo considered. "Nah."

"Over there!" Roz said in a panicked whisper. "Look!"

She pointed her horn across the moons-lit landscape, hugging Nin's urn tight. Higher on the hillside, an animal crept into view. Except it wasn't an animal.

It was a demon-beast, mottled white in the light of the four moons.

7

THE KUMIHO LOOKED like a pale jaguar and moved with a deadly grace. Even its nine tails were sinuous, a writhing dance of snakes swaying above its muscular butt. Only its long head looked bulky and awkward, more like a bloated rat face than anything feline.

Chibo couldn't have seen more than an ugly patch of whiteness, but he still gasped. "Oh, badness."

"Shh." Ji clamped a hand over Chibo's mouth. "It hasn't spotted us."

"Where are the others?" Roz mouthed.

Sally scanned the hills. "I can't see them."

The kumiho's snout swiveled and sniffed. Despite the distance, the sense of venomous evil made Ji's knees weak. He barely managed not to whimper. Heck, he barely managed not to faint. The kumiho's tails swayed. White fur glimmered and snake tongues tasted the air, trying to get a fix on Ji and the others.

Chibo made a soft, fearful noise.

"Shhh," Sally hissed.

The kumiho screamed and Ji's bones turned to jelly. The demon took a step—then spun, quick as a silverfish.

The water buffalo thundered forward. Two thousand pounds of horn-tipped muscle hurtled at the demon. The kumiho crouched low, snake tails coiled. The buffalo's massive head thrust closer like a battering ram, and his hooves pounded the earth.

At the last second, the fox-demon pounced. A blur of milky paleness flashed. Demon claws slashed, and snake fangs struck at the buffalo's hide.

A bellow of pain echoed across the valley. The water buffalo fell to his knees, toppled to his side, and lay still. It was over. The fight was already over. The kumiho had killed two thousand pounds of sheer muscle in three seconds.

Ji wanted to cry, but he needed to run. He needed to get away, to get everyone away. He didn't have a plan, he didn't have a clue. He didn't have anything except panic as he reached for Chibo's hand—and missed, because Chibo was wrapping his wings around Sally for comfort.

Sally's furry muzzle clenched and her eyes shone with unshed tears. "Poor buffalo."

"Cry later!" Ji snapped, grabbing again for Chibo. "Run now!"

"I'm not crying," Sally said.

"Well, I'm wetting my dragonpants," Ji said, dragging Chibo away. "Because that kumiho is going to kill us all! Go!"

"It's coming!" Roz said, an edge of panic in her gravelly voice. "It's coming!"

"Chibo, take off!" Ji rubbed his face. "All of you, get away. This is my fault, and I—" He gulped, and lied with utter sincerity: "I've got enough fire to roast it."

"You haven't," Roz said.

"I stole fire from that jewelry box! I drained the gems to fuel my flames and now I'll—"

Sally snorted. "You're such a liar."

"Run, Sal—*please!*"

"We need to think," Roz rumbled. "The 'pearls' are moons. So long as four moons shine, the kumiho are free to hunt, but once a single moon sets, they'll vanish."

"We can't make a moon set!" Ji said.

"Oh, yes we can," Sally told him, loping away from the kumiho. "C'mon!"

"What are we—"

"Move!" she called over her shoulder.

Ji scooped Chibo into his arms and raced after Sally, following her from the farm into a field, toward the pointy hill with the moon peeking from behind the peak. When another yowl sounded, Ji glanced over his shoulder. Higher on the hillside, the kumiho stared at them, its predatory eyes glimmering in the predawn light.

"It sees us," Ji said.

"Run!" Sally yelled.

The kumiho leaped to a charred patch of ground, and loped past farms and furrows in a mottled-white flash.

"It's too fast!" Ji said.

Sally sped toward the pointy hilltop. "Shut up and *run*!"

With Chibo whimpering in his arms, Ji leaped over a weedy hedge and past a pile of dung. His heart punched his throat and his vision narrowed in terror. Roz thundered along beside him, hugging Nin's urn tight, while Sally leaped ahead, forging the path.

"C'mon, c'mon," she barked. "This way, faster!"

As Ji scrambled around a mound of rice hulls, he caught a glimpse of the kumiho prowling past the hedge. From this close, it was even more horrific: its pelt looked like rotting meat and its fangs jutted and dripped.

Its dead eyes stared at Ji and he stumbled over a charred plow.

Roz shouted, and Ji threw Chibo into the air. "Fly!"

Green light tinted the world. The kumiho stopped and yowled ferociously, enraged at the sight of its prey escaping. As Chibo's light dimmed, the demon loped closer. Ji scrambled to his feet and started running faster than he'd ever run before.

"Almost there!" Sally shouted.

"Almost . . . where?" Roz panted.

"Just run!" Sally barked.

Even as he sprinted past a makeshift shed, Ji saw the truth: they couldn't outrun a demon-beast. They were all going to die on this hillside, with three moons glowing high and the fourth slowly setting, with frogs croaking and the scent of smoke in the air.

Except *no*. Not all of them. He couldn't let that happen.

He'd never done anything harder than slowing down with a vicious kumiho on his heels. Still, he wrestled with his terror until his sprint became a run and his run became a trot. Finally, he halted completely. His knees almost buckled and his heart definitely stopped, but he turned to face the demon. This was his fault. Everything was his fault, and he'd pay the price to make it right.

"K-keep running," he whispered, too softly for anyone to hear. "I've g-got this."

When the kumiho prowled closer, the moons-light dimmed. Ji wanted to scream, but his voice didn't work. His legs didn't work either, and his brain was producing panic instead of plans. The kumiho bared its teeth. Black saliva dripped to the ground. The beast crouched to pounce, and Ji prayed that the others would get away. . . .

Then Sally bounded in front of him, shouted, "Hey, maggot-mouth!" and galloped away on all fours.

When the kumiho spun toward Sally, Roz grabbed Ji's

arm from behind and yanked him backward. She dragged Ji into a drained paddy, slimy with mud and stinking of fish. The kumiho stalked closer, screaming in rage. Ji's feet smeared trails in the muck and his terrified gaze tracked the swaying of nine snake tails.

The demon-beast sprang, cutting through the air like an arrow. Claws extended. Jaws wide. Fangs dripping venom. Thirty feet away, twenty feet away, arcing toward Ji and Roz in a single leap.

At ten feet away, the demon's dirty pelt started shimmering like smoke. In midair, the blotchy snout and muscular chest turned vaporous. The nightmarish head blurred into a foggy haze. The pale body feathered into dozens of wispy tendrils—and, like smoke in a breeze, the kumiho dissolved in the fading moons-light.

Ji gaped in disbelief, his knees wobbling. "The—it—the—"

"Um," Chibo piped from behind him. "Where'd the fox-monster go?"

"It un-un-unraveled. . . ."

"I told you so!" Sally crowed, leaping in front of him. "I told you we could make the moon set!"

"What are you talking abo—" Ji gasped in amazement. "Sally! You're a genius!"

She laughed. "I know!"

Ji looked toward the pointy hilltop. The fourth moon was completely—but just barely—hidden behind the peak. If he'd been five feet higher uphill, a tiny splinter of white would still be visible. Once the kumiho had crossed that line, the moon "set" and the demon vanished. That was where Sally had been leading them!

"You clever hobgoblin!" he said. "You saved us!"

"Oh!" Roz rumbled. "Oh, I see! Well done, Sally!"

"I don't see!" Chibo piped, landing in the muddy field. "What happened?"

"If you're five feet farther uphill, there are four moons and a fox-demon," Ji told him. "But right here, there's only three moons and her." He pointed to Sally. "Dame Sally the Magnificent."

"I'm glad *someone* was thinking." Roz tilted her curved horn toward Ji, her eyes narrowing. "I can't believe you tried to sacrifice yourself like that."

"Um. You're welcome?"

"Jiyong!" she snapped. "That was very brave and very wrong of you. You cannot simply let a demon eat you to save the rest of us."

"I couldn't think of anything else to do," he explained.

"That's not an excuse."

He actually thought it was a pretty good excuse. "Sorry."

"I'm not angry."

"You look angry."

"I'm not. I just—" Roz wrapped Ji in a sudden, fierce hug. "Promise that you'll never try anything like that again!"

"Sure," he lied.

"Promise me for real," she demanded.

"I promise for real," he said, though honestly what was he supposed to do? Let the kumiho kill them all?

"Jiyong," she said. "The next time they appear, I expect—"

"The next time?" he asked. "What next time?"

"Oh. Well, if their power is linked to four moons, then every time a fourth moon rises . . ."

"They'll come back?"

"I expect so, yes."

Ji rubbed his face. "Until they catch us."

"That strikes me as probable."

"It strikes me as terrifying." Ji took a shaky breath. "There's only four moons every five or six days, though, right?"

"The moons are unpredictable."

Sally led them from the muddy field onto a rocky path, and Ji said, "We'll keep moving until we can find a place to talk to Ti-Lin-Su. Even if it means traveling during the days."

"Isn't that exactly what the Summer Queen wants?" Chibo asked.

"Yeah, but we can't do anything else. The only question is, where can we cast the spell?"

"Canals," Roz suggested. "Or waterways or fountains."

"Fountains with lots of spouts," Sally said.

"How about a place not in the middle of a town?" Ji thought for a second. "Who can we talk to about the rivers? Someone who'll tell us where the current is strong or strange or—" He stopped. "Fisherfolk."

"Ask fisherfolk about the currents?" Roz nodded. "That's a good idea."

Sally plucked a twig from her arm. "Not as good as the hidden-moon thing, though, right?"

"Not nearly," Ji assured her.

"The next question is," Roz said, "where do we find fisherfolk who won't run away from us?"

"Send in the human-faced boy," Sally said.

Ji ignored her. "We'll follow the river to a fishing village. They'll know about any weird currents or whirlpools."

"So that's the plan," Roz said. "First we find the river, then a fishing village."

"Then Ti-Lin-Su," Ji said, "who'll lead us to the Ice Witch."

"Who will break this spell and turn us human again," Sally said. "And *then* I'll stop getting mud in my tail."

"Oh, no!" Chibo cried.

Ji's heart clenched in fear. "Did you hear something? Knights? Demons?"

"What? No! I just realized that seeing four moons wasn't so lucky after all."

8

THE WOODS GREW sparser as the hills became sloping fields and meadows. When dawn lightened the sky, Ji yawned hugely and they stopped to gorge on squishy avocados—and fell asleep.

Roz shook them awake in a panic. She'd heard the tromp of soldiers in the distance. Still half asleep, Sally guided them into a chilly stream, trusting the water to hide their scent and lead them to the river.

They slept in snatches the next day, dreading the kumiho at sunset and the soldiers at dawn. Only two moons rose, though, and they didn't hear soldiers again. The following evening, Ji took sentry duty while the others rested. Crickets chirped and mice rustled and three moons rose.

Ji hugged his knees, daydreaming about pan-fried crickets and honey-glazed mouse until something tickled the back of his hand. When he looked down, he saw an ant lion standing there, with a yellow mane and a ferocious stinger. It was smaller than before, though, and a paler red: casting the spell had drained some of Nin's ogreness.

"Oh, no," he groaned. "Nin?"

The ant lion waved its antennae.

Ji's breath caught. "Are you there? Nin? Say something!"

The ant lion climbed off his hand and wandered toward the colony. Ji crawled to the urn and watched three ant lions repair a fallen mound of dirt. A few more stood aimlessly on the leaves. What if the transformation was complete? What if Nin's true self was gone and only mindless ant lions remained? Like the urn was a funeral urn, and Roz was just carrying Nin's body around.

Tears sprang to Ji's eyes. He still remembered the last thing Nin had ever told him: *Take care of everyone, stone-friend.*

"I'm trying," he whispered. "But I couldn't even take care of *you*."

The ant-lion colony didn't answer.

The next day, Ji and the others crested a hill and spotted farmland with wary llamas guarding herds of sheep. Beyond that, the stream widened into a river. A village sprawled across both banks. Dozens of houses stood on stilts and a wooden bridge with fluttering banners arched across the river.

"A village!" Sally said.

Ji smiled. "Fisherfolk."

"Don't see any hiding places."

"No trees?" Chibo asked.

"No trees," Sally told him.

Chibo sighed. "No good."

"No problem," Ji said.

"No complete sentences?" Roz raised the hood of her cloak. "Though we are beasts at the moment, we needn't speak like animals. I hope that we break this spell before we're reduced to grunts and snorts."

Sally grunted.

Ji snorted.

Chibo giggled.

"Shall we continue?" Roz asked, a hint of humor in her gruff voice. "Or wait until nightfall?"

"I don't know." Ji squinted toward the river. "We've been lucky with the moons so far, but if a fourth one rises tonight . . ."

Roz frowned. "We can't simply stroll into the village in the daylight."

"I can," Ji said. "If I raise my hood and keep my sleeves down."

"I'm not letting you go alone," Roz told him.

"That's stupid. If they see us, they'll send for the knights."

A rare stubborn glint showed in Roz's eyes. "Not after what you did with that kumiho, Jiyong. We need to stay together."

"Fine. I'll sneak ahead and snag a cart. You can hide in back, and I'll drive."

"Snag?" Sally flicked her tail. "You mean 'steal'—and you don't know how to drive a cart. And you're afraid of horses."

"I'm not afraid of them! They just scare me."

Sally's tufted ears pricked with amusement.

"Won't someone notice if you steal a cart?" Chibo asked.

"Not if I'm sneaky enough." Ji's shoulders slumped. "But Sally's right: I can't drive a cart."

"We'll sneak closer together," Sally said. "Then we'll hide while you ask the fisherfolk, um . . . I don't know. How do you ask about a complex current?"

Ji widened his eyes and pretended to speak to a villager: "'My brother said he'd meet me somewhere, but I forget what it's called. You know, that place where the water current is all doolally? Where *is* that?'"

"You're a trifle too good at lying," Roz rumbled.

Ji flashed a grin. "It'll work, though."

Keeping low, they crept to the river. The cool air smelled of mud, and voices rose on the breeze, along with

74

the distant sound of an ax chopping wood. Climbing to a shrubby rise, Ji looked toward the village. A steady flow of people crossed the bridge, and wooden boats drifted in the river. A single fisherman or fisherwoman stood in each boat, gently poling against the current, while a flock of sleek black birds swam and dove around them.

"Weird boats," Ji said.

"Weird how?" Chibo asked.

"Each one has these crooked posts sticking out. Like the legs of an upside-down cockroach."

"Those are perches for the birds," Roz rumbled. "The fisherfolk train the birds to catch fish. They take the bigger fish and reward the birds with the smaller ones."

"Sounds like nobles," Ji said.

"There!" Sally pointed downriver toward a clump of bushes. "That's the perfect hiding spot."

"Perfect," Ji agreed.

The mud oozed around Ji's ankles and made horrible squelching sounds every time he took a step. Roz sank in even deeper and made noises even more disgusting. Ji almost teased her, but she looked so mortified that he kept his mouth shut. And when they reached the hiding place, it *was* perfect.

So perfect that it was already occupied.

A mud-splattered kid of five or six crouched behind the bushes, chewing on a pickled eel.

Sally froze.

Roz froze.

The kid spun toward them and cried, "It wasn't me!"

"Of course not," Ji said soothingly, stepping in front of the others. "We won't tell—"

The kid didn't listen. She—or he—scrambled from the bushes and churned through the mud of the bank toward the village bridge.

"Wait!" Chibo trilled.

"Don't be afraid," Roz rumbled.

"We're friends!" Sally growled.

The kid squeaked in fear and veered to one side, directly into a deeper patch of muck. With a panicked yelp, he—or she—sank to the waist in the mud.

"Mommy!" the kid wailed, still sinking. "Help! Help, I'm stuck!"

On the bridge, a few villagers turned toward the screams. A skinny woman dropped her basket. Even from a hundred yards away, Ji saw the horror on her face. As the closest fisherfolk started poling toward the struggling kid, the skinny woman leaped off the bridge and landed with a splash in the river.

"They're too far," Roz said. "They won't reach her in time."

"I'll get her," Sally growled.

"I'll go!" Ji grabbed her arm. "You stay out of sight!"

"Help!" the kid screamed.

"Dorinda!" the skinny woman shouted, splashing slowly closer. "Hold on!"

The mud sucked at Ji's feet as he raced toward the kid; it clung to his pants and splashing his cloak. He lunged forward, his legs aching and lungs heaving. He grabbed the kid's wrist and yanked. She rose an inch and he sank two. An instant later she dropped even deeper—first to her chest, then to her shoulders.

"Pull, pull!" the skinny woman screamed at him, as villagers gathered on the bridge. "Dorinda!"

Ji tugged with all his might . . . and couldn't free the girl. "I *can't*!"

"That's my daughter!"

"Grab the pole!" Roz roared from behind Ji. "Get ready!"

She stood on the bank, her hands cupped in front of her . . . with Sally balanced on her interlaced fingers. Roz heaved, and Sally hurtled through the air, somersaulted twice, and landed in the closest fishing boat. The black birds squawked in alarm as Sally grabbed the fisherman's pole and thrust it like a lance toward Ji.

"I can't reach!" Ji bellowed as the mud reached the kid's chin.

A flash of green light swept from the sky. Chibo grabbed the pole and carried it across the water. Ji desperately snagged the wet end of the pole with the claws of one hand while his other hand gripped the sinking kid.

Still holding the pole, Chibo zoomed in a circle to Roz. She grabbed the dry end of the pole, braced herself, and tugged. With one hand on the pole and one hand on the

trapped girl, Ji felt his arms stretch to the point of snapping. He clenched his fists, whimpering in pain . . . and
with a great splotching sound, the girl squelched free.

Ji toppled backward. The girl scrambled across his
chest, trailing muck across his face. She crawled to the
weedy bank, and Roz dragged Ji after her.

"Are you okay?" Ji asked, finally releasing the pole.

The girl took a deep breath. "Monster! *Monster!*"

"No, no!" Ji yelped, putting his hood up. "It's just mud,
it's just—"

"Snake-monster!" the girl screamed, scrambling away.

"Get away from her!" the skinny woman yelled at Ji.
"Get away!"

"We saved her life!" Ji said.

"Don't touch her!" the woman screamed. "Don't you
touch her!"

"If I hadn't touched her, she'd be dead!"

"Monsters!" the fisherman shouted, standing in his
boat. "Ogres!"

The skinny woman wrapped the crying girl in her arms.
"Shh, you're safe, you're safe now."

Children wept and shrieked on the bridge; adults bran-
dished axes and paddles and screamed, "Call the guard!
Monsters! They tried to eat Dorinda!"

"We did not!" Sally bounded to the riverbank. "We're
not even hungry!"

"We have avocados!" Chibo fluted.

78

For some reason, that didn't calm the mob. "Kill them! Kill the beasts!" The villagers swarmed toward a riverside path, weapons in their hands and hate in their eyes. "Kill the beasts!"

"Spread your wings, Chibo!" Ji shouted, raising his arms until his sleeves fell to his shoulders. His scales glinted, thicker and darker than a week earlier. "Roz, roar! Sally . . . hobgoblin!" He stepped toward the villagers. "Stop! Stop right there!"

"Roar?" Roz suggested.

"Rozario!" Ji hissed. *Louder!*

She snapped the pole in half and gave a half-hearted "Roar!"

The villagers didn't even slow. They surged forward. Rocks and sticks whipped at Ji . . . until Sally, almost as scary as a kumiho, yowled behind him. The villagers seemed to hit an invisible wall. Fear sprang into a dozen pairs of eyes, and callused fingers tightened on oars and scythes.

"We don't want to hurt anyone," Ji told them.

"You tried to eat Dorinda," a long-haired villager muttered.

"We don't eat people," Chibo said.

"You jumped out at her," the villager said. "You trapped her in the quickmud."

The rest of the mob muttered, and the fear in their eyes tightened toward anger. Ji knew that look. He knew you couldn't reason with anger and fear.

"Yeah, but you—you chased us off!" Ji told the mob, backing slowly away. "We're running away. Heroes, that's what you are."

A few villagers paused to consider. "Heroes?"

"That's right," Ji said. "We're running away now, and you'll never see us again."

"All we wanted was to find a fountain," Sally said.

"Get out of here!" the long-haired villager snarled. "Filthy monsters."

"Beasts! Ogres!" other villagers shouted. "Animals!"

"There's no fountain hereabouts," the skinny woman murmured, rocking her muddy daughter in her arms. "But there's the water clock at the manor. Follow the north branch of the river. Now get out—your kind isn't wanted here."

9

THE JEERS AND taunts of the villagers chased them into the woods. When the shouts faded, Roz bandaged Chibo's bald head where a rock had cut him. Nobody talked much; they were all still reeling from the hate in the villagers' eyes. They weren't human anymore. They weren't welcome in the human world.

At least not until they broke this spell.

"Okay," Ji said, scraping mud from his cloak. "We need Ti-Lin-Su to find the Ice Witch—"

"And now we know how to find her." Roz smoothed her tattered dress. "We'll cast the spell at this water clock."

"What's a water clock?" Chibo asked.

"A sort of watery clock," Ji explained.

Roz huffed. "A water clock measures time using the

flow of water through various bowls and channels and casks. Gears and wheels direct the current into marked containers, where each mark represents a different interval of time."

"Like I said," Ji told Chibo. "A watery clock."

"Well . . . yes." Roz paused and looked northward. "I expect we're heading for Turtlewillow Manor."

Sally looked at her. "There's a manor called Turtlewillow?"

"It's known for its collection of clocks." Roz started through the woods. "I had no idea that we were so close."

"So this clock's on an estate?" Sally asked.

"Yes. Generations of barons and baronesses have installed clocks on Turtlewillow property."

"Nobles are weird," Chibo said.

"I've heard the water clock is remarkable," Roz told him. "If the spell works anywhere, it will work there."

Ji scratched the scales on his shoulder and plodded northward. *If the spell works anywhere.* What if Ti-Lin-Su didn't know where to find the Ice Witch? What if the Ice Witch refused to break the spell? What if they were already too late?

That evening, they ate the last of the avocados as they hiked across muddy pastures, following the river by the light of three moons. Ji scanned the horizon fearfully until one of the moons dipped behind the trees. With only two moons in the night sky, they finally slept.

"We're getting close to an estate," Sally said, the next afternoon. "I smell stables."

"How about knights?" Ji asked.

Sally's nostrils flared. "I don't think so. Not close, anyway."

"Not close is good," Chibo said.

"We need to cross the river," Sally said. "The manor's on the other side."

She found a shallow spot where flat rocks lined one bank. Roz dropped crushed snails into the urn for Nin's ant lions to eat. Chibo spread his wings and drifted over the river, his toes trailing in the current. Sally unfastened the belt cinching her oversized shirt around her waist, then groomed her tail on a shaded rock.

Ji rinsed his face and cloak, watching the homey scene. "After we convince the Ice Witch to break the spell, we'll live like this all the time."

"Splashing in a quiet river?" Chibo asked.

"With nobody chasing us."

"If only the witch wasn't so hard to find," Ji said.

Sally tugged at a tangle in her tail. "Yeah, why couldn't she be like the footmen back at Primstone Manor?"

Ji scrubbed his hair with his dragon-y fingernails and remembered the manor. He'd spent most of his time cleaning boots and scraping pots and pans, but there'd been good moments, too. He'd hung around with Sally and listened to Roz read stories. He'd plotted to rescue

Chibo and even played strategy games with Brace, despite being forbidden to make friends with a noble. Of course, he'd also bowed his head to Posey and Nichol. Still, while they'd bullied Brace, the twins had mostly ignored the servants—as long as the servants never made them wait.

"Imagine that," Chibo fluted. "Just ring a bell and the Ice Witch comes running."

"If only it were that easy," Roz rumbled, her eyes day-dream-y. "If only we could just say the word and she'd come fix everything."

Sally gazed into the distance and Chibo heaved a sigh. Ji wrung water from his cloak and enjoyed the fantasy: Blink your eyes and find yourself standing in front of the Ice Witch. Blink them again, and she'd break the Diadem Rite spell and return everything to normal.

Then Sally pointed at a lizard basking on the rocks. "Hey, Ji! That looks like you."

"At least I'm not a doorbell," he said.

"I'm not adorable!"

"Only on the outside. On the inside you're scary."

"Um," Roz said from farther across the river. "Erm."

"On the inside," Sally told Ji, "you're *scaly*."

"Pardon me?" Roz rumbled. "Help!"

When Ji looked at her, horror clamped his chest.

A green eel had climbed Roz's legs and wrapped around her waist. Rising sinuously from the water, it was as thick as Ji's wrist. Lumps dotted the creature's skin, and smaller eels sprouted from its body and clung to Roz's backpack and elbow and Nin's urn.

Ji shouted and lunged toward her. The rocky riverbed tripped him, and he splashed face-first into the water. He thrashed closer, terrified and urgent—and Sally slammed onto his back, between his shoulders. Her weight dunked his head underwater; then she launched herself off him, leaping to help Roz. Ji swallowed a mouthful of muddy water. His hands shoved at the riverbed and he rose, gasping . . . just in time to see Sally tearing the eels away from Roz.

Not eels. *Vines* were uncoiling from the stream. Seaweed-y vines covered with lumps that sprouted into spikes and tendrils.

Roz couldn't use her hands to free herself because she needed to keep Nin's urn above the water. Instead, she started climbing the opposite bank, straining to get away. A few strands of seaweed snapped, but others wrapped tightly around her legs.

Chibo shouted, "What's wrong? What's happening?" while Sally tore at the vines with her hands and ripped at them with her teeth.

"Get away from the river!" Ji barked at Chibo. "Hover above—not too high. Don't—"

He lost track of what he was saying when he reached Roz. He splashed onto his butt in the shallow water and slashed at her legs with his scaly feet. His claws cut through a slimy vine that Sally had loosened, and Roz burst free.

The seaweed fell away, retracted into the churning, muddy water, and vanished.

Roz stomped up the bank with Sally, and Ji scrambled after her, gasping and dripping. Chibo landed beside them, babbling questions, while Roz flopped to the grass in a sprawl of half-troll limbs.

"Are you okay?" Sally asked her. "Are you hurt?"

"What *was* that?" Chibo demanded.

"I'm f-fine," Roz said. "Only f-frightened."

"Was it a kumiho?" Chibo asked. "They can't come out in daylight!"

"Seaweed rose from the stream," Ji told him.

"And tried to strangle Roz," Sally growled. "I thought the queen was weak. She's supposed to be *weak*."

"That's what the ogres said," Ji told her as he crouched beside Roz. The whole reason Nin had snuck into the city was to wait for the Summer Queen to cast the Diadem Rite. The ogres believed that casting the rite would weaken the queen—and that was when they'd planned to attack, to sneak through goblin tunnels and overthrow the crown.

"If she's weak, how did she send killer seaweed?" Sally asked.

"I guess she's getting stronger," Ji said. "She's probably been tracking us since we cast the spell."

"And we're about to cast it again," Sally said.

"Yeah, but this time we'll do it right," he said, trying to

sound confident. "This time we'll find Ti-Lin-Su. Right, Roz?"

"I don't know." Roz's shoulders started shaking beneath her cloak. "I—I've never read about anything l-like this."

Sally cocked her head. "Are you sure you're okay?"

"Of course. My skin is thick. Too thick." Roz started to weep. "L-like a rhino's. I . . . I cannot take it anymore! My skin, my horn. D-did you see how those villagers looked at me? I can't bear it any longer."

All of Roz's dismay and dread—all her disgust at her transformation—came out in a rush of tears and words. She hated what Brace and the Summer Queen had done to her. She hated what she'd become.

As Chibo and Sally comforted Roz, a knot of anger formed in Ji's heart. He made a silent vow. He wasn't as smart as Roz, he wasn't as tough as Sally, he wasn't as curious as Chibo . . . but he was meaner than any of them. And he'd make the queen pay for hurting Roz. He'd make Brace pay. He'd make everyone pay.

When a cloud drifted in front of the sun, Ji forced himself to unclench his fists and scan the pastureland for threats. He didn't see any. He didn't see anything except a far-off tower rising above the hills.

"What's that?" he asked.

Sally narrowed her eyes. "A clock tower."

"Turtlewillow?" he asked Roz.

She sniffled and nodded. "I imagine we're already on the outskirts of the estate."

"Okay. Let's stay away from water until we reach the clock, just in case the queen has any more surprises."

"Why isn't she weak?" Roz asked, taking a shuddering breath.

Ji gave a sudden laugh. "Why are *we* so strong?"

"What?" Chibo fluted.

"We robbed a coach, we escaped a kumiho. We cast a spell. A spell! Us!"

Sally lifted her muzzle in a fierce grin. "We saved a kid and found the water clock."

"That's right," Ji said. "And now we're going talk to Ti-Lin-Su and find the Ice Witch. Everything's going to be okay."

"As long as nobody spots us," Roz said, gazing worriedly across the fields.

Nobody spotted them. Instead, they spotted the water clock.

An aqueduct sloped across the countryside toward a high, square platform of granite blocks. On top of the platform, nine black bowls dangled from ornate bronze beams. Beside the platform, three bronze tanks, engraved with scenes from history, revolved slowly to the sound of whirring and clicking and splashing. A mechanism like a weathervane tilted and spun between the tanks, its outstretched arms covered in bells and cymbals.

"How ingenious!" Roz breathed. "The water clock must chime different tones at different hours!"

"I haven't heard any chiming," Sally said.

"I suppose the gears are disengaged." Roz frowned. "I wonder why."

A dirt path led downhill from the water clock to a gently waving cornfield. Stairs zigzagged down from the granite platform toward a pretty little cottage shaded by palm trees. Coals and embers smoldered in a shallow fire pit near a mound of dirt. Bees buzzed around a bowl of fruit on a picnic table, while mango trees fluttered over a cheery chicken coop.

Ji assumed the clock workers lived in the cottage, but he didn't see any. Still, the whole place looked peaceful and welcoming.

"Where is everyone?" he asked.

Sally cocked her ears. "Nobody's here now."

Ji eyed the coals burning in the firepit. "They haven't been gone long."

When he trotted closer to the clock, the scent of mango trees made his mouth water.

"Soldiers came through yesterday." Sally gestured toward hoofprints on the ground. "That's probably what I'm smelling."

Ji peered at the barn. "You don't hear anything?"

"Nope. I smell grilled turkey in the cottage, though."

"Let's eat!" Chibo piped. "Except shouldn't we cast the spell first?"

"Maybe we should wait for a moon to rise," Ji said. "And eat mangos for a while."

"Let's try our luck with the sun," Roz said, heading for the stairs.

The top of the water clock offered a view of the rolling pastureland and the cornfields stretching toward Turtlewillow Manor. The aqueduct flowed into slowly spinning bronze tanks with beaklike spouts that triggered valves and spigots. Water splashed into the dangling black bowls. When full, they tilted and poured into a wide, shallow central basin.

"Looks complex to me," Ji said.

"This should work quite well." Roz propped Nin's urn on the edge of the basin. "Everyone hold hands and . . . take care not to lose too much of yourself."

A reflection of the sun glinted in the water. For some reason, daylight didn't feel as mermaid-y as moonlight had. Still, Ji squinted and thought of Ti-Lin-Su. He couldn't quite picture her face, but the gurgling of the basin reminded him of her water garden. The rippling pools, the splash of her tail . . .

He focused on the sounds. A minute passed, then two more. The blob of the sun's reflection wobbled in the water's flow, but nothing else happened.

"Doing this in the sunlight feels wrong," Sally said.

Valves opened and gears clattered with a *click-slosh-whirl*. Water gushed from pipes and dripped from channels. *Click-slosh-whirl*. Ji stared at the sun's reflection until his eyes stung. *Ti-Lin-Su, Ti-Lin-Su, we need you, we need your help. Click-slosh-whirl*. Bowls filled, then tilted, emptying into puddles that swirled through pipes.

"Use your wings," Ji told Chibo. "You have the most magic."

"I do?"

"Sprite power worked last time," Sally said.

"Not entirely," Roz said.

"I'll try," Chibo said, unfurling his wings.

"We're too afraid," Ji said. "We're not pouring enough of ourselves into the spell like we did the first—"

The instant Chibo's wings touched the basin, Ji felt as if he'd plunged into the swirling water. Without moving an inch, he was carried along like a twig in the rapids. His tongue thickened and his forehead itched. Claws sharpened from his toenails and—

"Shut up!" Sally said. "Listen!"

Ji didn't hear anything except the *click-slosh-whirl*. "Nobody's talking!"

"Shh!" said Roz.

"Oh!" said Chibo.

"Click slosh whirl," said the water clock.

"See?" said Sally.

"What?" said Ji.

"Whick closh swirl," said the water clock.

"That's Lady Ti-Lin-Su!" Roz told him. "I know her voice!"

"Wish ogrsh lan," the water gurgled. "Ays wish. Ice witch ogre lands."

"I *am* magic!" Chibo beamed, his green eyes shining. "Did she say 'Ogrelands'?"

In the basin, the sun's reflection shimmered into Ti-Lin-Su's face. "We heard you calling. . . . reached out at riverbank . . . help carry you . . . Shummer Queen heard too. Stay hidden. Wash fur traps. . . ."

"Fur traps?" Sally asked.

"*For* traps!" Ji snapped. "She's saying 'Watch for traps'!"

"Orgrelandsh." Ti-Lin-Su's faced distorted in the swirling current. "Search for Ice Witch in the Ogrelands. She issh . . ."

"She's where?" Ji asked. "Where in the Ogrelands?"

"Whee don't know her eshact locashun. You musht shearch high and deep. . . ."

The image faded and Roz gasped. "No!"

"What?" Ji asked, as the spell shattered. "What's wrong?"

"M-my fingers," Roz stammered. "My fingers."

She raised her three-fingered hands. Three-fingered, not four. Not anymore. She'd lost fingers, and her face looked more troll-like, her features coarser and her skin more granite flecked.

"This spell is a fire that burns our humanity for fuel," she whispered.

"I can't—" Sally growled. "I can't cover my claws anymore."

When Ji turned toward her, he almost whimpered. Her muzzle was longer and her legs were slightly crooked, like a dog's legs. And Chibo's shirt ripped as his hunchback swelled, while his eyes grew bigger than any human eyes.

Looking away, Ji touched his itchy forehead and felt lumps. "What's on my head? What are they?"

"Bumps," Sally told him, her voice more growly than ever. "Two little bumps."

Chibo spread a second pair of wings, and Ji's world narrowed into fear and disgust. Betrayed by their own bodies, warping into misshapen monsters. Losing fingers, growing horns. It was too much; the price they'd paid was too high. . . . And for a few minutes, horror won.

10

"EVERYONE BREATHE," ROZ finally said, stroking Chibo's bald head. "We learned how to fix this. We contacted Ti-Lin-Su and now we know to head for the Ogrelands."

"Except what happens once we're there?" Sally growled. "We still don't know how to find the Ice Witch."

"We'll talk to Ti-Lin-Su again, or we'll ask the ogres," Ji told her as he started down the stairs of the water clock. "For now, let's eat. I'm starving."

"That grilled turkey does smell good," she said.

While Sally prowled to the cottage, Ji frowned toward the mango trees. Three blue-bat boxes—which looked like crosses between birdhouses and beehives—hung from the trunks, with dozens of flower petals littering the ground beneath them. Weird.

"There are coconuts on the palm trees!" Roz said, lumbering past.

Ji squatted to look at the flower petals—and they weren't flower petals. "What the heck?"

"What's wrong?" Chibo asked.

"There are dead blue-bats on the ground," Ji told him. "Hundreds of dead blue-bats."

"Poor blue-bats," Chibo said, his huge eyes sad. "They're so little and so blue."

"The nobleman in the library coach said something about them dying off. That's why he was returning to his estate—"

"And there are papayas on the picnic table!" Roz called.

Ji raised his head, like a deer scenting wolves. "Wait."

"What's that?" Roz asked, glancing over her shoulder.

Ji looked at the tomatoes. He looked at the mound of dirt beside the cottage, then at the fresh papayas on the picnic table. Fresh fruit, and the delicious scent of grilled turkey? No people anywhere? And where had the mound of dirt come from?

"Stop!" he shouted. "Roz, wait—nobody move!"

"Beg pardon?" Roz asked, and took one more step toward the picnic table.

Her trollish foot, barely contained by a patched slipper, touched the ground . . . and disappeared. Her other foot and both legs followed, because that wasn't the ground: Roz had stepped onto a camouflaged sheet of canvas scattered with mango leaves.

Her cloak billowed and she disappeared from view, falling into a deep pit. A crash sounded and she shouted in pain.

Ji started running before he knew what he was seeing. The pit gaped in front of him—a trap big enough to hold a lion. The picnic table was gone, swallowed along with Roz. Nin's urn rolled to a halt beside the smoldering fire pit.

"I'm coming!" he yelled, but took only two steps before a yellow cloud erupted from the pit, filling the air. He skidded to a halt. "Roz! Roz?"

"I'm okay," she said, her voice shaky and muffled. "I—I landed on a sack of chalk dust or, or—"

"Chibo, get over here!" Ji yelled. "I'm lost in this dust! Roz, keep talking so we can find you."

"What shall I talk about?" Roz asked.

"Anything!"

"Um, I could tell the story of Mino and Mano?"

"I don't care! Just keep talking."

"Well, Mino and Mano were the first two mages. When the Summer Queen took the crown, she performed a ritual to give them fragments of her power."

"Sally!" Ji called. "Climb the clock and look out for trouble!"

"I'm on it!" Sally called from outside the dust cloud.

"What happened?" Chibo asked as a faint green wing

sliced through the swirling yellowness. "Roz fell in a hole?"

"A trap," Ji told him. "The Summer Queen knew we'd need a place like this."

"A place like what?"

"Like with crazy currents." Ji groped blindly forward. "She must've told her soldiers to dig a hole, and now Roz is stuck and—" A scary thought occurred to him. "And this yellow dust is a signal to them!"

"To who?"

"Her knights! I bet they're hiding far enough away that Sally can't hear them, just waiting for a big yellow cloud. Where are you?"

"Coming!" Chibo fluted from nearby.

"Yeah, and *they're* coming too. Keep talking, Roz!"

"We're almost at the pit," Chibo said, taking Ji's hand. "I can feel the edge with my wing."

"Um, Mino and Mano wished to please the queen by growing stronger," Roz said, her voice trembling. "Except they'd been granted power by the same spell. So, as Mino grew more powerful, Mano weakened. That's the price of Balance."

With the scaly toes of one foot, Ji felt the ground fall away. "We're here, Roz!" he called, kneeling at the edge. "Follow my voice. Can you reach my hand?"

A crash sounded. "It's too deep! I can't!"

"They're coming!" Sally growled. "I hear hoofbeats."

"Keep telling the story!" Ji told Roz, mostly to keep her calm. Well, mostly to keep *all* of them calm.

"Er, Mino gathered power," Roz said, "trying to save his husband. But the more power he used, the weaker Mano became. That is Balance. Remember how Isalida mastered woodland magic but lost her self and turned into a forest? Well, Mano died."

Ji chewed his knuckle as she spoke. Soldiers were galloping closer every second, but how do you get a half troll out of a pit trap?

"If you strengthen one part of a spell, you drain another," Roz continued. "You empty yourself, you lose yourself."

"I see them!" Sally yelped from above. "A dozen knights, riding fast!"

"I have a plan!" Ji shouted. "Chibo, fly out of here. Sally, tell him how to reach you!"

When a breeze thinned the dust cloud, Ji caught a glimpse of Chibo soaring away. In the pit, Roz stretched upward but her trollish hands couldn't reach the edge. Hoofbeats sounded, and a woman shouted orders. Ji couldn't make out her words as he sat on the edge of the hole, his legs dangling inside. *Okay. Here goes.*

"What's your plan?" Roz asked as he took a breath. "What are you—"

He slid in and landed on the cracked picnic table. He fell onto his butt and stared at the swirling yellow dust.

"Jiyong!" Roz said. "What on earth is your plan?"

"Ow," he told her.

"Now you're trapped too!"

Ji looked through the thinning dust toward the early evening sky. "Sally! Lead Chibo away! I'll stay with Roz!"

"Is that your plan?" Roz scowled at him. "If you haven't a plan, Jiyong, I warn you—"

"I have a plan!"

"What? To keep me company in a trap?"

"No!" he lied.

"If you get hurt . . ." Her eyes gleamed. "You have no right. You have no right to put yourself in danger for me."

"We're staying together. Sally was right. We stay together."

Roz snorted in angry amazement. "You just sent her and Chibo away!"

"That's different!"

"How is that possibly different?"

"Because shut your ricehole!" he explained.

"Jiyong," she rumbled, her voice soft and dangerous, "I cannot allow this. We know where the Ice Witch is! We can't let them catch us now. I'll lift you toward the edge, and you'll scramble out of here."

He frowned. "I'm not leaving you."

"You'll come back for me," she said, grabbing his arm. "You'd *better* come back for me."

"Hey!" he said, trying to tug away. "Let go!"

"I beg your pardon," she said. "But this is going to sting."

"Roz, don't—" he started, and she threw him from the hole.

The world spun: the sky, the cornfields, the sky, the water clock. Then he slammed to the ground ten feet from the fire pit. His arm ached and his side throbbed. Smoke stung his eyes, though most of the yellow dust was gone.

"Stupid troll," he groaned to Nin's urn.

"I heard that!" Roz said from inside the pit. "Now go and hide!"

A horse nickered nearby, and armor jangled. Ji didn't waste time looking for the knights, though. He wrapped Nin's urn in a tight hug, lifted it off the ground, staggered three steps, and—

Thunk.

An invisible hand shoved the urn. Ji lost his footing. As he stumbled toward the fire pit, he caught a glimpse of a crossbow bolt sticking from the urn. That was what had shoved him. Then he fell, and the urn, spewing dirt, rolled into the fire pit. Ji scrambled to pull it from the coals, but two more bolts stabbed the ground inches from his outstretched hand.

"By all the moons," a woman said behind him, "you look more monstrous than ever."

Ji knew that voice. Lady Nosey was the daughter of Baroness and Baron Primstone . . . except her name was actually Posey. Ji called her "Nosey" because she looked down her nose at servants. Her twin brother's name was

Nichol, but Ji called him "Pickle" because he was always sour.

She sat astride an evil-looking warhorse, idly reloading her crossbow. She was petite and pretty, with gold-painted braids in her jet-black hair. She was everything a young noblewoman should be, except kind. Well, and except jeweled: she wasn't wearing any jewelry, not a necklace or a bracelet or even a pinky ring. Nothing Ji could use to spark dragonfire.

Armored knights flanked Nosey. Two of them pointed crossbows at Ji's chest, and the others held coarsely woven nets.

"I give up!" Ji raised his hands in surrender. "Just let me pull my urn out of the fire."

"Perhaps if you ask properly," Nosey said.

Anger tightened Ji's stomach, but he didn't know how long ant lions could survive in burning coals, so he bowed his head. "May I please pull the urn out of the fire, Lady Posey?"

"That's not 'properly'!" she declared, her warhorse prancing beneath her. "Her Majesty decreed that if my brother and I caught you, she would make us a duke and a duchess. You should address me as 'Your Grace.'"

Ji stared at her. He was impressed despite himself. "No way. A duchess?"

"I know!" Nosey's smile looked almost human. "Can you believe it!"

"Wow. I mean . . . wow."

"Duchess Posey." She holstered her crossbow with a flourish. "My mother will be over the moons."

"That's kind of awesome. With an estate and everything?"

She nodded. "A few thousand acres."

"Whoa. You're evil, but that's cool."

"Evil?" she said. "Me? You're a beast and a traitor and a . . . beast! What is sprouting from your head, goat horns?"

"I'm not the one who's a traitor! I worked for your family for years, and now you're trying to kill me."

"A small price to pay to protect humanity."

"That's easy for you to say!" Ji sputtered. "They're going to kill Roz, too, and she's wellborn."

"Barely," Nosey said, though her gloved hand tightened on the reins. "She's barely wellborn."

"She never did anything wrong."

Nosey's face clouded. "Perhaps not, but . . . she must serve her queen."

"We don't want to die," Ji said. "Please—"

"And *we* don't want the realm to fall," Lord Pickle interrupted, trotting closer on a warhorse that matched his sister's. "We don't want tens of thousands of people to die."

"What would you do, if you were me?" Ji asked.

"I'd serve my queen."

"Keep telling yourself that," Ji murmured, before

raising his voice. "Please, Your Grace, may I drag the urn out of the fire?"

"Absolutely not. I've seen what you do with fire." Pickle turned to the knights. "Secure him!"

Three nets soared through the air at Ji. Heavy hooks whistled and spun. Ji scrambled sideways . . . too slowly. A line of fire burst along his back as the nets hooked into his flesh.

"This is the Winter Snake?" a knight in a crested helm asked.

The Winter Snake? They thought Ji was the Winter Snake? That wasn't even a real thing. It was a myth about a flesh-eating serpent, a devourer of children, a poisoner of wells. A threat to everything decent and good and alive.

Ji gasped with pain at the hooks. "I'm not . . . the Winter Snake."

"You're a hatchling," the knight said, "and our job is to make sure you never grow up."

"Now!" Sally yelled.

The knight half turned at the shout but still managed to whack Ji with her mailed fist. Pain burst in his head and the world spun into a wobbling blur. Swords whispered from sheaths, horses danced and whinnied. Dull impacts sounded. *Thump! Thump-thump!*

Ji blinked tears from his eyes and saw yellow-green rocks falling from the sky.

No, not rocks. Coconuts. One hit the ground a foot

from Ji, and emerald wings soared above.

"Eat coconuts, chuckle-knuckles!" Chibo fluted, dropping another coconut at a target he couldn't see.

"Get the urn," Ji mumbled, dizzy from the blow to his head. "Sally, get Nin!"

"Kind of"—she grunted—"busy at the moment."

Fine. He'd do it himself. With a whimper, he pulled a hook out of his side. Blood trickled and pain flared—and a snarling fur ball bounded past him. Sally ducked a sword, then leaped onto a saddle behind a knight. The horse reared and the knight crunched to the ground as Sally somersaulted away.

A dart whizzed past Sally's tail, and Nosey shouted, "Don't hurt her if you don't have to!"

Ji yanked another two hooks from his skin, his vision blurred with tears. Horses stomped and knights yelled. Crossbows twanged. Blows landed with *thunk*s and *clank*s.

"Catch that hobgoblin!" Nosey yelled at the knights. "She's half your size and— *Yiiiii!*"

"Sorry," Sally growled. "Were you using that?"

"My hair!" Nosey shrieked. "You beast!"

Sally grunted at a meaty *thud* and fell silent. A ragged cheer sounded from a couple of knights. When Ji's vision cleared, the nets wrapping his face seemed to divide the world into segments. Then something caught his eye: a skinny black-and-gold rope draped across one of the nets that wrapped him.

Not a rope! A braid.

A gold-painted braid that Sally must've cut from Posey's head. When Ji snorted a laugh, a knight smacked him again and his world turned black.

The final hook ripped from Ji's shoulder and he woke with a moan of pain. His teary eyes sprang open. The evening wavered around him. Muttered words and loud whinnies sounded, along with the crackle of the dying fire.

A sharp edge pricked Ji's neck, and a shape loomed over him. He blinked a few times. The nets were gone, but Lord Pickle was holding a sword to his throat.

Moving just his eyes, Ji peered around the water clock yard. Two moons hovered in the darkening sky. Chibo and Sally and Roz stood inside a ring of mounted knights. Chibo's lip was bloody, and leather cords bound Sally's front paws. Lady Nosey's horse cantered at the front of the knights pointing spears at Roz, who was wrapped in heavy chains. Also, Nosey was missing a few of her gold-painted braids—and one of them was in Ji's lap.

"Get moving," Lord Pickle said, tapping Ji's cheek with the flat of his sword.

Ji wrapped the gold-painted braid around his fist. He glanced at the fire pit as he stood, and his stomach curled at the sight of Nin's urn on the burning coals. A glut of dirt smoldered in the fire. No ant lions moved— but at least Ji didn't see any dead ones. Maybe they'd run off before they'd been burned.

He knew what he needed to do. He had a plan. A stupid plan, but a plan. His grip tightened on the gold-painted braid, and—

A strange wind rose. Hot and dry: a strong, whipping desert wind. The leaves of the coconut palms flapped. Embers swirled and warhorses nickered. The faint smoke of the fire thickened, blackened, then braided into a figure: a lanky teenager mounted on a warhorse and wearing smoky armor. Brace. Well, *Prince* Brace now, casting a spell to make himself appear in the smoke even though he was probably miles away. A moment later, another smoky figure appeared: a hulking man with broad shoulders and a bald head. That was Mr. Ioso, one of the queen's mages. The two of them rode smoky warhorses from the fire until they floated in the air above the pit.

"Good news, Prince Brace," Lady Nosey said, urging her horse closer. "The trap at the water clock worked perfectly."

Brace's smoky gaze swept the yard. "Well done, Lady Posey, Lord Nichol."

"Thank you, my prince," Lord Pickle said.

"You trapped us, Prince Brace," Roz said, her gruff voice gentle, "but you are trapped as well. If you order our deaths, you'll never escape from that. Once you're crowned, you'll live for hundreds of years knowing that you killed your friends."

Brace shifted on his saddle. "And saved my realm."

"What kind of realm turns you into a murderer?"

A muscle twitched in Brace's face. "The only one we have. Look at yourself, Roz. You're a horror."

"My prince," Mr. Ioso said, leaning closer to Brace, "I suggest that we drag the creatures to the river to finish the sacrifice immediately."

Ji's jaw clenched. If they reached the river, Brace would cast the Diadem Rite. A tree would rise from the water, with sharp branches to impale Ji and the others—branches that would drain their souls to feed Brace's crown. They'd die and he'd grow stronger: powerful enough to protect the human realm.

Except, at the word "sacrifice," Pickle had glanced at Sally and frowned. Like he didn't want to hurt Sally, like he cared about her. *Interesting*. Back at Primstone Manor, Ji had noticed that the twins had a soft spot for cuteness.

"Her Majesty prefers that we conclude the Diadem Rite in the Forbidden Palace," Brace told Mr. Ioso.

"Surely that was merely a suggestion, my lord," Mr. Ioso said.

"Sally!" Ji hissed. "Sally!"

One of her tufted ears twitched.

"Look cute," he whispered, too quietly for anyone without hobgoblin ears to hear. "Look cute for the twins!"

Sally glared at Ji, but then she widened her big eyes and shifted her tufted ears and fluffed her fluffy fur. And holy guacamole, Ji couldn't believe how adorable she looked when she tried.

"Now beg for our lives!" he said in an urgent undertone. "Cry big, fat, heartbreaking tears!"

"Have you no honor?" Sally growled to Brace. "Standing here talking about killing unarmed foes."

Ji scowled. She needed to whimper and purr, not talk like *Sally*! Still, when Lady Nosey and Lord Pickle saw her, he heard them gasp at her sheer adorability. They even glanced at each other, like maybe they agreed with her.

"That's what brigands do," Sally continued. "Not highborn nobles."

"Perhaps the creature has a point, my lord," Lady Posey told Brace, though her fascinated gaze kept drifting toward Sally.

"Bring them to the river," Mr. Ioso ordered, "so Prince Brace can complete the rite once and for all."

Lord Pickle cleared his throat. "Of course the *others* must be dealt with, Mage Ioso, but perhaps we should spare the hobgoblin—"

"I didn't ask you," Mr. Ioso said, sending a rope of smoke from his right hand to wrap around Pickle's neck like a noose.

Pickle made a horrible choking noise as the rope lifted him from his saddle.

"No!" Nosey shouted, spurring her horse toward her brother. "Stop!"

"Release him!" Brace told Mr. Ioso. "Her Majesty

108

prefers that the beasts be brought to the Forbidden Palace, so that is what we'll do."

"As you wish, my prince," Mr. Ioso said, and made a fist.

The smoky noose dropped Pickle, who fell gasping to the ground.

"You can't trust them," Sally growled to Nosey. "They'd kill your brother just as fast as they'd kill mine."

Pickle pushed himself to his knees and Nosey watched Mr. Ioso with a furious glare. At Primstone the twins had been selfish and mean, but they weren't killers. There was good in them. Surely they'd refuse to help Brace and the queen commit murder.

"Bring the beasts to the city, Lady Posey," Brace said, his voice soft. "Serve your queen well, and receive your reward."

After a moment, Nosey bowed. "Of course, my prince."

Ji felt his lip curl. So much for refusing to help with murders. The twins were utterly useless: they cared too much about being good, loyal, and obedient.

"You have no honor," Sally growled.

"Keep your mouth shut, animal," Brace said, and raised his right hand.

His smoky fingers wafted away in the breeze. The smoke that formed him and Mr. Ioso began swirling and shifting, breaking apart as he stopped casting the spell.

"Don't do this," Roz rumbled to Brace. "You're better than this."

"I'm sacrificing a handful of lives to save thousands. That makes me a hero."

"You're wrong. Killing us just makes you a killer."

For a moment, Brace simply looked at her, his smoky form unraveling.

"You used to have kindness, Brace," Roz rumbled. "You used to have heart."

"Now I have responsibility," Brace told her, and faded into a thread of smoke, like the final breath of a dying fire.

11

THE MANGO TREES shriveled and blackened. A silence fell. The only sounds were the gurgle of the water clock and the pop of embers. Brace and Mr. Ioso had vanished, but the knights remained—pointing spears at Roz and crossbows at Sally and Chibo.

"Get moving." Lord Nichol nudged Ji with the flat of his sword. "Join the others."

"You don't want to do this," Ji told him. "Look at Sally. *Look* at her. Do you really want them to kill her?"

Nichol sighed. "Of course not, but—"

"Please, let us go," Ji begged. "Please. We'll take off, we'll disappear—"

"—but we must obey our queen," Nichol finished. "We have to."

"In that case"—Ji took a breath—"I'm giving you one chance."

"One chance for what?"

"To stay uncooked," Ji told him, and lifted the gold-painted braid in his fist.

"Posey!" Nichol said, stepping backward. "The queen said not to let him near jewels or *precious metal*!"

"It's paint," Lady Posey said. "He's bluffing."

"*Gold* paint," Ji snarled. "Why do you think Sally threw it to me?"

"Adorable or not," Posey muttered, touching the spot where her missing braid had been, "that hobgoblin will pay."

"You saw what I did in Summer City," Ji told the knights. "And look at me now. I'm more snake than human. I'll burn you to ash."

A few of the knights cast nervous glances at one another, but the one who had punched Ji drew her sword. "The lizard is lying! The Winter Snake is also called the King of Lies! Serpent-Tongue, the Truthkiller."

"You have one chance," Ji said. "Leave this place before I count to ten, or suffer the consequences!" He deepened his voice. "For I am the Winter Snake and I command powers that you cannot imagine."

This time, even the knight who'd punched Ji looked worried—which was great, except for one thing. Posey was right. Ji was bluffing. *Of course* he wasn't the Winter

Snake. He couldn't raise a single spark from gold paint.

"It's not true," Posey said tentatively. "Grab him."

"YOU SHALL BURN!" Ji raised the gold-painted braid overhead. Because why not? He had nothing to lose. When they realized for sure that he was bluffing, they'd stomp him into mud . . . but that's exactly what would happen if he *didn't* bluff. "I CALL DOWN FIRE UPON YOU!"

Nothing happened, of course.

No fire sparked.

No smoke rose.

And worst of all, no knights fled.

"When I'm good and ready!" he continued. "After I count to ten . . ."

Posey glanced at Sally and looked almost disappointed. "Lock him in chains. We've a long journey to the Forbid—"

"Aiiiii!" A knight's cry cut her off. "My leg! Fire, fire!"

Two of the horses screamed and reared. Another knight yelled, and his horse made a horrible shrieking noise.

"Flames burn them!" Ji bellowed, keeping up his act. "Fire and ash at my command!"

Posey's horse squealed and spun. One rear hoof lashed out, barely missing Roz's face. Nichol screamed and Posey shrieked. The first knight galloped off wildly and four other knights followed, borne away by bolting horses. The remaining knights slashed at the air with swords and spears, as if they were beating back invisible flames.

Tears of pain ran down Posey's face. Her jaw clenched and her horse bucked. For one moment, she glanced at Sally with what looked like relief. Then she yelled, "Retreat! Retreat!"

Knights shouted, beat at their armor . . . and galloped away with Posey and Nichol, leaving Ji and the others alone at the water clock.

"Invisible flames!" Sally whistled. "Awesome!"

"I couldn't see them," Chibo said, sounding disappointed. "I missed the invisible flames."

"Nobody saw them!" Sally told him. "They're *invisible*."

"There were no flames," Roz rumbled. "Did you feel any heat? Ji, what on earth just happened?"

"I . . . don't know." Ji looked at his scaly hands. "Maybe dragons do that?"

Maybe ant lions do that, Sneakyji! a voice said inside his mind.

Ji's heart turned gleeful somersaults. That was Nin! A colony of ant lions couldn't talk out loud, so Nin communicated by speaking directly into the minds of the others who'd survived the Diadem Rite.

"Nin!" he shouted, tears of relief springing to his eyes.

Maybe ant lions crawl mouse-quiet onto horses and inside armor and buttsting all at once!

"He's back! They're back!"

Sally's muzzle raised in a smile. "Where are you? Say something!"

114

We're here, there, and everywhere, Sallynx!

"Holiest guacamoliest," Chibo breathed, his four wings spreading happily.

Ji laughed. "We thought you were dead, Nin, you stupid ogre!"

"Oh, thank goodness!" Roz rumbled, snapping her chains. "Oh, Nin. Oh, thank goodness!"

Ji looked at the blackened urn in the embers of the fire. "But—but where are you? Still in the urn?"

Only one of us is still urnside, Nin told Ji. *Too fieryhot for the rest. Most are creepycrawling in the tinymountain.*

Ji glanced at the mound of dirt, barely visible in the twilight. "Over there?"

And the rest are buttstinging horses and knights.

"Poor horses." Sally plopped to the ground, grabbed a fallen sword with one of her rear paws, and cut the leather cords binding her wrists. "I hope they're okay."

"They're warhorses." Ji paused. In the faint light of three moons, a speck launched from Nin's blackened urn and flew toward him. A single ant lion, glowing a dull red. "Is that the queen?"

The lionqueen egghatcher! The tiny ant lion landed on Ji's nose. *We needed—*

"Hot!" Ji batted at the ant lion. "Hot! My nose!"

We needed heat to hatch a queen. The ant lion flew off, zigzagging toward the mound of dirt. *Did Missroz put us on the blazefire? Clever Missroz!*

"I had no notion that ant-lion queens require heat to hatch," Roz said.

Of verycourse! How else could she hatch?

"I'm just so glad," Roz rumbled, beaming at the ant lions.

Ji scanned the freshly dug earth until he spotted the trail of ant lions. "C'mon, Roz, over here! Nin, gather all your . . . *yous* together. We'll fill Roz's backpack with dirt and plop you all inside."

Avocado rinds! Nin said when the first ant lions crawled into the backpack. *Our favoritemost food, after roast sweetbeets with spicy peppers. Are they called "rinds" or "skins"?*

"Rinds, I think," Roz said.

Or peelskins!

"Well, I suppose—"

Rindpeels?

While Nin chattered on, Ji scooped dirt into the backpack in the light of the three moons. Beside him, Sally dug like a dog with her front paws.

"Never tell me to look cute again," she said, too quietly.

"I don't know what your problem is."

"Jiyong," she said. "Just don't."

"Fine," he muttered, though he still didn't understand.

If *he* had to look cute to save everyone, he'd look cute. If he had to beg, he'd beg. If he had to steal or cheat or lie, he'd steal or cheat or lie. As far as he could tell, he'd do anything. Maybe that made him dishonorable. Maybe it made him monstrous like a Winter Snake. He didn't care. Roz had smarts and Sally had dreams, but Ji only had *them*, and he couldn't imagine a line he wouldn't cross for them.

When they finished filling the pack, Roz scooped ant lions onto the dirt. "Is that all of you, Nin? Are you comfortable?"

We're snug as a rugbug!

Ji grabbed the straps. "Now let's go."

Once we dig chambers, we'll be snugger than a mugger.

"We don't have time for—" Ji grunted, unable to lift the pack. "Stupid dirt."

With one three-fingered hand, Roz swept the pack onto her back. "You can't blame dirt for being heavy."

That's a cleverwise saying! Nin announced. *"You can't blame dirt for being heavy!"* You are wise as a troll, Missroz.

"She *is* a troll," Sally said.

A half troll, Nin told her. *Nobody is a truetroll until they Begin.*

"Begin what?"

Being truetrolls, Sallynx! The Beginning is a thunderclap passagerite that turns ogres into trolls. A grand ceremony of—

"The knights will come back soon," Ji interrupted. "We need to move. Is everyone ready?"

We were hatched ready, Nin said.

"Where are we going?" Sally asked Ji.

"The Ogrelands," he said.

"Wait!" Chibo pointed toward the horizon. "Is that what I think it is?"

Sally gasped and Roz groaned, but Ji didn't see anything scary, just a moon peeking over the hills. Then he realized: it was the *fourth* moon rising tonight.

The kumiho moon.

"I—I can't hear them," Sally said, lifting her head to the night sky.

"Not yet," Roz said, her voice shaking.

Sally's ears flattened. "If we reach the moon shadow of the hill behind us, they can't follow."

"Forget the hill." Ji grabbed Chibo's hand. "Run for the manor."

Roz grunted softly. "Are you sure?"

"We can't reach the manor before they catch us," Sally snarled. "It's too far."

"Come on!" Ji said, trotting toward Turtlewillow Manor with Chibo. "Move!"

"What are you thinking?" Roz asked.

"You heard Ti-Lin-Su. We need to get to the Ogrelands without being seen!"

"Oh, good plan!" Roz said, lumbering closer. "Everyone stick with Ji!"

"What plan?" Chibo asked her.

"Plan on dying," Sally growled, scanning the night for fox-demons.

"The Ice Witch is in the Ogrelands," Roz explained, trotting along the dirt path toward the cornfield. "And there's only one way to get there."

We can think of ten ways! Nin announced. *Fastmarch, bustleclimb, slithercrawl, amblestroll—*

"Without being seen," Roz added. "Or being caught by kumiho."

A prickle of fear sounded in Nin's mind-speak. *What about the Gravewoods?*

Sally frowned as she loped downhill beside Roz. "What's that?"

Humans call it the Shield Wall.

"Oh!" Roz said. "Is that actually real?"

Deadlyreal, Nin said. *Killingreal.*

"I've read legends about a Shield Wall." Roz steadied the jouncing backpack as she jogged. "They say that the first Summer Queen built a barrier around the Ogrelands, to protect the humans after the war."

The fearful prickle of Nin's mind-speak turned to sadness.

"Who cares?" Sally barked. "That doesn't explain why we're heading to the manor."

"We're heading for the goblins," Ji told her. "For the goblin pen at Turtlewillow. We'll use their tunnels to travel underground."

"And go straight to the Ogrelands without being seen!" Sally finished. "The kumiho can't follow us and the knights won't even think of the tunnels. That's actually a great idea."

"If we get there in time," Ji said.

Sally followed the path between cornfields, loping on all fours for a few steps before straightening. "And if the goblins help us," she said.

"They'll help us," Chibo fluted. "Goblins are polite that way."

When a hair-raising yowling sounded in the distant darkness, Sally veered from the dirt path. "This way!"

Cornstalks whipped Ji's face as he followed. He tightened his grip on Chibo's hand, staying close to the shadow of Roz's bulky form.

What's chasing us? Nin asked, from the backpack. *We can't smell them!*

"Kumiho," Sally said.

Kumiwho?

"Kumiho!" Roz rumbled.

Oh! Nin said. *Ho. Kumiwhat are kumiho?*

"Would you shut your mandibles?" Ji panted, stumbling on the uneven soil.

"Fox-demons," Roz explained. "Summoned by the queen to hunt us."

The queen is too weak to demoncall, Nin said. *After the Diadem Rite, it would take longmonths for her to summon again.*

"She seems to have recovered quickly," Roz said, flattening the cornstalks.

The shamoon said months and months.

"What's a shamoon?" Chibo asked.

"An ogre shaman," Roz said.

Not a shaman, Missroz! Not a shawoman, either! A shamoon.

"Well, either your shamoon's wrong," Ji said, "or Brace summoned them."

Sally raised her paw. "Shh! Horses."

Ji held his breath but only heard the crackle of cornstalks in the breeze. The lumps on his forehead itched. He peered toward the distant manor and saw the peaked tops of two clock towers.

"They're heading the other way," Sally said.

"At least we get to meet more ogres," Chibo fluted. "That's some aws."

"Some aws" was how Nin used to say "awesome." Ji snorted and told Chibo, "Just what we need. More numbskulls."

"Don't pretend you're not excited," Roz rumbled. "We all know how much you missed Nin. You sang lullabies to the urn every night."

"I did not," he said, tugging Chibo toward the manor.

"They weren't always lullabies," Chibo said.

"They weren't even singing," Sally added.

Chibo giggled.

Sally stepped from the cornstalks onto a fallow field.

The light of the lowest moon—the fourth moon—glinted off farm buildings. She sniffed the air, then slunk across the field into a terraced rock garden. The sound of wind chimes reminded Ji of the jangle of warhorses' harnesses. The kumiho didn't yowl again, though. Maybe they'd lost the scent, or maybe they were crouching in the shadows, ready to pounce.

"I smell goblins," Sally said, stalking into a dahlia garden. "The pen isn't far now."

"It will be a relief to be safe with goblins," Roz said.

Ji plucked corn silk from his hair. "That's the first time any human ever said *that*."

"They're lovely," Roz said. "And polite."

"That just means they say 'please' before eating you," he said, which wasn't really fair.

Goblins looked weird, with their four arms and beaver teeth and bobbly knees, but they'd always treated Ji kindly. The ones at Primstone Manor wore collars, dug trenches for the nobles, and loved good manners. And the ones in Summer City had helped Ji and the others escape after the Diadem Rite.

"There," Sally said, pointing across the garden with her snout.

A stone building squatted in a hollow past the garden. A heavy iron gate stood open in the nearest wall. Back at Primstone Manor, the goblins lived in a dirt-floored pen inside a "folly"—a small building constructed to look like a fake ruin—but this looked worse.

This looked like a prison.

Bamboo poles and coconut husks were piled in the yard. Ji didn't see any goblins. He didn't hear any, either. Nor birds, nor crickets, nor frogs. A strange silence strangled the night. Like the whole world was holding its breath. . . .

"Run," he whispered.

"Pardon?" Roz asked.

Sally's big eyes widened. "RUN!"

Roz lumbered across the garden, her heavy tread crunching on the pebbled path. Ji dragged Chibo behind him, terrified of every patch of shadow.

Ow, ow, ow! Nin said, as the backpack slammed up and down. *Rozquake!*

"Stop talking!" Ji snapped, stumbling onto a circular lawn in the center of the garden.

A fountain rose where six pebbled paths came together. Marble sundials bordered the lawn. The whole place shone with tranquillity—until Roz stopped short and seemed to growl and whimper at the same time.

Ji didn't growl. He didn't whimper. He didn't make a sound. He simply stared in frozen horror as a kumiho prowled from behind the fountain.

12

FISH-BELLY-WHITE FUR GLISTENED in the moons-light. Milky eyes gleamed above a mouth that drooled black goo. Muscular shoulders bunched like a jaguar's, and snake heads stared at Ji over the demon's sinewy body.

"Get back!" Roz roared, spreading her arms. "Back, back!"

Ji stumbled away, tugging a petrified Chibo with him. "We need to reach the goblins!"

"Stop!" Sally yelped. "There's another one behind us! There's barely any scent, but—"

The hissing of nine snakes silenced her. The sound shivered Ji's soul and he sent his dragonsenses into his chest, groping for the slightest ember of heat. Anything to spark a fire. He felt nothing but chill and dread—and Chibo's hand trembling in his.

"The—the goblin p-pen is up ahead," Ji stammered. "We can make it."

"We can't," Sally snarled. "We're not fast enough!"

"You are," Ji said.

Her tail lashed. "I won't—"

"Fly!" Ji grabbed Chibo around the waist and flung him upward. "Go!"

An emerald glow bathed the world and the snake-hissing stopped. The kumiho froze, white eyes staring.

"Sally, get to the goblins!" Ji snapped. "Nin, start butt-stinging!"

We are, Sneakyji! Overagain and overagain! We can't hurt it!

Shadows shifted when Chibo darted away through the air. The first kumiho licked its teeth with a thick tongue and pounced.

Sally leaped sideways, silent and shadowy.

Ji crashed frantically through the dahlias.

And Roz hurled a marble sundial at the demon.

The kumiho danced aside, dodging easily . . . but the sundial shattered on the paving stones. Chunks of marble flew. One sharp piece spun at the fox-demon and opened a wide gash in the creature's flank. The wound oozed black blood, and an anguished howl split the night.

Sprinting toward the pen, Ji caught sight of the second kumiho. "RUN!" he bellowed. "Runrunrun!"

Roz thundered toward the goblin pen. Ji scrambled behind her, his mind strobing with panic. He saw flashes of flowers—of Roz—of the path—of green wings against a moons-lit sky.

When the howling stopped, Ji glanced at the wounded kumiho and his heart froze. The fox-demon wasn't wounded anymore. The slash had already closed—completely healed—and the second kumiho stalked along beside the first.

Roz flung another sundial against the fountain. The two kumiho scattered to dodge the chunks of marble, and Ji fled.

Through the palm trees.

Down the slope.

Into the hollow.

Across the yard and toward the stone goblin pen.

His lungs burned, his clawed feet scraped the dirt. Fear flickered like lightning in his mind—but the gate was only thirty feet away. A green glow shone on the stone wall, which meant Chibo was nearby, while Sally crouched in the corner at a pile of bamboo poles.

And Roz faced the two kumiho, her tattered pink dress flapping around her, gripping a bulky tree limb like a cudgel.

Roz, who sipped hibiscus tea. Roz, who lost herself in books. Roz, who'd been raised to be a governess. Gentle Roz, clever Roz. The only measure of goodness that Ji ever needed. Protecting Sally and Chibo from two demonic horrors. Protecting Nin, who'd finally returned to them. Protecting *Ji*.

He didn't flinch when Sally touched his elbow and gave him the bamboo pole. He just nodded. She was right. Whatever happened, they'd stay together.

A moment later, he and Sally flanked Roz—Ji held the bamboo pole while Sally bared her hobgoblin claws. A half dozen kumiho tails hissed and Ji's knees turned to water. Fear gripped his throat, but he didn't flinch, not this time.

Sneakyji! One bite from their tails will deathslay any of you. How do we—

"Everyone move slowly toward the goblin pen," Ji murmured. "Once we're inside, we'll slam the gate—"

One kumiho sprang at Roz while the other charged Sally. Ji jabbed at the kumiho that was attacking Sally and missed by two feet. The kumiho tore the bamboo pole from his hands with jagged teeth and leaped for his throat.

"Yii!" he yelped, stumbling backward.

Too slow. A swiping claw slashed his leg. Pain flared and he fell to the ground, screaming in terror.

The kumiho opened its jaws, black spittle spraying. Ji couldn't see anything except teeth and a thick, ropy tongue. Then Sally landed on the kumiho's snout with both rear paws.

She drove its muzzle into the dirt and yelled at Ji: "RUN, YOU LAZY LIZARD!"

He scooted backward as she dodged the snapping jaws and swiping claws—and Roz smashed the second kumiho with her cudgel. Bone crunched and the demon skidded across the yard, scrambling for purchase.

Then it shook its head, its bones reknitting.

The first kumiho drove Sally toward Ji—toward the gate. Three bloody lines soaked Sally's torn sleeve where a claw had sliced through skin. She moved fast, though. Inhumanly fast, blocking slashes and bites, while Nin mind-shouted warnings. Ant lions swarmed the kumiho's eyes to block its vision, so the demon spun sideways to see with its tails. Snake heads hissed and snapped at Sally.

"Inside," Sally gasped, dodging wildly. "Chibo, inside! Shut the gate, Ji!"

The snake heads blurred at her. Nothing was as fast as a striking demon-snake, not even a hobgoblin. She couldn't beat those snakes much longer—

The kumiho thumped Sally's head with a powerful paw. She crumpled to the ground and moaned. The beast gave a victorious yowl and stood over her, mottled-white fur shining in the light of the four moons.

Sallynx! Nin blurted in mind-speak shrill with fear. *Scamperfast, scamperfast!*

A snake head lashed downward for the killing blow, and two things happened at once.

First, Ji lunged at Sally, trying to shove her away from the snake's deadly fangs.

And second, Chibo screamed, "Bad demons!" and, wings glowing fiercely, dive-bombed the kumiho.

Ji lost his balance and sprawled on top of Sally, while Chibo crash-landed five feet away and lay there moaning, his wings glowing steadily. Sally's furry body felt warm and muscular beneath Ji, but his skin crawled with a chill: the kumiho stood above him, snake tails hissing.

He imagined a burning puncture in his shoulder. He imagined venom flowing through him. Then the hissing quieted. And when Ji peeked at the kumiho, it was crouching away from him, teeth bared and tails lashing. It had retreated ten feet. Too far to reach him.

The other kumiho had done the same; it was pacing and snapping at Roz—from five feet away. Not attacking. Just stalking back and forth in the green glow of Chibo's wings. What the heck? Why had they stopped when they'd won the fight?

"Who cares?" he muttered to himself, rolling off Sally. "Roz, get Chibo!"

Roz grabbed Chibo, while Ji hefted Sally into his arms. Her furry little form was dense with muscle, and it almost yanked his arms from their sockets. Still, he managed to drag her toward the gate while the kumiho prowled in agitation, like they were trying to gather the courage to attack. . . .

The pain in Ji's shoulder radiated into his chest. He stumbled through the gateway into the goblin pen and collapsed, spilling Sally onto the dirt floor.

She grunted at the impact, and her eyes sprang open. "What—"

"The gate!" Ji gasped to Roz. "Close the . . ."

Chibo fainted in Roz's arms and his wings disappeared into his hunchback. As the night darkened, the kumiho howled and bounded forward in a sudden attack—

Roz slammed the gate down, and venomous snake tails slashed and snapped through the bars. They missed Roz by inches as she stumbled backward. The demons couldn't break through the gate, but that wasn't what had stopped them earlier. Ji didn't know what had stopped them. He tried to think about it, but the inside of the goblin pen kept swaying and shifting around him.

Are you stonesafe, Missroz? Nin asked urgently. *Is everyone oh and kay?*

"I'm fine," Roz rumbled, her voice shaking. "Chibo fainted. Is—is everyone else unhurt?"

"Yeah," Ji whispered, as the world dimmed.

"No," Sally growled.

"What's wrong?" Roz asked.

"It's Ji." Sally stared at his shoulder. "He's been bitten."

"Silly fuzzface," he told her. "If they bit me, I'd be dead."

Then he proceeded to die.

13

DIRT PACKED THE stillness of Ji's grave. A fierce itch irritated his skin as scales erupted from his flesh. His knees cracked and his spine unfurled into terrible new shapes. His skull lengthened, his torso stretched, his legs fused. Poison swirled in his veins and his heart hungered for treasure, for gems.

Even their names thrummed with power:

Amethyst.

Lapis lazuli.

Beryl.

Citrine.

Malachite.

Turquoise, topaz, emerald.

Ji felt them in the tunnels beyond his grave, in the damp

131

subterranean dark. He hungered to snatch flames from the gemstones, to warm his belly as if drinking spiced wine from a bejeweled goblet. He sensed animals scurrying in the tunnels. Warm-blooded creatures with souls that shone like opals and burned like rubies. Souls that flowed and shifted like fire. His crimson eyes weighed the souls and wanted to drink them, too. Golden antlers branched from the bony ridges on his brow and ten thousand scales shimmered on his body.

A dragon, a pearl, a diamond. Garnet and gold—

Death was surprisingly uncomfortable. First a chill seeped into Ji's bones; then he burned or boiled. Maybe baked. There was a lot of jostling, and the sound of a hundred sheep coughing, *ka-ka-ka*. Finally, a sharp pain prodded Ji's shoulder and water splashed his face and dripped in his throat.

Also, his nose itched.

Darkness swelled. Darkness tinged with torchlight. Darkness etched with spiraling patterns, strange designs carved into a stone wall. And some buttonhead kept groaning: *Ooooaah, oooooaaah.* Then Roz's face appeared, except with a squarer jaw and sharper cheekbones, granite-flecked skin and a curved horn. But her eyes shone with a *Rozziness* that warmed Ji like a bonfire on a winter's night. She looked anxious, though. Ji wanted to squeeze her hand and tell her not to worry, but he couldn't move or speak.

"He's awake!" Roz said, from a hundred miles away. "He's awake, he's alive!"

Ooooaaah, the groaner replied.

Sally's fuzzy snout appeared. She looked at Ji with her big, adorable eyes and burst into tears. Which didn't make sense. Sally never cried.

Ooooaaah, the groaner said.

"Dragons heal," Roz rumbled, like a prayer. "Dragons heal."

Oooh, the groaner agreed.

"Stupid boy." Sally pressed her furry forehead against Ji's lumpy horns. "Jumping in front of a kumiho."

"You can't blame dirt for being heavy," Chibo said.

Trickles of water glinted with torchlight. A droplet trembled, and Ji trembled too. Shivering and sweating at the same time. The groaner started up again, making a noise like a depressed cow—and Ji realized it was *him* groaning.

When his sad mooing quieted, he heard voices: Roz's rumble, Sally's growl, and Chibo's fluting. And Nin's mind-speak: *We like shroomfood. It's not tastybeet, though.*

"It's not tastyrice, either," Chibo said.

"You're ant lions, Nin," Sally said. "Of course you don't mind mushrooms for the tenth meal in a row."

"I'm grateful they're feeding us at all," Roz said. "Especially considering how unlike the other goblins they are."

"Unlike?" Sally said. "You mean 'unfriendly.'"

"They're not that bad," Chibo fluted. "At least they're leading us to the ogres."

"Yes, that is quite magnanimous of them," Roz said.

Magnanimous? A fiery rodent?

"No, Nin, you doolally insects," Sally said. "She doesn't mean they're a fiery rodent."

Magnanimous, Nin said. *Magma plus mouse.*

Ji blinked at the spiraling designs covering the rock wall in front of him. To his right a lantern illuminated the backpack full of Nin's ant lions. Roz sat on the ground with her legs tucked to one side, picking at a bowl of soggy leaves. Chibo hugged his knees, four wing tips peeking from his hunchback, and one of Sally's ears was notched—a cut from a kumiho's claw.

Sneakyji! An ant lion crept onto Ji's nose. *Cub's awake! They're awake, she's awake!*

"*He's* awake," Sally said, a smile splitting her muzzle.

That too! All of them are awake—sillybeet humans!

Sally gave Ji a fierce and fuzzy hug. "Stupid boot boy."

"What—" he croaked. "Where?"

Roz took his hand. "We reached the goblin pen. We closed the gate—"

"You closed the gate," Chibo told her. "I mostly fainted."

"We all did, except Roz," Sally said. "Well, and Nin."

"Taking us to oogers?" Ji asked, his voice not quite working. "Orges?"

Roz nodded. "The goblins are leading us to the mountains."

"That's where ogres come from!" Chibo fluted, as Ji closed his eyes again.

And barelyrarely leave, Nin said with a note of sadness.

"Shh," Roz said. "He's falling back asleep."

Ji smiled softly, wrapped in a blanket of satisfaction. They'd done it. They'd escaped the kumiho and knights, and were on the way to the Ogrelands to find the Ice Witch. To break the spell at last.

The shamoon say we invaded the human realm long ago, Nin continued, in a muffled sort of mind-speak, *to seize more hillfoots and—*

"Why?" Chibo whispered to a couple of ant lions carrying dead pill bugs toward the backpack. "Why'd you need more hills?"

Greedy! Greedy ogres! We lost and humans trapsnared us behind the Gravewoods. We cannot freewander, so now only a few of us are left.

Ji didn't know what Nin was talking about, but that was nothing new. He didn't understand Nin half the time even when he *wasn't* falling asleep.

"That's why ogres are attacking the Summer Realm?" Sally purred softly. "To get the foothills back?"

Yes. We must backgrab them and stop the evilqueen. You are puresure she is strong again, Missroz?

Sleep swirled around Ji. They were in the goblin

tunnels heading for the Ogrelands, he understood that. Something else still nagged at him, though. Something about stealing fire from treasure—*emerald, amethyst, malachite*—or reshaping souls. He couldn't quite remember. Had he dreamed of being a full-blooded dragon? Yes. Yes, a dragon who didn't only fuel his fire with gemstones but fueled his magic with people's souls.

The darkness swam with the scent of sapphires and rubies, beryl and citrine. . . .

The next time Ji woke, a tunnel wall was sliding past his face and he was wrapped in a cocoon.

No, not a cocoon: a curtain. A threadbare, filthy curtain. Three ant lions untangled themselves from his hair and waggled antennae at him.

Cub's awake! Nin announced, then told Ji, *We've been peekseeing you, Sneakyji!*

"Muh," Ji said, which meant, "Good morning."

You're the fifth cutemost sleeper we ever peeked!

"Guh," Ji said, which meant, "I bet Sally's the top four."

We don't really sleep. We dream, though. Did you dream? Are you feeling happystronger? Sallynx drips squeezewater into your mouth for you to lickswallow, and . . .

As Nin nattered on, a shape came into focus: Roz was marching in front of Ji, holding the edges of the curtain.

She smiled over her shoulder. "Good morning!"

Oh. The curtain was a stretcher! He was being carried

in a stretcher made of cloth. Ji tilted his head to see who was holding the other side—and almost screamed.

Goblins were ugly enough from a distance, but only one foot away and carrying your stretcher? They were terrifying. They had beady eyes, wrinkly skin, and teeth like beavers. And two pairs of arms: one short, muscular pair with shovel-claws and one spindly pair that sprouted from their bellies.

"Yaa-hi!" He changed his half scream into a greeting. "Hi there! Hello!"

The goblins didn't answer. Which was weird. Goblins prided themselves on having excellent manners.

Ji cleared his throat. "It's good to meet you."

The goblins trooped grimly ahead, not even glancing at him.

"To meet Kultultul again, I mean," Ji continued, hoping that using the goblin word for "goblins" might help. "We have goblin friends in the city. I know one who collects combs. For a shrine? Very pretty—"

One of the goblins chuffed dismissively.

"Our new friends," Roz told Ji, in a brittle sort of voice, "prefer extremely . . . distinct shrines."

Distinctly lumpyboring, Nin said.

Ji peered at the tunnel wall, expecting tidy niches packed with ribbons or feathers or pebbles. Instead, he saw a hole containing what looked like a single misshapen potato.

"What a beautiful shrine!" he lied.

The goblins gargled and scowled.

"Our new 'friends,'" Sally said, prowling closer, "are full of awe."

They are awful! Sallynx means they are awful!

"They care," Roz said with a polite smile, "about more than beauty."

"They do?" Ji asked. "I mean, that's good! Nothing's more important than politeness, after all."

The goblins glared at him with beady eyes. Sheesh. He must be in pretty bad shape if even goblins saw though his lies.

"Er"—Ji looked at Roz—"how long have I been sleeping?"

"Three days."

"What?"

"Almost four." Chibo ambled beside the stretcher, his glowing wings brushing both sides of the tunnel. "You had a fever most of the time."

"You're extremely fortunate," Roz said. "Nothing survives kumiho venom. Except, apparently, half dragons."

"You're a lucky lizard," Sally said.

Resilient reptile!

"Sturdy snake," Chibo said.

An ant lion on the stretcher shook its mane. *Gutsy gecko!*

"And even so," Roz continued, "it was touch and go. You gave us a scare, Jiyong."

"Sorry," he said.

"You also saved Sally's life."

He snorted. "She'd saved mine two seconds earlier."

"That's what I keep telling them," Sally growled.

"How long before we reach the ogre mountains?"

"Another few days, I think," Roz rumbled. "I'm not sure. Our new friends are . . ."

Scowl-eyed and closemouthed, Nin said, and Ji was glad once again that nobody could hear Nin's mind-speak except the five of them.

". . . quiet and thoughtful," Roz finished, with a nod to a nearby goblin.

Missroz told us to drop eaves on them when they don't know we're listening—

"Drop what?"

Eaves. To listen.

Oh, eavesdrop! "Any luck?"

No. They talk in Goblish, which we don't standunder.

"Yes!" Roz glanced warningly at the goblins. "Yes, we're very lucky. They offered to help us. They are eka-stremely ka-ind."

Sally snorted. "Extremely."

"Not really," Chibo whispered to Ji. "Not this bunch. But they're bringing us to the Ogrelands anyway. We don't know why."

The rocking stretcher lulled Ji. He drowsed for hours, rousing occasionally to watch the goblins and sleepily feel the tug of distant gemstones through the tunnel walls. His dragonsenses probed the ground more powerfully than ever. Maybe because he'd lost another chunk of humanity, or maybe because he was underground. Maybe both.

He didn't wake fully until the goblins stopped to sleep in a cavern with rows of wall shrines. In the torch-lit darkness, he gazed at the misshapen pink potato shapes in the niches. If only they were *real* potatoes: roasted, boiled, mashed. The thought made his mouth water. He wolfed down a few slimy mushrooms instead, and eyed the goblins across the cavern. Two of them squatted a few feet apart, pushing rocks back and forth on the ground with all four hands.

"What're they doing?" Ji asked.

"Playing Seven Pebbles," Roz told him.

"What's that?"

"A goblin game—but don't call it a game!"

"When I did," Sally growled, "they looked like they wanted to gnaw my head off."

"They claim Seven Pebbles is a contest of pure skill," Roz told Ji. "A subtle, strategic competition, not a game."

"Huh," Ji said around a mouthful of mushroom.

The rules make nonsense, Nin said. *It's a rumblejumble of doolallyness.*

"Look who's talking," Sally said. "The Kingqueen of Rumblejumb."

Ant lions climbed the stalagmites to act as sentries, while Ji peered at the goblins. A burly one glowered at

Roz, while smaller ones snuck glances at Sally and Chibo. Ji didn't know much about Kultultul—except that "Kultultul" actually meant "the People," which was what the goblins called themselves—but he recognized furtive looks and ill-concealed hostility.

Something was wrong.

After most of the goblins fell asleep, Ji finally got up from his stretcher. He held Roz's rock-hard elbow and walked around the cavern to build his strength. The snakebite throbbed on his shoulder, and he flinched every time he touched it.

So of course he kept touching it.

On his third lap, he murmured, "I don't trust these goblins."

"Neither do I," Roz rumbled. "But how else can we reach the Ogrelands without being seen?"

"There's no way." Ji rubbed his aching shoulder. "I need gemstones so I can shoot fire if anything happens."

"Can you sense any nearby?" Roz asked.

"Just barely. Gems come from underground, right?"

"Of course!"

"Yeah. I thought so." He leaned more weight on her. "I'll keep sniffing for them. If I find any, we'll need Nin—"

We're right here! Nin said, and an ant lion peeked around Roz's horn.

"—and Sally to dig them up."

"Without being seen," Roz murmured, casting a worried

141

glance toward the goblins.

Ji managed two more laps before flopping down beside Sally. They chatted for a while; then Ji groped with his mind for any trace of gemstones. No luck. But when Chibo and Roz started snoring, he smiled. Sure, they still needed to reach the Ogrelands and find the Ice Witch—and convince her to break the spell—but at least they were alive.

"Stop scratching," Sally whispered.

Ji dropped his hand from his snakebite. "It itches."

"That's what happens when you get chomped by a demon-snake."

"Yeah." He looked at the stalactites overhead. "I wonder how far underground we are."

Sally's ears drooped. "I'm not thinking about that."

"At least we're safe," he said. "We'll reach the Ogrelands soon, and find the Ice Witch."

"How?"

He wrinkled his nose. "Maybe the ogres know where she is."

"Nin doesn't," Sally said. "And these goblins are bad news."

"Well . . ." Ji lowered his voice. "I'll keep sniffing for gems, just in case."

Sally twitched a tufted ear. "The knights think you're the Winter Snake."

"That's doolally."

"Is it?"

"Of course it is."

"Don't you want to be the Winter Snake?"

"What are you talking about? Do I want to be an evil serpent that eats babies? No, Sally—I'll stick with tamales, you jerk."

Her ears flattened. "It's different for you."

"What is?"

"All *this*." Her tail lashed in the firelight. "You still look almost human. I'm turning into an animal." She looked away. "I keep catching myself walking on all fours like a dog. I won't stay human much longer. And Chibo's eyes are big as grapefruits and he's got two sets of wings. Nin's a bunch of bugs and Roz is . . . She cries in her sleep."

Ji looked toward Roz, her broad shoulders rising and falling with her breath. "She does?"

"You didn't notice?"

"I—" Ji swallowed. "No."

"Chibo doesn't even boast about flying anymore. He's sick of being this way. We all are."

"That's why we're looking for the Ice Witch—so she can change us back to humans once and for all."

"Except you! You're not sick of it. You don't care! You're happy like this."

He peered at her. "Is that why you're mad at me?"

"No!" She shrugged. "Maybe."

"You're mad because my face didn't change much?"

"That should make *you* mad."

"Ha ha."

"Because you've still got the same dork face."

"Yeah, I get it, Sally." He scratched his snakebite. "You're mad that I'm not furry or troll-y."

"Plus, you don't care about being human."

"Of course I care!"

"Stop scratching."

He dropped his hand. "I'm trying break the spell, Sal. What else am I supposed to do?"

"You're supposed to hate it! Look at your chicken feet!"

He peered at the scales covering his ankles and toes. "Huh. They do look a little like chicken feet. I bet I'd taste delicious in pepper sauce."

"Shut up," she grumbled. "You don't have to sound like you're okay with it. That's exactly the problem."

"We're going to find the Ice Witch," he told her. "We're going to break the spell. I won't have chicken feet forever, and you won't have big cute eyes and fluffy ears—"

"I'm serious," she said, glaring at him.

A flare of anger warmed Ji's cheeks. "You think I want to be a lizard? All I want is to be free. We escaped Primstone Manor, we escaped the queen, and for what? Look at us. We're trapped inside our own skin." He raised one scaly hand. "How do we get free of *this*? We're freaks, we're monsters. If we show our faces, we make children cry and fisherfolk scream. I hate this, Sally, but what else am I supposed to do? We have to keep heading for the Ice

Witch, because that's the only way we'll ever get our lives back."

When he stopped talking, the silence felt deep. His breath came fast and hard, like he'd been running. Of course he didn't want to stay a beast forever. How could he live as a half reptile? How could anyone?

"That's better," Sally said.

"I'm glad you're happy that I'm sad," he grumbled.

"You're not *that* sad." She rolled away from him. "You don't even get burrs in your tail."

14

THE NEXT MORNING, Sally wasn't angry anymore. Maybe she'd just needed to snap at him. Even better, he didn't need the stretcher anymore. He trudged along, still weak, but able to stay on his feet.

The tunnels stretched for endless miles. Shrines with pink potato shapes appeared regularly, but everything else changed. Straight tunnels wiggled into crazy curves. Walls rose, then fell; the stone floor felt smooth, then rocky—then dry, then wet.

And Ji felt the tug of gemstones calling him. So softly that he barely noticed it at first. But as the hours passed, he probed deeper into the rock, stretching his dragon-senses farther and farther—yet he still couldn't pinpoint any gems.

"They're too far away," he grumbled. "I can only feel ten feet through the dirt."

"Keep trying," Roz said.

Ji stumbled past underground waterfalls, pushing his dragonhunger deeper into the earth. Mushroom-covered walls rose around him and glowing fish splashed in chilly pools. He barely saw them, his attention burrowing through the surrounding rock until he felt the sharp tug of jade.

"Oh!"

Roz glanced at him. "A gem?"

"Jade." He nodded at the tunnel wall. "Fifteen feet through there."

"Jiyong," she said gently, "we can't dig that deep with goblins watching."

"Oh, right."

He spent the rest of the day sweeping the tunnels with his dragonhunger like a bloodhound sniffing after a trail. He could sense gems through the rock—ten feet, twenty feet, even thirty feet in—but nothing close enough to help them.

"At least you're getting stronger," Chibo offered.

Ji grunted. "It's not helping."

And the evilqueen's stronger, too, Nin said. *Or at least not weaker. We need to find the ogres and warnscare them not to attack. If they do, the evilqueen will slaykill them all.*

"We'll warn them," Ji promised.

We must! Nin's mind-speak hummed with urgency. *Or our family will die. Our mothers and fathers, all our tribes.*

Ji swallowed, feeling the weight of Nin's desperation. He raised his voice and called to a goblin, "I beg your pardon, but please can you tell us about the ogres?"

The goblin chuffed under its breath.

"We heard that you're working together," Ji said. "That goblins are digging tunnels from the mountains to the city? For a surprise ogre attac-ka on the queen?"

The goblin turned away sourly, one of its belly-arms scratching its bare neck. Which was another weird thing: these goblins didn't wear collars, even though they'd lived in a pen. Of course, sometimes goblins shared collars. That way, while none of them was completely free, none was always enslaved.

Ji asked another goblin about the ogres. It didn't answer. Ji flattered a third goblin, lied to a fourth, and offered to play Seven Pebbles with two more. Running out of options, he even tried singing—just in case goblins like music. None of them told him anything useful. They barely said a dozen words to him and most of those were "patient" and "wait" and "stop singing, it hurts my ears."

So he followed them into the gloom, keeping his songs to himself and sniffing for gemstones.

The next morning, a sudden clatter sounded from the

tunnels ahead. The goblins veered into a side tunnel to avoid whatever was coming.

"Nin," Ji muttered to the ant lion on his collar. "See what's making that noise."

A few ant lions must've peered around the corner, because a minute later Nin reported, *A crowd of goblins is scurrywalking toward the human realm.*

"Why are they heading that way?"

Roz's granite-flecked brow furrowed. "And why are they keeping us apart?"

We can't tell. But the crowd is tremblescared and weepcrying. They look extremely able to miser.

"Able to what?" Ji asked.

To miser, Nin repeated.

"Miserable," Roz translated, tapping her elongated horn.

"What's wrong?" Chibo asked.

Goblin guards are kickshoving them onward.

"Perhaps we're wrong to think of all goblins as being alike," Roz said.

Sally snorted. "Goblins are goblins are goblins."

"People aren't all the same," Chibo said.

"Yeah they are," Ji said darkly.

Over the next few hours, the tunnels widened. The hum of gemstones faded, even as Ji's ability to sniff them out extended deeper into the bedrock. Torches flickered beside wall shrines displaying the pink potato-shaped

149

rocks, and spiral designs gleamed in the walls.

Then Sally's ears pricked. "There's a big open space ahead."

"Everyone watch out," Ji murmured. "If the goblins are lying about bringing us to the Ogrelands, it may be a trap."

A faint roar sounded, like a distant waterfall. The goblins bustled around a corner and gestured toward a flight of stone stairs leading upward, wide enough for two carriages.

"Whoa," Ji said.

Chibo's emerald wings spread out from his hunchback. "Are those stairs?"

"Yeah," Sally growled. "And that's the sound of goblins. Hundreds of them. Thousands."

"Wh-what about ogres?" Ji asked.

"Just goblins, I think."

One of their goblin escorts knee-wobbled toward Roz. "The White Worm will see you now."

"That is . . . very kind." Roz fiddled with the hem of her cloak. "And of course one should know of the White Worm. However, I'm sorry to admit that I do not. Who is—"

"Our ka-ing!" the goblin said. "Our ka-aptain. Our ka-mmander."

"There's a king?" Chibo fluted under his breath.

"What an honor!" Roz rumbled to the goblin. "And will His Royal Highness, erm—"

"Will he lead us to the ogres?" Sally demanded.

"His Deepness," the goblin chuffed.

"His Deepness, of ka-orse," Roz said. "I beg your pardon."

"Also called His Politeness," the goblin said.

"That's a lovely title."

"And His Brutality."

"P-pardon?" Roz asked, while Sally's tail lashed.

"His Deepness will guide you." The goblin gestured toward the stairs with a belly-arm. "We do not ka-eep the White Worm waiting."

Roz's lips narrowed as she looked at Ji. Sally's nose twitched and Chibo, nervous and edgy, prodded a wall shrine with the tip of one glowing wing. But they'd come too far to turn back—and they didn't have anywhere else to go—so Ji politely bared his teeth to the goblin.

"Than-ka you very much," he said. "We are eager to meet His Politeness."

The goblins climbed the uneven steps. Ji stumbled when he followed, because his human—or half-human— feet couldn't pivot into the lopsided stair slots. Still, he eventually stepped through the archway at the top.

Beside him, Roz whispered, "Goodness me."

"What?" Chibo said. "What is it?"

"We're on a stairway," Sally said, "carved high into the wall of a cavern."

"Not simply a cavern," Roz said. "There's an entire underground city spread out beneath us."

White marble streets wound around white marble

domes with oval doors and round windows. White marble towers rose from the ground like gigantic stalagmites with stairs spiraling upward on their walls, while white marble upside-down towers hung from the ceiling like gigantic stalactites, connected to the regular towers with walkways. Goblins hunched and slouched everywhere, their knees bobbling and their belly-arms waving. Shafts of daylight fell from above, where wide circles opened to the upper world.

"That's a lot of goblins," Sally growled.

Roz pointed toward the middle of the city. "Look at the banner."

Wavy white columns encircled a stadium carved into the cavern floor. A massive throne rose at the far end of the stadium, and frost touched Ji's heart when he saw the banner behind it. He couldn't make out any details, but the design looked an awful lot like a picture of a tree with the rising sun.

"That's . . ." Sally cleared her throat. "That's the symbol of the Summer Queen."

"Where?" Chibo squeaked. "Here? Where? Why?"

Ji swallowed. "Hanging over the throne."

"Perhaps it's the spoils of war," Roz said with a gruff nervousness. "Perhaps the goblins won it in a battle."

Warspoils, Nin said in agreement. *Goblins aren't ogrestrong, but in battle they burst from underground and* fwoomf! *The earth gulpswallows dozens of their enemies.*

"Fwoomf," Chibo repeated.

"You ka-ome to the bowl," a goblin said, and started down a stairway leading into the city.

In the streets, goblins chuffed and barked at the sight of Ji and the others. Vendors sold strange fungus-foods from strange carts and goblin kids peered at them from strange doorways. Goblin soldiers knee-wobbled from alleys and joined the procession. Just a few at first. Then a few dozen. By the time they reached the wavy columns that stood sentry above the sunken stadium, hundreds of goblins marched behind them.

"I thought we were meeting ogres," Chibo fluted. "To lead us to the Ogrelands."

"Maybe we are," Ji said, taking his hand.

Sally's tufted ears flattened. "Maybe."

Past the wavy columns, the stadium opened in the floor, revealing an oval bowl big enough to hold hundreds of goblins. Twenty or thirty goblins knelt on mushroom-shaped stools, gnawing at rocks. Stone chips speckled the floor, the falling bits sounding like gravelly rain, and burly goblins surrounded the barn-sized throne, wielding clubs with jagged heads.

"Elite guards," Sally growled.

"Perhaps elite *guides*," Roz said faintly.

"Yeah, that's why they've got clubs." Sally's muzzle twitched. "To guide."

Halfway down the ramp into the bowl, Ji caught Roz frowning at a row of bars lining one wall. Prison cells.

She didn't say anything, though. The goblins zigzagged around mushroom-shaped stools, heading across the stadium. When they reached the huge throne, Ji craned his neck, looking toward the top. It was way too big for a goblin. Way too big for an ogre. Was the White Worm a giant? Where *was* he?

"Kneel before the White Worm," one of the goblin guards barked.

Ji knelt. "Uh . . ."

"We are honored," Roz told the guard.

"Speak for yourself," Sally murmured.

"Where is he?" Chibo asked. "Can you see him? I can't see him."

"I'm not sure," Ji told him. "I can't—"

"He is before you!" the goblin guard announced.

Ji peered higher. The seat of the throne was twenty feet overhead, and it looked as empty as a sack of nothing.

"His Deepness is ka-ind indeed to see us," he said, because it sounded like the sort of thing you told a huge empty throne. "So generous! We are beyond happy to—"

"I AM THE WHITE WORM," a voice boomed from above. "GAZE UPON MY POWER AND TREMBLE!"

The voice made Ji's bones vibrate, and he tried to obey, he tried to gaze at the White Worm's power—but he still didn't see anything. He did tremble, though. That voice sounded like a giant chewing on piglets: he trembled plenty.

"YOU KA-AME INTO MY HOLY PRESENCE TO

BEG A BOON FROM THE WHITE WORM?"

Beg a boon? Nin asked. *Yes! We need to warnstop the ogres.*

"And find the Ice Witch," Chibo whispered.

"Y-yes, Your Deepness." Roz pressed one hand to her chest. "We are friends to the goblins in the human city, and we as-ka that you—"

"SPEA-KA UP, HALF HUMAN! I KA-ANNOT HEAR A WORD YOU ARE MUTTERING."

"I beg your pardon, Your Politeness!" Roz said, raising her voice. "We beg a boon! We hope that you will favor us with—"

"IS YOUR HEAD INSIDE A SAC-KA OF FEATH-ERS? ARE YOU CHEWING A DUNG-SHROOM? I STILL KA-ANNOT HEAR YOU!"

Ji chewed his lower lip. Should they run? They couldn't: not with a hundred goblins in the bowl, a thousand in the city, and a huge, invisible, furious goblin king on the throne.

"We beg a boon, Your Deepness!" Roz shouted. "We beg that you'll lead us to the Ogrelands!"

"WHO DARES SHOUT AT THE WHITE WORM?" the voice demanded. "RUDE! RUDE BEAST!"

"I'm sorry, I—"

"OFF WITH THEIR HEADS!" the White Worm bellowed. "CHOP THEIR NEC-KAS! FEED THE FUNGUS WITH THEIR BLOOD!"

15

THE GOBLIN GUARDS bobbled forward, clubs raised. Sally tensed, Chibo spread his wings, and Ji jumped to his feet.

"We're sorry!" Ji yelped. "We come in peace! We love Kultultul! We chew rocks for fun!"

A squeal of laughter sounded from the throne; then a high-pitched voice said, "I'm ka-idding! Just ka-idding! Let them stay fully headed!"

The goblin guards stopped and woofled. A few showed their teeth. Laughing? Hungry? Both?

"Oh, did you see their faces?" the high-pitched voice continued. "I thought the scaly one was going to wet his widdershins!" The voice paused. "No? That is not the human saying?"

Ji squinted toward the throne and saw a weird goblin

standing at the edge of the seat. Even weirder than the average goblin: smaller and rounder, with six arms instead of four. Also, it was pink. Bright pink. Actually, it looked a lot like the misshapen pink potatoes in the wall shrines.

"Send them up!" the pink goblin said, chuffing merrily. "With heads still attached for now!"

The goblin guards woofled. "We obey, Your Deepness."

Ji gaped. That shrimpy six-armed pink goblin was the White Worm? How had such a booming voice come from such a little mouth, and changed to such a high-pitched squeal?

The guards prodded Ji and the others toward a marble staircase that rose to the second level of the throne. At the top, a polished marble expanse stretched toward another throne—a regular-sized throne that stood atop the massive throne's seat. More mushroom-stools dotted the throne floor, and goblins in white tunics clustered around the pink goblin.

"So! You are the former humans!" The White Worm bustled forward to greet them, six arms spreading in welcome. "Transformed into something better. But only halfway. Too bad! Poor ka-reatures. You wish you'd been changed into *goblins*, you unluc-ka-y half humans!"

"Y-yes, your majesty," Roz stuttered. "If only—"

The White Worm clapped his middle set of arms. "Offer our guests a seat!"

Three white-clad goblins gestured toward mushroom-stools at the foot of the throne. Roz curtsied politely before sitting, while Ji perched on a stool near two goblins playing a furious game of Seven Pebbles. His mind whirled with questions. Where were the mountains? Where were the ogres? Why was the White Worm pink?

The White Worm climbed onto the regular-sized throne, crossed four of his arms, scratched his belly with a fifth, and held a stone scepter with a sixth. "Tell me your tale, half humans, and I will help you or swallow you whole."

"Is he kidding again?" Chibo whispered.

"No idea," Ji said.

He's too small to wholeswallow you, Nin said. *He'd have to chopslice you first, or pastegrind you into a chewy marmalade.*

Ji shot a stern look at the backpack, even though—thankfully—the goblins couldn't hear Nin's mind-speak.

Roz told the White Worm about the Diadem Rite, the transformation, and their escape. "And now we must beg for your help. We need the Ice Witch to break this spell. We plan to ask the ogres how to find her—unless perhaps Your Politeness knows where she is?"

The goblin king's pink skin turned fish-belly white and his voice boomed out: "THE WHITE WORM KNOWS ALL!"

"Yes, of course!" Roz blurted. "I'm sorry!"

White! Nin said, as Ji's heart thumped in his chest. *We don't like him when he's white!*

The king snapped his stone scepter in two. "NEVER DOUBT MY KNOWLEDGE, HALF HUMANS!"

"I beg your pardon. I meant no offense!"

The White Worm turned pink again and snatched a new scepter from a stack beside his throne. "No need to apologize," he told Roz in his squeakier voice. "It's ka-wite all right. So, you need help reaching the Ogrelands?"

Roz gulped. "Y-yes, Your Deepness."

"And what do you offer in return?"

"Ah," Roz said. "Er."

"How ka-an we serve you?" Ji asked.

"An eka-cellent question, Scalyboots! That is the perfect thing to as-ka. How *ka-an* you serve me?"

Trying to look eager and obedient, Ji watched the White Worm attentively. When the goblin didn't continue, he said, "However Your Deepness wishes?"

"Another good answer!" The White Worm rubbed his beaver teeth and asked Roz, "Do you know the rules of Seven Pebbles?"

"I am sorry to say that we do not," she said.

"*I* am sorry to say that *you* do not!"

"Er, well, to our great regret—"

"To *my* great regret!"

"Um," Roz rumbled.

"We'd love to learn, Your Deepness," Ji said. "Although

we hear it's a very subtle and complex g—" He coughed into his fist. "Strategic challenge."

"Eka-stremely challenging. Far beyond the ability of mere half humans." The White Worm gestured toward the two goblins playing in front of them. "Observe. Look. And also . . ."

"Yes, your majesty?" Roz asked when the goblin king trailed off.

"*Watch*," he finished.

A spiral pattern of lumps—the game board—was carved into the floor between the two goblins. Each goblin held one pebble in each of its four hands. The first goblin placed a pebble on a lump, then took a pebble from another position. It placed two more and moved three. The other goblin placed four pebbles, one of which slid down a lump.

"No doubt you are terribly jealous that you ka-annot understand!" the White Worm said. "You are filled with unshed tears?"

"Y-yes." Ji swallowed, thinking fast. He needed this blithering weirdo to help them reach the Ogrelands, which meant he needed to play along. "We would love to learn the rules, Your Majesty. If it's allowed?"

"Ha!" The White Worm hopped down from his throne. "You aim too high! Finding ogres is easier than ka-ompeting in Seven Pebbles."

"We beg your pardon—" Roz started.

"But I am a good and generous ka-ing! So I shall show you. The rules are simple. Each ka-ontest of Seven Pebbles uses fifteen pebbles."

"But then—" Chibo fluted, "why is it called Seven Pebbles?"

"Foolish half human!" The White Worm stared at Chibo. "What are *you* ka-alled?"

"Me? I'm Chibo."

"And how many pebbles do you have?"

His huge eyes widening, Chibo gazed at the White Worm. "Zero?"

"But you are not ka-alled 'Zero Pebbles'! You are ka-alled 'Chibo.' It is ka-alled 'Seven Pebbles' because that is its name." The White Worm squeaked a laugh. "The rules! Listen ka-losely. You ka-an play a pebble from any of your hands, but you must play only those pebbles that weren't played in any of the last three turns, unless one of them was played twice by one of your left hands in the previous eight turns, or five turns if your opponent's teeth are shorter than yours, or if it is a pebble you played seven turns ago, or plan to play seven turns in the future—or six turns, in the lower tunnels—unless, of ka-ourse, it is one of your first five ka-ontests—in which ka-ase you withdraw three or one or two pebbles from the board, depending on the score and the pebbles and the moons."

Ji stared at the king in bafflement. He made even less sense than Nin talking about a pickled beet. Heck, he made less sense than a pickled beet talking about Nin.

"That is merely the first rule," the White Worm announced. "We ka-all it 'Rule Six.'"

Chibo giggled, a little hysterically.

"A fascinating ka-ontest, and such a ka-lear explanation!" Ji enthused, reaching for a pebble. "So with my two hands, I can pick up two pebbles—"

"DO NOT TOUCH!" the White Worm bellowed, paling to a milky color. "FILTHY HALF HUMAN! "

Ji jerked his hand back. "Sorry! Sorry!"

"OFF WITH HIS HANDS! OFF WITH HIS WRISTS! OFF WITH HIS FINGERS!"

"Wait—" Ji blurted when a goblin guard shuffled toward him. "No! I didn't touch anything!"

"Oh, that is ka-wite fine, then." The White Worm pinkened and waved the guard away. "Let Scalyboots ka-eep his hands. He only has two, after all! Two hands. Poor humans."

"Th-thanks," Ji stammered. "I didn't know."

"Of ka-ourse you cannot touch pebbles without an invitation!" the White Worm scoffed. "Only goblins truly understand Seven Pebbles. Too ka-omplex for your simple minds."

"Yes, Your Majesty."

The White Worm gestured to the game being played on the ground. "And some goblins play terribly! Loo-ka at these two dolts. Disgraceful. Terrible! Chop off their heads if they ka-annot play better." When the guards merely gazed at him, he said, "Chop-chop! Start chopping!"

The guards grabbed the two goblins and dragged them away.

"Surely you can't execute them because . . ." Roz gave a weak smile. "Are you jesting again, Your Politeness?"

"Ha ha!" the White Worm said. "No."

"You cannot—" Roz started.

"Seven Pebbles is a serious ka-ontest! And when played with the royal pebbles? The world itself shakes!"

"The—the royal pebbles?" Ji asked.

The goblin king pointed his stone scepter directly overhead, at a stalactite jutting down from the cavern roof. A dozen strings dangled from the stalactite, swaying in the air sixty feet above the throne. No. *Fifteen* strings, each one knotted around an angular stone that looked like a cloudy quartz crystal.

"Behold the most glorious set of pebbles in the underground realm!" the White Worm declared. "As I am the best player." He peered at Ji. "Ah! You like-a them, don't you, Scalyboots?"

"Yeah." Ji stared at the pebbles. They didn't look like much, but there *was* something royal about them. "I mean, yes, Your Goblinificence."

"They are royal." Swirls of white appeared on the White Worm's skin. "ANYONE WHO WISHES TO RULE

MUST BEAT ME IN SEVEN PEBBLES!" The swirls faded. "If they win, they are the new ka-ing. And if they lose . . ."

"You chop off their heads?" Ji guessed.

"And their nec-kas," the White Worm agreed.

Ask about the ogres! Nin said. *We need to warnscare them not to attack the city now that the evilqueen is strong again!*

"Ask about the Ice Witch," Sally murmured.

"We should not waste your majesty's time," Roz told the White Worm, with a tremulous smile. "If you'd just point us toward the ogres, we'll be on our way."

"Of ka-orse!" the White Worm said grandly. "You wish to find the ogres? Simple! Just ka-limb from the city and head toward the mountains until . . ."

"Until what?" Chibo asked, learning forward.

"Until you reach the mountains!" The White Worm chuffed a laugh. "There is only one problem."

"What's that, Your Deepness?" Roz asked.

"I obey the Summer Queen," he said, his pink skin paling to white. "AND SHE TOLD ME TO LOC-KA YOU UP."

Ji gasped—and the goblin guards attacked.

16

JI WOKE INSIDE one of the stone cells that lined the bowl, his head aching from getting bashed with a stone club. He groaned and rolled onto his side.

"Here," someone said, and gave him a damp cloth. "This will help."

"Thanks," Ji said.

"Than-ka you for than-ka-ing me," the voice said.

A goblin! A goblin was bending over him—and getting ready to smash the rest of his head in!

"Hey!" Ji scrambled to his feet. "Get away from me!"

"I am sorry to say that I ka-annot," the goblin chuffed, gesturing with a belly-arm. "I am a prisoner too, I beg pardon."

"Oh." Ji unballed his fists. "What did you do?"

The goblin showed his chipped teeth nervously. "Gave you a wet rag? Perhaps too wet? Not wet enough?"

"No, I mean, why are you locked up? Did—" Ji stopped and scanned the cell. "Where are my friends?"

Dozens of goblins huddled on the ground and dozens more hunched in neighboring cells. To Ji's relief, a furry heap of hobgoblin snored in his own cell. Chibo lay beside Sally, while Roz slumped unconscious in a section of the cell with heavier bars, a metal chest on the ground near her.

"Sally!" Ji trotted closer. "Roz! Are you okay?"

"They are alive, I am happy to say," the chip-toothed goblin told him, following along. "But, I am less happy to say, they are only alive be-ka-ause the White Worm—"

"Mighty worm, powerful worm," the other goblins murmured.

"—plans to hand you over to the ka-ween's soldiers."

"Well, he won't," Ji said, kneeling beside Sally. She was breathing steadily, and when he prodded one of her ears, it twitched.

The goblin cocked its head. "I beg your pardon?"

"We'll stop him."

"The White Worm—"

"His Deepness, His Brutality," the other goblins murmured.

"—always gets what he wants."

Chibo was shivering, so Ji asked the goblins for a blanket

to cover him, then checked on Roz. Ji dimly remembered that she'd knocked a dozen goblin guards aside before the White Worm joined the fray. When he turned white, he was even stronger than a troll.

"Roz?" Ji asked, fear squeezing his chest. "Are you okay?"

She took a shuddering breath in her cell-within-a-cell.

"Roz, say something!"

"Muh," she moaned, raising her head. "Ji?"

"Hush," he told her. "Go back to sleep. You rest. I've got this."

"Yuh," she said, lowering her head.

Ji watched her and wanted to cry. From anger, from helplessness. From coming so far and ending up in a cell. They'd escaped knights and kumiho—and a stupid pink potato-shaped goblin caught them? Why did the White Worm obey the Summer Queen anyway? Didn't he know she enslaved goblins? And where was Nin?

Ji wiped his face and knocked on the metal chest. "Nin? Are you in there?"

Sneakyji! Are you in there?

"What? No. I'm right here."

We're right here too! Where is here?

"You're locked in a chest inside a goblin prison. Are you okay?"

We are snug as a skunk in a trunk. Also, we are tremble-scared and terrified.

"Me, too," Ji said. "I'd wet my widdershins, if I knew what that meant."

You will find a way out.

"There are bars so thick that even Roz can't smash them."

You are not Smashyji, Nin told him. *You are Sneakyji.*

Except how was he supposed to sneak out of a dungeon in the middle of a goblin city? Ji paced in the cell, weaving past clusters of frightened goblins. He glowered through the bars at the White Worm, who stood at a banquet table stuffing his face with three of his hands while a fourth scratched his bottom and the last two scolded one of his attendants. Then the royal pebbles caught Ji's attention. Fifteen pebbles dangled in the air a hundred feet away, like the most boring wind chimes in the world.

"How long before the queen's soldiers get here?" he asked Chiptooth. "It must take days just to tell her we're here."

"I am very sorry," Chiptooth told him. "They are already on the way. The White Worm—"

"All-knowing Worm," the other goblins murmured.

"—sent messengers days ago, while you were in the tunnels."

"They're already coming?" Ji rubbed his face. "Do they even know the way?"

"Yes, the human ka-ween visits every several years."

"The queen comes here? The Summer Queen? Why?"

168

"To chec-ka on the White Worm—"

"Glorious Worm, ka-lever Worm," the others muttered.

"—and tell him how many goblins to send."

"To send where?"

"To the humans."

Ji frowned. "What? Why?"

"To wor-ka in the human mines and ka-rypts and tunnels," Chiptooth chuffed sadly. "That is why we are here. The ka-ing chose us to serve, and now he will give us to the humans."

"Forever," the other goblins murmured. "And our children, and their children . . ."

A gasp sounded from Roz's cage-within-a-cage. "The king gives goblins to the Summer Queen?" she asked, rising to her knees. "He betrays his own people for her?"

"Every goblin ka-ing does this," Chiptooth said, bobbing its head. "Sends thousands of goblins to wor-ka for the humans. That is the price of peace."

"That's not peace," Ji said, and watched the goblin king waddle in front of his throne. The White Worm looked like a fool, but this was no joke. Sending goblins to live in pens, to die in slavery? This was evil.

"In every generation," Chiptooth said, "the Summer Ka-ween grants a new White Worm—"

"Terrible Worm, brutal Worm," the other goblins muttered.

"—the strength to rule us. In the olden days we were

many tribes, and free. Now there is only one tribe. And the rebels."

"What rebels?" Sally asked, sitting up with Chibo's head in her lap.

"Goblins who wor-ka against both thrones."

"You mean the goblins who are helping the ogres?" Roz asked Chiptooth. "They're rebels? They don't follow the king?"

"Yes. They fight to stop the human ka-ween, so the White Worm—"

"Greedy and treacherous Worm."

"—will fall. If the ogres attac-ka soon, they will be vika-torious. She is wea-ka."

Roz bowed her head. "I'm sorry, but the queen's not weak anymore. She's become strong again."

The goblin prisoners waved their belly-arms in horror, and Chiptooth said, "Please tell us this is not the truth! Please! She is still wea-ka!"

"We're pretty sure she's strong again," Ji said. "Though we don't know how."

"Er." Roz cleared her throat. "We have a theory."

"We do?" Ji asked.

"To grow stronger, the queen must weaken someone else. That is how her magic works."

"Right," Sally growled. "Balance."

"Do you recall the nobleman in the library coach talking about a blue-bat plague? And all the dead blue-bats at the water clock?"

"Poor little guys," Chibo fluted sadly.

"You think she killed them," Sally growled to Roz. "You think the queen wiped out the blue-bats and drained their power to strengthen herself."

"Yes."

"Why them?" Chibo asked, almost wailing. "Why blue-bats?"

"Perhaps she needed the sort of magic they have? Or perhaps they were simply the easiest targets."

A wordless feeling of despair came from Nin. *So she is realtruly strong again? Ogres will not survive if we don't warnscare them. The ogres will not survive.*

Roz rumbled softly to Nin, while Sally lashed her tail. Chibo spoke with the goblins, who woofled in reply. Asking questions, offering comfort. A few of the younger goblins wept, but Ji turned away, his gaze sweeping the white marble stadium through the cell bars. How long before the queen's soldiers came? And who would lead them? Posey and Nichol? Mr. Ioso and Prince Brace? All of them together?

It didn't matter. Once they arrived, Ji and the others didn't have a chance. They'd be sacrificed to strengthen the Summer Realm—to keep the goblins enslaved, the ogres beaten, and the crown forever triumphant.

The sunlight streaming through the holes in the cavern roof dimmed as dusk fell in the world outside. Torches flickered to life around the marble city. Chuffed songs echoed in the streets and a busy woofling came from the marketplace.

But in the cells, fearful silence reigned. The goblins hunched together. Roz and Chibo dozed off, still weakened from the fight, while Sally picked flecks of gravel from her tail. Soon only Ji was awake. He rested his lumpy forehead on a cell bar and watched bonfires blaze across the goblin city, casting a dull yellow light.

The fires roared higher. Flames spewed like snake tails. A booming voice shouted, "Off with his neck!"

Six giant hands played Seven Pebbles—and Ji was one of the pebbles, scraping across a playing board. Chunks of diamond slid across the lumpy spirals—

Ji woke with start, his face pressed to the bars.

Dawn's light glowed through the holes in the roof. Ji used the trench in the corner, ate some mushrooms, and returned to the bars. For a moment, he glowered toward the White Worm, who was polishing his teeth atop the giant throne. Then Ji's gaze lingered on the dangling royal pebbles. He didn't know why. Seven Pebbles couldn't help them, despite his stupid dream. Nothing could help them, with the Summer Queen's soldiers galloping closer every minute. Fear dug a pit in his stomach, a hollow ache behind his belly button. A greedy, needy, hungry feeling . . .

"Oh," he breathed. "I guess sniffing those rocks paid off after all."

"He said something!" Sally called to Roz.

Ji jerked in surprise. He hadn't seen Sally standing beside him.

"And what, pray tell," Roz asked, "did he say?"

"Something about sniffing rocks."

Rocks sniffsmell delicious! Nin said.

Ji's pulse pounded in his chest. "I need to challenge the White Worm to a game."

"Of Seven Pebbles?" Sally asked.

"Hey!" Ji shouted toward the throne. "Hey, White Worm!"

Sally grabbed his arm. "If you lose, they'll chop your head off."

"I won't lose," he said. "Hey! Wormy!"

"Do you know how to play?" Chibo fluted, gliding beside him.

"Of course not," Ji scoffed. "Now help me get his attention!"

Sally lashed her tail and called to Roz. "Should we help him?"

"Jiyong, what—" Roz started.

"Wormy!" Ji yelled. "Hey, potato-face! You look like a turnip and you smell like a beet!"

Beets smell fishexcellent, Nin said. *And insulting a skullnumb goblin king is not exactly brilly ant.*

"Jiyong!" Roz rumbled. "The king is the best player among the goblins, and he has six arms!" She turned to

Chiptooth. "You cannot win against someone with more arms, right?"

"You are right, I'm sorry to say," Chiptooth said. "It is impossible to beat the White Worm—"

"Cunning Worm, evil Worm," the others muttered.

"—at Seven Pebbles, even with four arms."

"I challenge you to a game of Seven Pebbles!" Ji hollered across the bowl.

"WHO DARES?" the White Worm boomed, so loud that the goblins near him fell to their knees. "WHO DARES INSULT THE MIGHTY WHITE WORM!"

"I'll mash you like a pink potato!" Ji shouted—which was not a sentence he'd ever dreamed he'd bellow at a goblin king across an underground city.

Still, it seemed to work. A dozen elite guards marched toward him, clubbing any goblin who got in the way. In a minute, they clustered outside his cell, barking in Goblish. The goblin prisoners knelt while a mean-looking guard pulled a key ring from its belt and unlocked the door.

"Sally, that one," Ji said, staring at the mean-looking guard. "Remember that goblin."

Her ears twitched. "Why?"

"Because that's the one with the key," he whispered, and turned toward the goblin guards. "I need Sally to come with me."

The mean-looking goblin made a rude gesture and barked at the other guards, who grabbed Ji.

"I need her," he repeated as they were pulled from the cell. "For the challenge!"

"Let me come!" Sally growled.

The guards slammed the door in her face and dragged Ji away. Fortunately, the mean-looking guard stayed with him as they crossed the bowl and climbed to the throne platform. Less fortunately, it shoved Ji to the marble floor. "Kneel before His Deepness!"

"Sure," Ji said, ignoring the pain in his knees. "Then I'll crush His Creepness at Seven Pebbles."

The White Worm lightened to the color of spoiled cream. "LOWER THE ROYAL PEBBLES AND WATCH YOUR KA-ING DESTROY"—he pinkened—"this foolish half human and chop him into eleven pieces!"

Ji swayed fearfully. "Eleven pieces" was way too specific. It sounded like the White Worm had chopped people into ten and twelve pieces, but hadn't been quite satisfied. Also, Ji had thought he had a great plan but now he wasn't so sure: his life depended on the royal pebbles.

"I've defeated a hundred masters of Seven Pebbles," the White Worm snarled, twirling his scepter with three of his arms. "When I beat the old White Worm, I won his throne. He was the best player in a century. Until me."

"And you were the best," Ji said, his voice barely wavering, "until me."

A white-clad courtier stepped behind the throne and turned a crank, which lowered the royal pebbles from the stalactite. Sixty feet overhead. Fifty feet. When they were at forty feet, Ji felt a surge of relief so strong that he barely noticed the pebbles being lowered the rest of the way to the throne.

But a minute later, two goblins arranged the pebbles on a black tray and offered them to the White Worm. "Your choice to choose, all-knowing Worm," they chanted in unison.

"With six mighty limbs, I choose six pebbles," the White Worm told Ji. "With two feeble twigs, you choose two. I will beat you in four turns."

"I'll win in three," Ji said, feeling a thrum of power in his chest.

The White Worm giggled. "Nobody wins in three! Three is not possible!"

"You'll see."

"I'll see you chopped into pieces," the White Worm replied. "And you will fertilize the fungus farms."

The goblin king plucked a pebble from the black tray, a roundish stone that looked like dirty quartz, cloudy and angular.

Except it wasn't quartz.

Not even close.

The king chose another pebble, then another. "Does the half human even know how to choose? Which are best to ka-pture, and which to slide?"

Ji kept his eyes on the tray. "Different pebbles do different things?"

176

A scornful woofling sounded. A few goblins muttered "foolish two-arms" and "half-human halfwit."

"You know nothing!" the White Worm chortled, and chose the rest of his pebbles.

"My turn?" Ji asked, his heart beating fast.

"Yes, yes!" the White Worm chuffed. "Try your best, you gormless gekko."

Of the initial fifteen pebbles, only nine remained. Ji choose the nearest one, and a mocking mutter spread through the spectators.

"Not *that* one!" the White Worm scoffed. "That is the worst of the bunch."

Ji tested the weight of the pebble in his palm. "Feels okay to me."

"Four turns," the White Worm said, his beady eye gleaming. "And then eleven pieces."

That time, Ji didn't feel a shiver of fear. He grabbed his second pebble and scanned the crowd for the mean-looking goblin, his heart beating with a slow *thump thud, thump thud.*

"My move," the White Worm said, sliding a pebble onto the board.

The crowd said, "Ooooh."

With a trembling hand, Ji placed one of his pebbles.

The crowd said, "Ka!"

The White Worm dropped another pebble onto the board.

The crowd said, "Ahhhh!"

Ji plucked two pebbles from the board.

"That is not allowed!" the White Worm said.

"No?" Ji swiped a handful of pebbles from the tray. "Then how about *this*?"

The White Worm paled. "You thin-ka you can cheat the glorious White Worm? CHOP HIM NOW! YOUR KA-APTAIN KA-MMANDS YOU!"

17

Ji CLOSED HIS fists around the pebbles . . . except they weren't pebbles.

They were diamonds.

After he'd honed his dragonhunger in the goblin tunnels, he'd been able to sense them from his cell. At least, he'd *thought* they were gems. But now heat surged through his arms, lava boiled his blood—and a fireball erupted from his eyes.

The blast caught the goblin king in the chest and flung him off the throne. Six white arms flailed as the White Worm hurtled across the stadium. He slammed to the ground, ricocheted off a half dozen mushroom-stools, and lay still except for a vague waving of his belly-arms.

The elite guards swarmed at Ji, shouting in Goblish.

Two more diamonds turned black in Ji's hands as he swept eye-flames at the guards.

They dove aside, screaming in Goblish.

"Behind you!" Sally yelled from the cell. "Duck!"

Ji fell to the ground and a club whistled past his head. When he spun, his eye-flames scorched a char mark across the throne before sweeping at the goblin who'd attacked him.

The stone club glowed cherry red in the goblin's fist. The goblin howled and fled, and another diamond crumbled in Ji's hands. Two more cracked when he swept his burning gaze around the fleeing, terrified guards. Then he spotted the mean-looking one with the keys.

"You!" he shouted. "Stop right there!"

The mean-looking goblin leaped away, but a fireball blasted it to the ground.

"Give me the keys," Ji snarled.

The goblin fainted.

"That works," Ji said, and tugged the key ring from its belt.

Panicked woofles sounded across the city, along with the uneven clatter of running goblins. A gong—maybe a warning bell—echoed through the cavern, and the keys jingled in Ji's hand. His fists throbbed. He wanted to *burn*. He wanted to set fire to the stone and drink the souls of his enemies. A fathomless dragonhunger seized his heart, and he teetered on the edge of forgetting himself.

"Jiyong!" Roz called.

Ji shook himself. *Right. The cell.* He trotted down the throne stairs to the cell, ash trailing between his fingers as diamonds crumbled in his palms.

"The pebbles were *gems*?" Sally asked from inside the bars.

"Diamonds," he told her.

Her ears flattened. "You knew? You knew they were diamonds all this time and didn't say anything?"

"I didn't know!" Ji's hand shook when he shoved the key in the lock. "Not for sure. Not until I got close."

"You *didn't* know?" she growled. "That's even worse. You risked playing that stupid game without knowing the pebbles were diamonds?"

He unlocked the cell door. "Sort of."

"I'm going to chop your head off myself!" Sally grabbed the keys from his hand and bounded deeper into the cell to free Roz.

A wave of weakness made Ji's legs tremble. Using dragonfire exhausted him. He scanned the throne and stadium, afraid of a goblin attack, afraid of the White Worm—and afraid of himself. A smoky haze covered the city, drifting past domes and towers. He heard chuffing sobs over the fearful woofling and the echoing gong. The weeping sounded like goblin children, and nausea coiled in Ji's stomach.

A *crack* sounded inside the cell as Roz broke the metal

chest to free Nin. Ji gripped the remaining diamonds harder. Heat scalded his palms and spread into his heart. He eyed the soldiers gathering at the top of the stadium ramp. He stoked his fire even though he was already dizzy, already weak.

Roz stepped beside him, adjusting the straps of Nin's dirt-filled backpack. Emerald-green light flickered as Chibo landed beside him and Sally followed, her hackles raised and her claws flexing.

"How do we get out of here?" she growled.

Roz pointed her horn toward the stalagmite towers. "I presume we climb one of those. Though they don't seem to reach the roof."

"You must ka-limb to the top of that tower." Chiptooth's belly-arm pointed to an upside-down tower. "Past the marka-tplace, aka-ross that bridge there. You will find a glowhole to the surface."

"Thanks," Chibo piped.

"C'mon," Sally growled. "Let's move."

Roz smiled at Chiptooth and helped Ji toward the ramp rising to the city streets. Nin babbled mind-speak that Ji couldn't take in over the roar of fire in his ears, while Sally suddenly looked backward.

She tossed the key ring to Chiptooth. "Unlock the other prisoners."

"You are ka-ind," Chiptooth told her. "And your heart is mighty."

Sally scowled with embarrassment. "Thanks."

"I will free them," Chiptooth promised. "We will join the rebels."

"That's very brave."

"It's very necessary."

"I'm—" Sally stood a little straighter. "I'm glad to meet someone fighting for what matters. Fighting with honor."

"Honor," Chiptooth said, showing both belly-palms to Sally, "is the highest form of politeness."

She mirrored the gesture with her paws. "Good luck-ka."

After Chiptooth rushed off to unlock the cells, Roz glanced at Sally. "Apparently all goblins *aren't* alike."

Sally grunted at her, then prowled up the ramp toward the city streets. She led the way past the wavy columns, toward a wide intersection—and frowned at the soldiers gathering in the crossroads.

Watch out! Three ant lions crawled from the backpack onto Roz's shoulder. *More goblinfighters ahead!*

"Stop right there!" Sally barked at the goblins. "Or the lizard cooks you!"

With a spark of panic, Ji sent flames roaring upward. The soldiers in the crossroads chuffed and raised their belly-arms in surrender.

"Yeah," Sally snarled at them. "That's what I thought."

Ji lowered his head and opened his fists. A pile of ashes filled one palm and a single half-burned diamond nestled in the other: only enough for one final blast.

Farther into the city, goblin parents stood with goblin children in marble doorways. Vendors trembled at stalls, and a silence fell—except for the sound of the gong. Nobody bothered them. Not at the squares, not at the marketplace. Not as they climbed up the first tower or crossed a bridge to the downward-facing tower. Uneven steps—built for goblin knees—zigzagged upward, past wall niches displaying pink potatoes.

"Maybe that's why the goblins in that crossroads didn't attack," Roz rumbled. "Because the White Worm is not able to lead them."

"Either that," Sally said, "or they're scared of Ji's eyeballs."

He showed her the last cracked diamond in his hand. "Good thing they don't know I'm almost out of gems."

"What?" she growled. "You were bluffing?"

"Nah," he said. "*You* were bluffing."

"And you say I'm a bad liar," she said, her muzzle lifting in a grin.

In a round chamber at the top of the tower, a hole opened in the ceiling: an exit to the surface. "Where's the ladder?" Chibo fluted. "I don't see a ladder."

"Neither do we," Ji told him.

Sally growled. "Sounds like the White Worm is conscious again. The goblin army is gathering. We need to go before—"

"Never fear!" Chibo piped, and flew through the hole in the ceiling.

"Get back here!" Sally yelled after him.

"Chibo?" Roz rumbled. "Chibo!"

Silence from above.

"Chibo!" Sally shouted.

"Roz," Ji said, "can you throw Sally through the—"

A ladder fell through the hole; then Chibo's face appeared. "Sprites do that."

When Ji reached the top of the ladder, the sunlight brought tears to his eyes. A squat, ramshackle watchtower stood above him in the middle of a lifeless plain. A few other towers rose nearby, each with a ladder descending into a skylight of the goblin city.

He took a steadying breath. The breeze smelled fresh after the sickly-sweet air of the goblin city, and the cracked earth was a reddish brown. A few clusters of cacti broke up the flatness. Mountains rose in the distance, over green foothills and a wide band of what looked like dirty snow.

"What is this place?" Sally asked, her ears twitching.

"The Clay Plains," Roz rumbled, struggling up the ladder behind her. "We're no longer in the Summer Realm. The Clay Plains! I never imagined I'd see them."

"What do they look like?" Chibo asked, hovering overhead. "All I see is a big flat nothing."

"That's what they look like," Sally told him.

The redflats? Nin asked, with a thrill of excitement. *We are not far from the Ogrelands! When we were a cublet, we used to sit outside our mother's ridge and peeksee the redflats!*

"Which way are the ogres?" Ji asked, scratching the lumps on his forehead.

Roz pointed. "East."

Just past the Gravewoods.

"That's what ogres call the Shield Wall, yes?" Roz asked.

One of the ant lions on her backpack nodded. *But we ogres are ashamed to chattalk about the Gravewoods.*

"At least tell us what kind of wall it is," Ji said.

The evilmagic kind.

"Are the goblins chasing us?" Chibo landed and retracted his wings. "Can you see the mountains? Did I totally save the day?"

Ji looked away from the ant lions on the backpack. "No, yes, and totally."

Chibo beamed. "Cool."

"The White Worm's coming," Sally said. "There's nowhere to hide for miles and Ji's out of gems."

"He has one diamond left, I believe." Roz gestured toward the wooden towers. "Enough to burn the towers and ladders so the goblins can't follow us."

Ji drew on the last scraps of power in the diamond. Heat scorched through his arm to his chest and exploded

186

from his eyes. The rough-hewn logs of the tower charred, but didn't catch fire.

"C'mon, Ji!" Sally growled. "You couldn't toast bread with that much flame. You couldn't light a candle."

"You couldn't wilt a lettuce leaf!" Chibo piped.

You couldn't sleepylull a baby! Nin said.

"Um," Sally said. "Ogres lull babies to sleep with fire?"

Not with feeblesparks like that*!*

"Would you shut your mouths?" Ji grunted, blasting more dragonfire through his eyes.

The watchtower burst into flames like a haystack in a lava flow. As Ji set fire to the other towers, the diamond turned to dust in his fist. He opened his hand to watch the last of the ashes—the last gem—waft away.

"Very thorough," Roz said, a little too calmly. "However, there is a slight drawback."

"What *now*?" Ji demanded, weak from shooting fire.

"Well, the queen's troops will see the smoke."

Ji cursed, and Chibo piped, "They'll find us! We've got to run, we've got to fly! They'll know exactly where we are!"

"No, they'll know exactly where we *were*." Sally gazed across the plain. "I don't see them yet. We just have to reach the mountains before they catch us."

The red-brown earth grew lighter as they hiked eastward, away from the plumes of smoke. After an hour, a coarse bluish grass covered the cracked ground. Roz said that a long time ago the Clay Plain had been a marsh, until the Summer Queen seized power. Then the water dried, the plants withered, and nothing remained but layers of terra-cotta.

"Like the warriors in the city?" Sally asked.

Roz nodded. "Some claim that Summer Queens shape terra-cotta warriors from this soil. Others say they use holy magic to bind their most dangerous enemies into their service."

Which turns them into clayfighters? Nin asked.

"There are rumors of a spell that transforms the queens' enemies into mindless lumps of obedience."

"Wait," Sally said, her ears swiveling. "I hear them. They're coming!"

"Who?" Chibo asked. "The goblins?"

"No." She pointed toward the Summer Realm. "The queen's soldiers. A lot of them—a whole army."

When Ji shaded his eyes to look, an ant lion hopped from his hair to his sleeve. In the distance, a flock of birds wheeled around a stand of cacti. Nothing else moved.

"How far away are they?" he asked.

"I don't know," Sally said. "Maybe half a day?"

"Have they seen us?"

"I don't think so. They're riding toward the goblin city. But we kind of stand out on this flat field of nothing."

Like the ogres say, Nin told them. *Nothing hides in the redflats except clay and melons. Golly!*

Ji blinked at the backpack. "Golly?"

Melons. Golly.

"Melancholy?" Roz suggested. "Nothing hides in the redflats except clay and melancholy. That's rather poetic."

"Forget poetry," Ji said. "Keep moving before the army spots us."

"Not *us*," Roz rumbled, hunching her shoulders. "They won't spot *us*. They'll spot me. The big, lumbering, ungainly troll."

Ji glowered at Roz and marched toward the foothills. Even without a gem, he felt inflamed and overheated. Stupid Roz. Like it was her fault for being tall. Like any of them thought for a second that she was a burden.

The big lumbergainly half *troll,* Nin said. *Nobody is a truetroll until Beginning.*

"Beginning *what*?" Sally asked.

"Beginning" is passagerite, a ceremony that turns the wisest ogres into trolls.

"A troll is just a wise ogre?" Chibo questioned.

All cubs turn into ogres. Some ogres turn into trolls. When an ogre's wisdom flows pure, the tribe gathers for a passagerite of Beginning. A thunderclap ceremony, a grandsolemn test of the soul.

"So Roz isn't a true troll because she wasn't clapped by thunder?" Chibo asked.

"If a troll is just a wise ogre," Sally asked Nin, "how come they look different?"

When cubs choose female or male, Nin explained, *they change into ogres. When wisdom chooses ogres? They also change.*

"Ogres are weird," Sally said.

Clouds gathered overhead. Gritty air stung Ji's nose. When the crunching of the red-brown plain ended, the ground turned softer. The sun dipped toward the horizon, and the scent of the foothills rose on the breeze: the sweet perfume of black soil and flowering trees. Dusk fell and a gentle slope rose toward meadows and woods.

Eventually Ji and the others made camp in the light of two quarter-moons. Only two moons, thankfully. There was nowhere to hide if the kumiho appeared.

Ji slept fitfully until Roz shook him awake. "Good morning!"

He peered at the predawn light. "Not morning yet."

"Not good, either." Sally frowned toward the Clay Plains. "The queen's army is still following us. And there's troublenews bigbad."

Troublebad bignews, Nin corrected, as two ant lions waggled their antennae.

Ji sat up. "What's wrong?"

"The goblin army is above ground, and they're also heading this way."

"No way," Chibo said, rubbing his eyes. "They're *both* after us?"

"A few armies don't matter," Ji said. "We just need to find the Ice Witch."

190

"A few armies don't matter?" Sally peered at Ji. "Did you really just say that?"

"They don't matter at all," Ji told her with a grin. "Not if they can't catch us."

18

THE WOODS THICKENED as they traveled higher into the foothills. Monkeys chattered and insects darted through the dappled shade. Meadows stretched beneath the mountains, and the band of "dirty snow" that Ji had spotted from the goblin watchtower looked like pale marble.

Like the goblin city.

"What's the white stuff?" he asked.

An ant lion climbed into Ji's hair. *The Gravewoods.*

"That's the Shield Wall?" Roz furrowed her heavy brow. "But it's not a wall at all! It looks miles wide and no higher than the treetops."

Only humans call it the Shield Wall, Nin said. *It is realtruly the Gravewoods.*

"You said it's evilmagic?" Roz asked.

Nin didn't answer for a moment. *We don't chattalk about the Gravewoods. Ogres are full of shame.*

"You're ashamed of the Gravewoods?" Roz asked. "Why?"

We did wrong, Nin said, then changed the subject. *The Gravewoods are terrible dangerous unless ogres guide us through.*

"Dangerous how? We need to know what's ahead of us, Nin."

"I don't know what's ahead of us," Sally growled. "But Brace is behind us."

"Can you smell him?" Ji asked.

"Not exactly."

"Then how do you know it's him?"

"Because grass is dying around the army. Entire fields are shriveling."

"He's casting a spell," Chibo remarked, his grip tightening on Ji's hand.

Fear drove them faster uphill. Ji stumbled but didn't slow, keeping Chibo close while Roz forged a path ahead.

"How far . . . ," Ji panted, "are the Ogrelands?"

"Do you see the highest mountain?" Roz asked, shading her eyes with a three-fingered hand.

Ji followed her gaze. "One mountain is twice as tall as the rest," he told Chibo. "The top half is all snow."

"That's Mount Atra." Roz shifted the weight of her backpack. "It's on the far side of the Ogrelands, so we're quite close. We'll see the Shield Wall any moment—I mean, the Gravewoods."

The Gravewoods, Nin repeated with an edge of fear.

"Would you tell us what that is?" Ji asked an ant lion on his shoulder.

"Yeah," Sally said, "and how we're supposed to get through it, if it's so scary."

Ogres will guide us on safepaths, Nin said.

"Safe from what? What are you tal—" Sally's ears swiveled. "Whoa. That's not right."

"Oh, boy," Chibo said. "What now?"

Sally loped into a wooded grove and stopped at a ginkgo tree with wildly fluttering golden leaves.

"Oh," Ji said, slowing behind her. "Yeah."

Roz cleared her throat. "That is quite . . . out of the ordinary."

"The tree?" Chibo asked. "It's just a tree."

"The leaves are moving," Sally told him. "For no reason."

"There's a reason," Roz rumbled. "There's just no wind."

"Why did we walk *toward* the scary tree?" Ji asked.

The leaves spun and twirled into the shape of a face. Brace's face, twenty feet high and fifteen feet wide and made of ginkgo leaves.

"If you can hear me," the tree-face said in a woody sort of voice, "you must stop right now."

Ji gaped at the huge leafy nose and the massive mouth

that moved when Brace spoke. Because holy guacamole, that was a *huge leafy nose and a massive mouth that moved when Brace spoke.*

A shiver ran through the leaves. "Jiyong, Miss Roz, and—you others, please listen."

"That jerk still doesn't know my name," Sally muttered.

"If you venture too deep into the Shield Wall," the leaves said, "you will die."

"And you want us alive," Sally growled, her ears flat. "So you can kill us."

"If you hear me," Brace said, "stop running. I know that one of your"—the leafy face paused—"'friends' was an ogre, but that will not save you."

Roz glanced at an ant lion on her sleeve. "You must tell us about the Gravewoods, Nin."

"The ogres are gathering in goblin tunnels outside Summer City," the leafy Brace said. "They think Her Majesty doesn't know, but her terra-cotta warriors are waiting. They'll slaughter the ogres before they reach the Forbidden Palace."

Slaughter! Nin said, cub's mind-speak shuddering with horror. *We must warnscare them!*

"Once ogres form war parties," Brace continued, "they become violent and mindless. After the ogres—"

"They're our friends!" Chibo interjected.

"—start marching to battle, they lash out like rabid beasts. They'll kill you long before the Shield Wall finishes

195

turning you into—" Brace's face blurred, the leafy gaze looking to his left. "What's that, Ioso? The *goblins*? You must—"

The magic stopped. The huge face slackened into normal leaves and branches . . . for a moment. Then the leaves curled and blackened and fell to the ground.

"Um," Ji said, after a few seconds. "What's this about ogres getting violent and rabid?"

"A war party is a squad of ogres who vow to fight to the death," Roz rumbled slowly. "Ogre war parties are known for their ferocity, but I'm not sure that Prince Brace is telling the whole truth."

The clayfighters are waiting, Nin said. *That much sounds wholetrue. The ogres will be slaughterkilled.*

"Nin's right," Sally growled, prowling past a boulder. "If they attack, the queen's terra-cotta soldiers will wipe them out."

Chibo spread his wings nervously. "We need to warn them."

"We will." Ji followed Sally toward the hilltop. "And Nin will tell us about this stupid Shield Wall."

A few ant lions crawled higher on the backpack straps. *The Gravewoods.*

"I don't care what you call it!" Ji snapped. "Just tell us about it!"

No, we mean right there. The ant lions pointed their antennae. *The Gravewoods.*

A higher hill rose on the other side of a gully. No meadows or grass grew on the facing slope, because the white "band" wasn't dirty snow or marble buildings: it was a range of foothills covered with jagged stone pillars and bizarre stone sculptures.

"A petrified forest," Roz breathed.

Sally's tail lashed. "A what?"

"Trees and bushes—a whole forest—turned to stone."

This is what keeps the ogres feebleweak, Nin said.

Roz lifted an ant lion on her finger. "The Gravewoods does?"

The ant lion nodded. *Our hillfoots are turned to stone. We spoketold you this!*

"You did not," Ji said.

We did! A deep sense of shame curdled Nin's mindspeak. *We spoketold you the whole sadstory.*

"I guess we weren't listening," Ji said, giving an ant lion a sympathetic look. "Tell us again?"

Nobody safecrosses the Gravewoods unless guided by ogres . . . or mages.

"Nobody crosses safely?" Ji squinted at the petrified forest. "What happens if you try?"

First your skin scabflakes. Then your throat parches, your eyes dry and crack. Every step, more full of pain. Every step, more parchdry and rockfleshed.

"Rock fleshed? You turn to stone?"

Over miles and miles. Step by step.

Roz cleared her throat. "Unless you're guided by ogres?"

Or mages. Then maybe safecross.

"Maybe?" Ji asked.

Longago, a spell was cast that turns flesh to stone if you try to leave the Ogrelands—or enter. A powerful and terrible spell.

"I suppose that's why the humans call it 'the Shield Wall,'" Roz said. "Because it keeps the ogres from invading."

"But ogres can still leave," Ji said.

Snailcarefully, Nin said. *And not safely. Even for ogres on the safepaths, the Gravewoods are dangerous.*

"So we need ogres to lead us across?" Sally asked after Nin trailed off. "Let's find some."

"Awesome," Chibo fluted, clearly trying to cheer Nin up. "I love ogres."

"I'll love if they'll tell us how to find the Ice Witch," Ji grumbled. "And I'll dance a jig when she breaks this spell."

Goodnews! Nin said. *And badnews.*

"What bad news?" Ji asked, as Chibo said, "I love good news!"

A few ant lions pointed toward a dozen huge shapes moving among the crumbling stone trees across the gully. Ji caught the flash of glossy red skin and curving white horns through the gloom of the petrified forest. Quick glimpses that looked like the bulls and lions and gorillas he'd seen in Roz's books—except utterly different.

Those are ogres! Nin announced. *Grownfull ogres! We found them!*

"What's the bad news?" Ji asked again.

Oh, well, Nin said, with a hint of nervousness. *They peeksee like a warparty. Brace spoke the realtruth. The ogres are marching to war, protecting the borders, and . . .*

"And what?" Roz asked.

If we enter the Gravewoods, Nin said, abashed, *they will attack.*

"Attack who?" Sally growled. "Attack *us?*"

A warparty will haltstomp anyone who comes scary-close to the Ogrelands.

"We're not scary," Chibo said. "We're scared."

Once ogres join together in a warparty, they grow eagerkeen to do battle.

Ji kicked a stump. "You mean they're looking for a fight."

"They won't hurt us!" Chibo insisted. "We're with Nin. And we're not a threat or anything. Just five kids lost in the woods."

"Ye-es," Roz said, rubbing her horn. "However, Nin knows ogres."

"We don't have a choice," Ji said. "There's two armies behind us."

Maybe Chibald is right. Maybe they'll listen to us. We're an ogre, after all.

"But they won't know you're you," Sally said. "They can't hear when you mind-speak."

"The ogres might stomp us," Ji said, "but the humans and goblins definitely will."

"That's what being a half human means," Chibo said, his huge green eyes sad. "Everyone hates you."

"We'll break the spell soon," Roz promised, taking Chibo's hand.

Ji scanned the Gravewoods. Nothing moved among the petrified trees. No shadowy shapes, no war party. He frowned and started down the gully below the last green hill before the stone trees started. Even if the ogres guided them across the Gravewoods—instead of stomping them into salsa—they still needed to find the Ice Witch and convince her to help . . . before the armies caught them.

When he reached the petrified forest, his breath caught. The line between the stone trees and the living ones was sharp as a boundary drawn on a map with a razor. One half of an ancient pine tree rose like a stone sculpture from rocky roots, with eerily perfect bark carvings. On the other half, narrow trunks grew from living roots, twisting and twining toward the sky.

Ji's palms itched. The stillness of the petrified woods unnerved him.

"Hello?" he called. "Ogres? We're here with a cub. A cub named Nin!"

No response.

"We need help crossing the Gravewoods!"

Sally prowled beside him. "They're not close anymore."

"They left?"

She shrugged. "I guess."

They want us to follow, Nin said.

"Why?" Roz asked.

"To give the Gravewoods time to weaken us," Ji told her. "Before they start stomping."

"Oh," she said in a little voice.

Ji ran his fingertips along the pebbled bark of the pine tree. How long before the spell of the Gravewoods seeped into his skin? How long before his eyes turned to stone and his lungs to rocks? He swallowed, then made himself take three steps into the petrified woods. The ground crunched like gravel underfoot. Because it *was* gravel, the remains of fallen stone branches and shattered leaves.

Roz touched his elbow. "The ogres will help us."

"Next time," he told her, "let's not get turned into beasts and captured by goblins and chased by two armies into a deadly forest."

"Would you rather be cleaning boots?" she asked.

"Yes!" he said.

She arched a disbelieving eyebrow. "I know you better than that."

"Boots never turned me to stone." He looked into the Gravewoods. "Okay, let's go talk to some ogres about a witch."

A faint trail led deeper into the forest. No birds sang. No bees buzzed, no monkeys hooted, no crickets chirped. Ji's skin tingled. He climbed over shattered logs and he slunk past fallen tangles of stone branches.

"Where *are* they?" Sally asked, her ears swiveling. "They were right here twenty minutes ago."

Nobody answered.

The magic of the lifeless stone forest made Ji's lips crack. His fingers ached and his eyes throbbed.

"I bet they're preparing a welcome feast!" Chibo piped. "Ogres would never hurt us."

No-o-o-o, Nin said hesitantly. *But a warparty might. They rockvow to protect the Ogrelands against all dangers.*

"We're not a danger," Roz rumbled. "Although I suppose we *are* leading two armies this way."

Nin gave a blurt of nervous mind-speak: *And they might ponderthink that Chibald is a mage.*

"Why him?" Sally asked.

No hair, Nin said. *Like Mysterioso.*

"Like Mr. Ioso?" Ji glanced at an ant lion. "Are all mages bald?"

Also, Nin said, ignoring Ji's question, *they'll see that we are not ogres.*

"Well!" Chibo said, after an unhappy pause. "At least there was only one moon last night."

"There were two," Sally told him.

"Well, there weren't four. No kumiho. That's all that matters."

Sally hopped over a clump of stone grass, sharp enough to stab. "Finding the Ice Witch and breaking the spell is all that matters."

Warning the ogres not to attack Summer City and saving them from the clayfighters, Nin said. *That's also all that matters.*

"Don't forget escaping the Summer Queen and White Worm," Roz rumbled. "And avoiding being turned to stone by the Gravewoods. That's all that matters too."

"And not getting stomped by ogres," Ji said, looking into the jagged woods. "Where are they?"

"Watching us, probably," Sally said. "Leading us into a trap."

"If this was a trap," Ji said, "you'd think they'd lead us onto a wider path."

Twelve seconds later, a wider path opened in front of them: a broad trail covered in the dust of petrified wood crushed by ogre feet.

Ji gulped. "Oh."

"What shall we do?" Roz asked.

"My skin's burning and my tongue's dry," Ji told her. "And we're only a mile into the woods. We need to find the ogres fast."

Sally followed the path uphill, moving on all fours. She prowled between shattered stone bushes and crumbling stone trees. A clay-tinged breeze brought the jingle of weapons from behind them: the sound of the Summer Army approaching. Chibo whimpered and Roz tsk-tsked, but Sally just kept stalking deeper into the woods.

Then Ji heard something else, a faint splash of water. "What's that?" he croaked.

The river, Nin said, and two ant lions dropped from the backpack.

They landed with a faint *tink*, and Ji saw two tiny statues, two stone ant lions, lying on a bed of stone moss.

"Nin!" he said. "You're turning to stone!"

Only a few of us. Like your hairtips.

"My what?" Ji raised his hand and felt the pinpricks of his stony hair. Just the very ends, not even as wide as a blade of grass. Still, he groaned. "The spell's already taking hold."

Sally broke a petrified strand from her tail. "It's just a little fur."

"Yeah, but what about Nin?" Ji crouched beside the stone ant lions. "How long before your queen dies?"

Days and days, Nin said.

"You're a worse liar than Sally," Ji said, scooping the stone ant lions into his palm.

Over the next hour, the splashing of the river grew steadily louder. Ji licked his cracked, flinty lips, while Chibo scratched his scabby neck until he bled. Sally started coughing, and even Roz's breath turned ragged and harsh.

Finally, Sally raised a furry fist. "I hear them."

"It's only the river," Ji croaked.

"No." She stepped onto a stone plateau fringed with petrified rosebushes. "Look."

A sheer cliff dropped from the far end of the plateau, and a river frothed at the bottom. A group of ogres roamed the stone-wooded hill beyond the crashing river. Ten or fifteen of them, stalking through the petrified whiteness.

Full-grown ogres, not cubs like Nin.

No two of them were alike, except for their bright red skin and yellow hair. Or yellow *manes*. Some of them looked like bulls: a thousand pounds of ogre with four legs and sharp horns and broad shoulders. Some walked on their knuckles like gorillas; others raised curved tusks and peered horribly around. A few looked almost human, except for their monstrous faces—with pointed ears and fangs—and claws. Stone rings dangled from most of the ogres' ears and noses.

"What?" Chibo asked, his wings fluttering. "What do they look like?"

"They're large," Roz said. "They're quite emphatically large."

"They're on the other side of the river—" Sally started.

The ogres caught sight of them and swarmed forward with huge leaps, bounding like a herd of agile buffalo. Without any hesitation, they leaped across the river and scrambled up the cliffside toward the plateau.

"Well"—Sally gulped—"we wanted to meet the ogres."

Ji's heart fluttered like a kite in a hurricane. "Nin! What do we do now?"

Tell them we're us! Tell them you're you! Tell them the evilqueen is strong again, and not to attack!

"Nin!" Ji yelled to the first ogre climbing onto the plateau. "We're friends of Nin! The cub, the ogre cub you sent to Summer City!"

The ogre roared in Ogrish, and five more swarmed from the cliffside.

Ji stepped forward. "Nin sent us to the Ogrelands with a message."

A gorilla-looking ogre rose onto its feet and roared so loudly that Ji's ears rang.

"I—I couldn't agree more," Ji heard himself say. "Ha ha! You know Nin. Er, but do you speak a little human? It's okay if you don't! I know a little Ogrish."

Tell them "Grkratck owkhteckcrrtat!" Nin urged.

"Gratack ow quit ratatat!" Ji announced.

The gorilla-looking ogre backhanded Ji across the plateau.

19

IT FELT LIKE being smacked by a mountain. Ji hurtled twenty feet and crashed into a stone rosebush, his feet tangled in his ears and his butt throbbing.

Roz stepped forward. "There is no need for that sort of—"

The gorilla-ogre swiped at her with his huge paw, aiming a blow strong enough to crack a boulder.

Roz caught his wrist and roared in his face, her curved horn an inch from his throat.

The gorilla-ogre jerked backward, then spun and slammed her chin with his other paw.

Roz shook off the blow and punched him so hard that he flew off the cliff.

A moment later, a splash sounded from the river.

"You mess with the governess," Sally growled, "you get governed."

At least, that's what Ji thought she said. He couldn't hear much over the ringing in his ears. He watched through teary eyes as the ogres spread out, facing Roz warily. Sally stalked beside her and Chibo unfurled his wings. Green light brushed against red skin and yellow hair and gleaming tusks.

"Jiyong!" Roz called, without looking toward him. "Are you hurt?"

"Hardest rosebush ever," he groaned.

"You behaved abominably," Roz told the ogres. "Nin is mortified for you, and I hope that you are sensible enough to feel remorse!"

A bull-like ogre rumbled at her, and a vaguely human one cracked its knuckles.

They understand a tinylittle Humanish, Nin said, *but they do not speak Rozlish.*

"I bring news from the human realm," Roz told the ogres. "Nin wants me to inform you that the Summer Queen is strong again. Do you understand?"

The bull-like ogre pawed the ground.

They do not! Nin blurted. *They do not standunder!*

"After the Diadem Rite," Roz said, weirdly calm, considering all the ogres, "your ogre shaman—that is, your shamoon—expected the Summer Queen to weaken, yes? However, she is strong again. If the ogres attack, the queen will kill them. You must tell them not to attack."

The ogres roared like an avalanche.

Tell them "Grkratck owkhteckcrrtat," Missroz! But don't say it like Sneakyji. He said that they lick regretful toenails.

"I cannot pronounce that," Roz told Nin. "We shall have to muddle through without—"

She stopped when the ogres shambled closer to her. They were so big that Roz only came to their shoulders. The dripping-wet gorilla-ogre bounded onto the plateau and the bull-like one turned its horned head toward the Clay Plain and snorted quizzically.

"I bet he's asking about the armies," Sally said.

She's a she! Nin said. *Silly Sallynx! And yes, that is what she ponderasks. If we're leading the invading army to destroy the Ogrelands.*

"Of course we're not," Sally told the ogres. "Those armies aren't our friends."

Chibo nodded. "They kind of want to kill us."

"You'd better listen!" When Sally snarled at the bullish ogre, she looked like a kitten scolding a boulder. "The Summer Queen sucked the spirit out of every blue-bat in the realm—"

"Poor little guys," Chibo murmured.

"—and she's stronger than ever." Sally glowered up at the ogres. "And Prince Brace is pretty nasty too."

"We are friends of Nin's," Roz added. "The cub you sent to the human city."

"We're *stone*friends of Nin's," Ji said, limping closer.

Roz nodded. "Nin wants you to know that an attack on Summer City will fail horribly, at great cost."

The ogres glanced at each other. The bull-ogre grunted, and one that looked almost human growled. Yellow eyes narrowed and red paws scratched at ivory tusks.

They start to believe you! Nin said, sparkling with relief. *Tell them again! Then beg them to safeguide us through the Gravewoo—*

A sudden clash of human weapons echoed through the petrified forest. Harsh voices shouted and stone trees fell with a bone-shaking *crash.* Plumes of dust rose through the lifeless canopy below the plateau, and the ogres stomped in sudden anger and suspicion.

"You are spyguides." The gorilla-ogre scowled at Roz. "Half-human scouts."

"Lead evilarmy to ogrehome," the bull-ogre grunted. "Friends of Summer."

"We're not the queen's friends!" Ji told the ogres, spreading his arms. "We're her enemies."

"We're running from them," Sally growled to the ogres. "Not leading them!"

A gravelly *crash* sounded in the distance. Horses screamed and soldiers bellowed.

"Protect ogrehome!" the bull-ogre roared.

"Stop humonsters!" the gorilla-ogre grunted. "Rock-vow."

Broad red shoulders tensed. Yellow eyes narrowed. Fangs flashed and tusks shook—

"Wait—" Roz started.

They're going to stomp! Scamperfast! The warparty is going to stomp!

"Run!" Ji shouted. "Into the river and—"

"NO!" Roz prodded the bull-like ogre in the chest with one finger. "I will not have it! You are acting dreadfully! Like spoiled children throwing a tantrum. You should be ashamed of yourselves! First you hit Jiyong and now you—"

The humanlike ogre raised a massive fist. "Tckrachgo ogwachka!"

"Enough!" Roz snapped, not even flinching. "Enough! We came as friends! We came to help you, with a message from Nin—from one of your own!—yet you attacked us. And now you threaten more violence? Is *this* how ogres behave? Is this how low you have sunk? Are you truly monsters? Mindless brutes?"

Ji gaped. The ogres gaped too. Partly because of Roz's impassioned words, but mostly because bushes were flowering across the plateau. Stone buds swelled and blossomed, unfurling into stone roses. A few petals shed from delicate blooms and shattered on the ground.

Roz looked from one ogre to the next, her voice gentler. "You are better than this. I know you are, because I know Nin, who is a cub with a sweet soul, an engaging humor, and a lively mind. I expected more of you. I expected better."

The bull-like ogre shifted and the gorilla-ogre fell to one knee.

"We must speak together as friends," Roz continued, ignoring the chime of shattering rose petals behind her. "As *family*, because Nin is our sibling. Did you understand the message we brought? The ogres in the tunnels must not attack Summer City. They must not invade or they will die. Grkratck owkhteckcrrtat!"

Ji had no idea what that meant, but the ogres all bowed to Roz, their yellow eyes lowering and gleaming tusks dipping. The bullish ones knelt on front legs, touching their horns to the ground, while the gorilla-looking one ducked her head.

"What are they doing?" Chibo asked. "Are they bowing?"

"Yeah," Sally said. "To Roz."

They are claimgreeting Missroz as a truetroll.

"A true troll?" Ji asked. "What did— Those roses— *Why*?"

This is a Beginning, Nin said.

"This is the grand rite of passage you were talking about?" Sally asked in disbelief. "She's just scolding them! *This* is a solemn thunderclap soul rite?"

Not usually— Nin started.

"Grkratck owkhteckcrrtat," a pot-bellied ogre with three eyes repeated.

An ogre with a face like a wild boar's nodded. "Grkratck owkhteckcrrtat!"

With a bellow, the ogres started stampeding in a frenzy around the plateau. Red skin gleaming, yellow hair streaming, they thundered past Ji. Breath snorted from flaring nostrils, while clawed feet and sharp hooves pounded the ground. Red hands plucked stone roses, and then the ogres started bounding off the cliff to the river-bank.

"Wait, they're leaving?" Ji said. "No, stop! Stop! We need your help!"

"Stay here!" Sally leaped in front of a charging bull-ogre. "You have to guide us!"

The ogre hurdled her like an ox leaping over a hamster. The wind of the ogre stampede ruffled Ji's hair. Then the last few ogres leaped the river and vanished into the petri-fied forest.

"Come back!" Ji yelled after them. "Come back, you stupid ogres!"

"Great," Sally growled, her ears drooping. "Now who's going to guide us?"

"I think," Roz rumbled, "that I am."

Ji spun toward her. "What, because now you're a true troll?"

Now she's a truetroll!

"That was a Beginning?" Sally asked.

That was a Beginning!

"You don't look different," Ji told Roz.

"I don't feel different," Roz said. "But I feel . . . more." She crouched and touched the gravel with her thick fin-gers. "Trolls aren't mages or shamoon. We're simply ogres."

213

Trollwise ogres, Nin said.

"Rozario Songarza," Ji said, enjoying scolding her for once. "You made stone roses bloom. What else can you do?"

"I can *feel*. Trolls haven't any powers beyond an awareness of the earth."

"How do you even know that? You've only been a true troll for two seconds!"

"I'm just . . . aware of it."

He snorted. "Are you aware that we're dying in the Gravewoods?"

"Are we?" she asked.

"Yeah, my skin is burning, my hair's turning to stone, and my eyes . . ." Except his skin wasn't burning anymore, and his eyes felt fine. "Oh."

"They only left," she said, "because they know I can guide us safely through the Gravewoods. I'll feel the safest paths and . . . soften the effect of the spell, at least briefly."

"Where'd they go?" Chibo asked her.

"To warn the ogre armies not to attack Summer City," Roz said.

Wordless relief burbled in Nin's mind-speak, bubbling with such happiness that nobody spoke for a moment.

"What does that even mean?" Sally growled. "That thing you said in Ogrish. Gratatack owlecrat."

"I've no notion. I don't speak Ogrish," Roz said.

"Ha!" Ji said. "Little Miss Truetroll isn't aware of *that*."

A *rough translation is "We met Nin in Summer City and were dragtaken to the Forbidden Palace, where Sneakyji ruined the Diadem Rite before we were spellchanged into ant lions and troll and sprite and hobgoblin and dragon, and we escaped the rite then peeksaw that the evilqueen is still strong in magic and clayfighters so we ran to warn the ogres not to attack—"*

"Are you telling me," Ji interrupted, "that 'gracklefat artifact-hat' means all of that?"

Also, it asks about the Ice Witch.

"No way! Did they tell us where to find her?"

Through the Ogrelands toward the topmountains. They don't know more.

"Do you?" Ji asked Roz.

"No," she said, shaking her head. "But I know I can lead us through the Gravewoods."

"One step closer to the Ice Witch." A slow smile spread across Ji's face. "One step closer to breaking this spell. We're just a bunch of servants, an almost-governess, and an ogre cub—and look as us now. We weren't even supposed to survive the Diadem Rite."

"Takes more'n that to stop us," Sally purred.

Ji felt his smile widen. "Takes more than fox-demons."

"Takes more than an underground city!" Chibo piped, his green eyes glowing.

Roz laughed. "It takes more than Brace and the Gravewoods."

More than a warparty and an evilqueen!

"They thought we didn't matter," Ji said. "They thought we'd die without a murmur and they'd go on to greater things. But look at us now. When we're together, there's nothing we can't do."

20

Another clash of weapons sounded and an ant lion nipped Ji's forearm.

There's something *we can't do!* Nin said. *We can't win a battle against knights.*

"Ow!" Ji rubbed his arm. "That hurt!"

We need to scamperrun to the Ogrelands before the armies catch us!

"They're getting closer," Sally warned.

"Then let's scamper and run," Ji said, trotting across the plateau. "We've come too far to get caught now."

Sally jumped off the cliff, landed on a ridge, then leaped to a rocky shelf, heading for the river as easily as strolling down a staircase. Chibo giggled in glee, spread all four wings, and glided to the riverbank thirty feet below. Ji and

Roz looked at the cliff, then looked at each other—then looked at the cliff again.

"This would be a good time for some troll magic," he said.

"I can't cast spells," Roz told him. "That's the power of shamoon, not of trolls."

"Then what *can* you do?"

"Trolls simply gain an awareness of the earth's immensity," she said. "We curse the mountain for blocking our path, yet the mountain is the path."

"Yeah," he said. "I've got no idea what you're talking about."

She looked toward her feet. "I simply feel the strength of this cliff, and the height."

"Believe me," he told her, "I feel the height too."

He also felt the armies marching closer through the petrified forest. They needed to run, even if that meant climbing down a cliff. He worried more for Roz than himself, though: at least he didn't have fingers as thick as sausages. If she fell, "awareness of the earth" wasn't going to save her.

"Get back up here, you chuckle-knuckles!" he yelled at Chibo and Sally. "And carry Nin's backpack down! Does Roz have to do everything?"

With a sweep of his four wings, Chibo followed the cliffside upward, soaring a few feet from the rock face so he could see. Sally bounded along beside him like a squirrel hopping up a rock pile. When she reached the top, she took the backpack from Roz and staggered from the weight.

"Ooof," she said. "Heavy."

"You ready, Nin?" Ji asked.

We're solidfirm! Nin said.

Sally and Chibo lowered the pack down the cliff as Ji scooted over the edge, his legs dangling. He groped with his scaly toes until he felt the ridge. Then he shuffled to a jagged crack in the rock, his lizard feet finding a solid grip.

Pebbles bounced off his head, and Roz rumbled, "Sorry!"

He peered up at her. "Are you okay?"

"I am fine, thank you," she said from a ledge closer to the top. "In fact, I think I shall simply . . ."

She jumped off the cliff.

She fell to the riverbank, her cloak flapping and her hair streaming behind her. Ji yelped as the stone ground cracked under Roz's feet. She brushed dust from her dress, then smiled at him, her trollish eyes twinkling. A moment later, Sally and Chibo reached the bottom and gave her the backpack.

Then all three of them watched Ji pick his way slowly downward. Sweat dripped into his eyes, and he muttered, "Stupid cliffs."

After about a thousand years, he reached the stony

riverbank. The water crashed, white and frothing. Droplets of mist cooled Ji's face. He lay on his belly, cupped his hands, and drank, while Sally lapped beside him, her ears pricked for danger.

"The battle stopped," she said. "And the army's closer."

"What were the knights fighting?" Ji asked.

"I don't know. The goblins?"

"But the goblins obey the queen."

Roz made a face. "The White Worm has a temper. Perhaps he hates Ji more than he fears the queen."

"Great," Sally said. "The humans want to eat our souls and the goblins want to chop us into pieces."

"They're both going to be disappointed." Ji looked at Roz. "Which way?"

"We'll head upstream," she said. "That's safest."

"Safest is good."

And upstream is happybest, Nin said in an approving tone. *Faster into the Ogrelands.*

"And farther from the armies," Chibo said.

The river poured out of a narrow gorge. The current crashed, spewing mist and spray, and then the river widened again. Stone trees lined the bank, with drooping stone branches that dangled to the ground like poncho fringes.

Ji eyed the quiet, jagged woods and asked Sally, "Do you hear anything?"

"Just the humans."

"Perhaps the goblins can't cross the Gravewoods?" Roz

suggested. "They haven't a mage protecting them."

Sally jumped a mound of overturned stone-roots. "Maybe. At least knights can't gallop through a stone forest. They'll move slowly."

"I wish they'd turn to stone," Ji grumbled.

"Brace and Mr. Ioso will protect them," Roz said.

"So only one army is chasing us now," Chibo piped. "Things are already looking up!"

"As long as the Ice Witch breaks the spell," Ji said, "before we run out of time."

The slope steepened as they followed the river into the mountains. Darkness crept across the petrified forest. Only one moon rose through the stony branches, and a few hours later Sally heard the human army making camp. Roz found a safe grotto, where they shared the last of the mushrooms before falling into exhausted sleep.

The next morning, the river led higher through the gray landscape. The lumps on Ji's forehead ached and dust of the petrified forest turned to paste in his mouth. Still, at least his skin didn't crack. Chibo probed stone spiderwebs with his wings and Sally kept dropping to all fours, but Ji didn't say anything. Nobody did.

"Humans are coming," Sally called at midday from her perch on a boulder. "Closer than ever."

Ji rubbed his forehead. "How many?"

"Does that matter?" Roz asked. "Ten knights or a hundred, we still cannot beat them."

"Sally could beat ten knights by herself," Ji said.

"Eleven," Sally purred.

"And you can throw pinecones at the rest," he told Roz.

"Plus, I've mastered swoopflying," Chibo reported.

We've mastered buttstinging, Nin said.

"We're so dead," Ji said.

"Maybe fifty knights," Sally said. "Plus a hundred foot soldiers."

"Not to mention Brace and Mr. Ioso," Roz said.

Mysterioso, Nin said.

"I think I hear digging, too," Sally growled.

"Oh! Is that what I feel?" Roz asked. "The goblins are digging beneath the Gravewoods. They're going underneath the spell."

Chibo wrinkled his nose. "So we're back to two armies chasing us."

"How close are they, Sal?" Ji asked. "How much time do we have?"

"They're still halfway across—*no*." Her ruff raised. "That's not possible!"

"What?"

"Brace is using magic to muffle the noise," she said, following the river around a bend. "They're only fifteen minutes behind us. Maybe twenty if—" She stopped suddenly. "Whoa!"

When Ji followed her gaze, he stared in awe. Because, around the river bend, the petrified forest ended.

The world turned blue and purple and green. No pale

trees, no stony earth. Sharp peaks loomed high above, magnificent and lofty. A lake spread in front of them, deep blue under the clear sky, gentle waves lapping. Birds bobbed in the water, and a coyote watched from the far shore, then vanished into the underbrush. Fields of purple clover covered the nearest mountainside, swaying in the breeze like the coat of a dreaming dog. The closer mountains were light green, while more distant ones were darker. Except for Mount Atra, which loomed above the rest, its white snowcap almost blinding in the sunlight.

Roz said, "Gracious me!"

A flock of parrots took flight, filling the air with swirls of color. Ji followed Sally to the lakeshore, which felt soft underfoot after the stone woods. The smell of fresh water and sun-warmed weeds filled the air. Chibo spun in circles, trailing his wing tips in the lake, like he'd momentarily forgotten the danger of the pursuing army.

"Look!" Sally pointed. "Jujubes!"

"I adore jujubes," Roz rumbled happily, like she'd also momentarily forgotten the danger of the pursuing army.

Chibo piped, "Last one there is a rotten egg!"

We adore rotten eggs! Nin said.

"I adore not getting killed," Ji said, like he *hadn't* momentarily forgotten the danger of the pursuing army. "There are soldiers closing in, remember?"

"The earth!" Roz fell to her knees on the lakeside. "It's so alive."

"And we're so dead," Ji told her. "We only got fifteen minutes!"

Roz pressed her palms into the sand. "Can you feel that?"

"All I feel is scared, Roz! What are you talking about?" A crash sounded in the stone woods. "There's an army—"

Two armies!

"—right behind us. I don't care about the stupid earth."

Sally gazed at the lake. "That's a lot of water."

"I don't care about the stupid water, either!"

"Maybe we should cast the spell again," Chibo suggested to Ji. "That's what Sally means."

"What can a mermaid do?" Ji demanded. "Other than turn us more beastly?"

Chibo's wings drooped. "She . . . could tell us where to find the Ice Witch?"

"We don't have time! Even if we knew where she was, we're out of time! Unless Ti-Lin-Su can reach across the realm with her fishy fingers and poke Brace in the eye—"

"Jiyong!" Roz gaped at him. "That's it!"

"If you tell me not to be rude," he said, "I'll scream."

Roz gazed across the lake, her eyes glimmering with wonder. "Everything's connected. The rivers and oceans, the mountains and valleys, the sun and moons—"

"The fishy fingers," Ji said.

She laughed. "Exactly! Mermaids. Seaweed. *Fingers.*"

"Stop talking like Nin!"

"I am not speaking like Nin!" Roz said primly. "And for your information, I find cub's manner of speech charming. Furthermore, seaweed is the solution to our problem."

"Either that," he said, "or your horn is crowding out your brain."

"This way, quickly!" She bustled into a stream that flowed down the mountainside. "There's an underground spring nearby, and a slow seep of water in the earth."

Ji trotted splashily after her. "Where are you going? You can feel underground streams now?"

"Trolls are attuned to the earth," she told him as she waded higher uphill. "Like dragons are to gemstones, I suppose. There are a thousand rivulets and streams within fifty yards of us." Roz sloshed against the current, her dress sticking to her calves. "This is far more complex than any water clock."

"Rozario Songarza!" Ji demanded. "What are you doing?"

She looked over her shoulder. "Remember the seaweed that sprouted from the river outside Turtlewillow?"

"Nobody forgets killer seaweed, Roz," Sally said.

"And do you recall what we were discussing at the time?"

"*I* do!" Chibo said, drifting over the stream. "We were daydreaming about ringing a bell to call the Ice Witch."

"Indeed." Roz stopped in a marshy patch where the stream widened. "I suspect that our longing—our desire—inadvertently called the mermaids."

"We daydreamed the *spell*?" Sally growled.

"You mean Ti-Lin-Su heard us?" Ji asked.

"Something like that," Roz said.

"And she sent seaweed to drown you?" Ji snorted. "She wouldn't do that."

"Perhaps the mermaids haven't mastered the spell." Roz splashed toward the center of the marsh. "Yet they felt our desperation and attempted to help. Do you remember what Ti-Lin-Su told us at the water clock?"

"Sure," Sally said. "To search for the Ice Witch in the Ogrelands."

"What else?"

"Nothing." Sally's ears pricked. "Oh! That they 'reached out' for us at a riverbank, right?"

"To 'help carry' us . . . ," Ji said slowly.

A smile cracked Roz's trollish face. "Everything is connected. Dragon and gems, trolls and the earth. Moons and kumiho. Mermaids and seaweed. *Seaweed* is mermaid magic."

"Are you sure?" Ji asked.

"Remember the seaweed mosaic outside Ti-Lin-Su's house in the city? Remember the seaweed in her ponds? No, I'm not sure—but it makes perfect sense." Roz nodded firmly. "Ti-Lin-Su responded to our need once. She will again."

Ji scratched the scales on his cheek. "So if we contact

her, the mermaids will send seaweed to help us?"

To awaycarry us! Nin said. *To escape the armies!*

Roz nodded. "I think they'll try."

"Magic hasn't worked that great so far," Ji said.

"No, but . . ." Roz trailed off when a *crash* sounded from the petrified forest.

Horses neighed and armor jingled. Soldiers shouted. Plumes of dust rose through the stony canopy of the Gravewoods.

Ji grunted. "We don't have a choice."

"We do have a choice," Roz said. "And we must choose carefully. We'll pay for this spell with our humanity."

And our ogreanity, Nin said.

"With our selves." Roz raised her three-fingered hands. "And we haven't much left. If we do this, we may lose our original selves completely."

For a long moment, nobody spoke. Sally pulled Chibo close, and he wrapped his emerald wings around her. Even Nin fell quiet. Then hoofbeats splashed and a group of knights, coated in gray powder, emerged from the Gravewoods. They hadn't spotted Roz yet, but it wouldn't be long.

"The army," Ji said, his breath catching. "They're almost here."

"I'd rather go down fighting," Sally said, a rasp in her voice, "than lose my soul."

Ji didn't like either of those options. He almost snapped

at Sally, but then he saw the gleam in her eyes. She wanted to fight, to face the enemy like a soldier. She'd followed him and Roz across the realm and she'd never shied from danger. She'd never hesitated to fight for him, for Roz, for Chibo or Nin. For what was right. She'd followed, but it was time for her to lead.

She deserved that. She deserved a whole lot more. Ji glanced at Roz, who nodded to him: as always, she knew exactly what he was thinking.

"If you want to stay and fight," Ji told Sally, "we'll stay and fight."

"We'll lose," she said.

"Yeah." He hunched a shoulder. "But with honor."

She peered at him. "You'd do that for me?"

"You're my best friend."

"Maybe honor *is* stupid," she growled. "Maybe it's like Seven Pebbles, a stupid, meaningless game with stupid, meaningless rules."

"Brace's honor is like that—" Ji paused as more knights galloped out of the Gravewoods. "But not yours, Sally. When you say 'honor,' you mean 'justice.'"

"We could use a little justice right about now," Roz said, touching Sally's shoulder.

Ji waited quietly for Sally's decision. Maybe he didn't understand honor, but he understood Sally. He trusted her. If she wanted to make a stand, he'd stand beside her. If she wanted to fight, he'd fight.

She watched the knights gathering at the lakeside. She'd always dreamed of riding with them, of thundering into battle on a warhorse, her armor glinting and her sword slashing. She'd dreamed of blood and victory, and vanquishing beasts in the service of the realm.

"Everyone into a circle," she growled, grabbing Roz and Ji's hands. "And think of the mermaid."

"We—we're not fighting?" Chibo asked.

"One day we'll crush them," Sally snarled. "But right now we're getting out of here."

Roz bowed her head while Ji stared at the broken reflection of the sun in the grassy marsh and silently begged for Ti-Lin-Su to appear. *The knights are coming. The knights are here. We need help fast, Ti-Lin-Su! Fast, fast—*

Ji tightened his grip on Sally's warm paw, feeling her rough pads and sharp claws. In his other hand, Roz's fingers felt cool and hard as marble. Think of the mermaid? Forget that. If Ji needed to put *himself* into the spell, he'd think of Roz and Sally.

Hoofbeats pounded closer. A knight shouted, "There they are!" and a crossbow twanged. The first hint of a rippling face appeared in the water of the marsh. Ji begged even harder. *Help us, Ti-Lin-Su! Bring us to the Ice Witch! The knights are here, they're here! Help us now, now, now!*

"Chibo," Sally said. "Get your wings in the water!"

21

EMERALD LIGHT FLARED from Chibo's back and touched the water.

Magic flooded the air, and strands of seaweed rose from the marsh, almost like reflections of Chibo's wings—except they wrapped around Roz's legs and were as thick and shiny as pythons. Smaller vines sprouted from the dripping seaweed, clinging to Sally and Ji and Chibo.

A half dozen strands unfurled higher, gripping Roz's thick wrists. "Lady Ti-Lin-Su!" she yelped. "It's us, it's us!"

"What is she—" A vine grabbed Ji's ankle. "Hey!"

"Roz!" Sally grabbed a tendril sprouting toward Chibo's neck. "Is this mermaids?"

Arrows flew overhead. One chunked into the thick strand of seaweed coiling around Ji's wrists and tugging him to his knees.

"It's not Ti-Lin-Su!" he cried. "It's not her!"

Sally yowled and slashed at the seaweed as the water whipped around her. Roz roared and ripped vines from her shoulders until a dozen more strands dragged her upstream, tumbling against the current. The weeds towed Ji behind Roz. Water filled his nose, and he caught a glimpse of Sally and Chibo, both wrapped in vines, struggling and sputtering. Ji's clawed feet scrambled in the streambed as icy water slapped his face.

Then the seaweed grew into a thick circle surrounding him and the others—dozens of stalks as heavy as tree trunks, each sprouting hundreds of slender vines that joined overhead into a dome that blocked the sky.

Darkness fell. Vines bound Ji's wrists to the slimy inner wall of a globe of seaweed the size of a stagecoach. Sally struggled against her bonds beside him, while Chibo spread his wings for light. Despite being shackled to the wall by thick seaweed, Roz shifted, keeping Nin's backpack above water and—

A geyser spouted in front of them, and Ji's stomach dropped. Was this it? Would the Summer Queen pierce them with watery branches and steal their souls?

But instead of shaping into a tree, the water formed a liquid face. "Miss Roz? Can you hear me?"

"I know that voice," Chibo fluted.

"Lady Ti-Lin-Su!" Roz said. "Oh, thank goodness!"

Laughter sounded like wind chimes. "You called, didn't you? We've been trying to reach you for days." The geyser solidified into a replica of Ti-Lin-Su's face, which peered curiously at the inside of the seaweed globe. "Where on earth are you?"

"Inside a . . . a chamber made of seaweed," Roz told her.

Tell her we're here too! Introduce us! Lady Mer-Lin-Su! Hello! O greetings to you, my lady!

"You dragged us upstream," Sally growled, twitching an ear at Nin's backpack. "Your seaweed landed us like fish."

"Oh!" Ti-Lin-Su said. "That is not supposed to happen. We're still learning this spell, I'm afraid."

"You're supposed to know everything," Sally grumbled.

"I'm a scholar, not a mage."

"We thought you were the queen," Chibo piped. "Trying to catch us."

"I'm quite sorry." Ti-Lin-Su smiled at Chibo, then asked Roz, "Tell me, have you reached the Ogrelands? We've been searchi—" The watery head sloshed, losing its shape. "Been ser-benz-benz . . ."

"My lady?" Roz asked, nervously.

The head re-formed. "Sorry! Magic is tricky! Where are you? What's happened?"

"We're in the Ogrelands," Roz told her. "We escaped the White Worm—do you know of him?—and crossed the Gravewoods."

"That is excellent news—"

"We still need the Ice Witch," Ji interrupted, tugging at his viny manacles. "And the queen's army is about ten seconds away. So maybe less chatting and more help?"

Ti-Lin-Su's watery head swung toward him. "Ah, there you are! Hello, Jiyong. I missed your draconic demands."

Oooh, Nin said. *Draconic.*

"My sisters and I consulted the ancient corals about the Ice Wit—" Ti-Lin-Su's watery face warped again, the geyser wobbling. "—to your former—"

"You're sloshing again!" Ji told her. "Get us out of here!"

"If you would be so kind," Roz added, shooting a governess-y look at Ji. "We are already in your debt, my lady."

"Nonsense," Ti-Lin-Su said, her face re-forming. "I'm in yours. This is the most fascinating time since the first Summer Queen rose to power by gathering all human magic into herself—"

"We know how she rose," Sally said as an arrow chunked into the outside of the seaweed chamber. "But how will she fall?"

"She's too powerful to fall. The combined strength of all the nations couldn't topple her. Only a full-blooded dragon might break the crown."

"Ji's a dragon!" Chibo fluted.

Ti-Lin-Su smiled gently. "He's merely a shadow of a half dragon, Chibo. He's remarkable, but he is to a true dragon what an acorn is to an oak tree."

Tinysmall and wearing a goofy cap? Nin asked.

"So where do we find a full-blooded dragon?" Sally asked.

"In the pages of history. They no longer exist. However—" An arrowhead poked through the seaweed globe three inches from Ji's cheek. "Oh! We're running out of time."

"GET US OUT OF HERE!" Ji bellowed.

"The spell is weakening. . . ." Ti-Lin-Su's geyser-face turned clear and watery. "You'll find the Ice Witch on the peak of Mount Atra."

"On top of the tallest mountain in the world?" Sally growled. "We can't get there before the armies catch us."

"Perhaps if we focus on the spell and—" Ti-Lin-Su started, before her face collapsed with a splash.

"What now?" Ji asked, tugging at his viny shackles as arrows thudded into the globe of seaweed. "We're wrapped like sushi for Brace to gobble. Stupid mermaids."

"Jiyong!" Roz rumbled. "Mind your manners!"

A damp ant lion on Ji's forearm waggled its antennae sternly. *Stop being so draconic!*

"What's 'draconic'?" Chibo asked.

Dragon plus moronic.

"It is not 'dragon plus moronic'!" Ji told the ant lion. "At least I don't think—"

The knobby green globe jerked. Ji's head slammed against the seaweed wall behind him, and only the vines around his arms kept him upright. Chibo squeaked in

234

shock and Sally yelped. The globe spun upside down, then twirled like a top—or a tornado—splashing and coursing upstream.

"Lady Ti-Lin-Su!" Roz rumbled. "Stop!"

The seaweed chafed Ji's wrists and tugged at his ankles. "I'm going to be sick."

"Wahooooooo!" Chibo fluted. "Faster, faster!"

The globe bobbed and tilted and finally turned upright. Ji slumped in relief—until the globe started spinning again. Slowly at first, then stomach-churningly fast. He squeezed his eyes closed to keep from losing his lunch while the hollow seaweed chamber tilted and scraped, shaking and jumping and spraying water.

Thunk! Thud! Rattle!

The globe hopped and lurched higher over rocks and rapids. Ji's eyes sprang open at a sudden heave. Roz rumbled a prayer, Sally bared her teeth, and Chibo whooped and hollered, his glowing green wings slicing wildly across the inside of the globe.

After twenty-seven terrified lifetimes, the seaweed ball finally jerked to a halt.

Water dripped and rasps of breath sounded.

"Some aws!" Chibo exulted. "Can we do that again?"

The seaweed globe collapsed into a mound of slimy vines. Sunlight blinded Ji. He staggered a few steps, still dizzy but no longer held upright by his bonds. Fresh air swirled around him. He blinked, then focused on a wide trail that crossed the rocky hillside in front of him.

"Oh, my!" Roz gasped. "Look!"

Ji turned. "Whoa."

"Yrr," Sally growled.

"Wow," Chibo said. "Even *I* can see the wow."

Far below them, the gorgeous blue lake and hills of purple clover spread at the foot of the mountain. Far, *far* below them. The petrified forest looked small and almost pretty, and past the foothills the Clay Plain extended into the distance.

Sniffsmells like ogrehome! Nin said. *We're here!*

"My . . . my hands," Roz said. Then her voice sharpened. "Sally! Are you hurt?"

For a terrible moment, Ji didn't recognize Sally. She'd condensed and widened and . . . twisted. She stood on all fours, her rear legs crooked like a wolf's and her muzzle long and predatory.

"I'm okay." She rose unsteadily to her hind feet like a bear. "What's wrong with your hands?"

"Two fingers. I only have two fingers on each hand." Roz took an unhappy breath. "I think I will soon have hooves."

"Did I change?" Chibo piped. "I don't feel different."

Roz touched his shoulder gently. "Your eyes are bigger and . . ."

"You're shorter," Ji told him. "A lot shorter."

"Check your legs," Sally said.

Chibo lifted his pants to reveal a pair of tiny, shrunken legs. "They're disappearing. They're just disappearing." He whimpered and looked at Roz. "Do real sprites even *have* legs?"

"They don't," she said. "I'm sorry."

Chibo gave a tremulous smile. "I guess we don't need them. We fly and, and . . ."

"And I suspect that sprites are the natural enemy of the kumiho," Roz offered, trying to cheer him up.

"The natural enemy?" he asked, his oversized eyes widening.

"Think back," Roz told him. "The kumiho cowered every time they saw your wings. Remember outside the goblin pen at Turtlewillow? They stayed away until you fainted."

"I guess," Chibo said, wrinkling his nose. "But they've got fangs and venom, and sprites don't have anything."

"It doesn't matter," Ji said. "Because the Ice Witch is going to break the spell."

When Roz looked toward him, she pressed her hand to her chest in surprise. Chibo gasped, his huge eyes widening, and Sally shambled closer.

She peered at him. "Your face is totally scaly now."

"I figured." Ji raised his hand halfway to his forehead. "The lumps are horns?"

"Antlers."

"Antlers?"

She nodded. "Tiny ones."

"Great, now I'm a reindeer." He tried to ignore the disgust twisting in his stomach. "Where's Mount Atra?"

"Farther in the mountain range." Roz looked toward the snowy peak that touched the clouds. "We're already halfway there."

"Where are all the ogres?" Sally asked, shaking to dry her fur.

"Hey!" Chibo said as droplets of water flew at him.

We don't call her Mount Atra, Nin said. *We call her Dkeruckgctut.*

Ji eyed the ant lions. "Ducker yucky cut?"

"Ignore Sillyji," Roz told Nin. "Does that mean something in Humanish?"

Of verycourse! It means "The Winter Stone We Don't Talk About, Where the Coldsnow Never Melts No Matter How the Sun Shines, the White-Capped Topmountain Loomrising above the Old Mines Deep in the Ogrelands, the Site of a Terribattle When the Evilhumans Invaded after the—"

"Okay, okay!" Ji said, turning away. "We get the idea."

"Winter stone?" Sally stroked her whiskers. "That's kind of like the Winter Snake."

Ji was about to answer when he noticed tiny shapes gathering along the shore of the lake that bordered the Gravewoods far below them. Metal glinted in the sun and banners flapped in the wind.

"Look," he said. "The Summer Army."

Lady Mer-Lin-Su saved us! Nin said, and a few ant lions on the tip of Roz's horn shook their manes.

"Unless they ride a seaweed ball," Sally growled, "they're a full day behind us now."

"And the goblins . . ." Roz squinted at the ground. "Hmm. The goblins tunneled beneath the Gravewoods. They're taking a shortcut through the mountain."

Shortcut? Nin said. *That's a funny word.*

"C'mon," Ji said, kneeling in front of Chibo. "We've got a long walk to an icy witch."

"I hope she's nice," Chibo said, climbing onto his back.

"With a name like 'the Ice Witch'? Of course she's nice."

"Yeah." Sally loped on all fours toward the mountainside trail. "It's not like she's called anything scary."

The trail wound through a field of crooked shrubs. Despite the distant snowy peak of Mount Atra, the wind felt warm. Ji gave Chibo's skinny legs a reassuring squeeze as he followed Sally.

"I've long wondered what was icy about the Ice Witch," Roz said.

"What's the story with her?" Chibo asked.

"The myth says that she traveled the realm after the first Summer Queen died. She treated the sick with potions and ointments."

"That's non-icy of her," Chibo said. "I wonder if she healed eyesight."

Roz glanced at Chibo. "Perhaps."

"It doesn't matter," Chibo said.

Sally grunted, then headed onto a zigzagging path that led deeper into the mountains.

"The Ice Witch didn't just heal people, though," Roz continued. "She also talked to them. About the wars, about the ogres and goblins, the bugbears and sprites and hobgoblins."

Did she talk about ant lions?

"I don't think she knew about them," Roz said. "She hated the nonhumans for starting the war, but she also hated the humans for what they did once they won it."

"So she hated *everyone*?" Sally asked, leading them onto a path that clung to a steep mountainside. "Sounds like Ji."

"I don't hate everyone! I don't hate anyone." Ji glanced at the sharp drop-off six inches from his left foot. "Except heights."

He gripped Chibo tighter and tried not to look down as he shuffled along the ledge. Sally trotted fearlessly ahead, but Ji scraped his shoulder against the cliff face. Roz edged sideways along the path, testing every step before she shifted her weight.

She didn't sound nervous when she spoke, though. "The myth says that the Ice Witch traveled the realm for years before she came across a group of captured ogres and starving goblins. She freed them and fed them."

"That's nice for an icy witch," Chibo piped.

"I would agree," Roz said, "except that she killed an entire battalion of guards in the process."

"Oh. I bet the queen didn't like that."

"The queen drove her from the realm," Roz said, "and locked her in a magical prison."

None of them spoke for a while, too focused on not plunging to their death. Finally, the path broadened again, and it ushered them into a wooded highland beneath the white spire of Mount Atra.

"That's the whole myth?" Ji asked.

"There's not much to it," Sally said.

Roz brushed aside a low-hanging branch. "You can see why Lady Ti-Lin-Su wasn't convinced it was true."

"So the witch is like a thousand years old?" Ji asked. "That doesn't sound right."

"Perhaps there have been many Ice Witches," Roz suggested. "Perhaps it's a title, like 'Summer Queen.'"

When Sally led them from the woods, the midday sun glowed on a mountainside scene that took Ji's breath away. Ornate shrubs covered overgrown terraces, and brilliant wildflowers splashed color across the slopes, while tumbling waterfalls glinted merrily in the light.

"Lovely!" Roz said.

"What?" Chibo asked.

"There are ledges in the mountainside," Sally told him. "And they're covered in flowers."

Ridges, not ledges, Nin said. *Like bull aardvarks in human cities—*

"Boulevards," Roz rumbled.

—with shops and homes and houses and stalls. This is an ogretown.

Ji took a deep breath of the sweetest air he'd ever smelled. Streams trickled along elaborate channels on the mountainside, collecting in fountains outside cave entrances. Overgrown bushes and vines spilled from higher to lower ridges. Yet other than the waterfalls, nothing moved but a flock of birds and two goats watching with cautious yellow eyes.

"Where is everyone?" Ji asked.

Most of the ogretowns are empty, Nin said, a hint of grief in cub's mind-speak. *Once there were a hundred towns, the shamoons say. But now? Only three, and all are shrinkfailing.*

"What happened?" Roz asked.

The first evilqueen turned the hillfoots into the Gravewoods, and we started withering like a waterless tree.

"So after the Summer Queen created the Gravewoods, the whole ogre nation started shrinking?"

Greedy, greedy ogres! Nin said angrily.

"It's not your fault," Chibo said.

We started the war. And then . . . the shamoons helped the evilqueen's spell.

Chibo's wings flared in surprise. "No way!"

Very way, Nin told Chibo. *This is why we are so full of shame. Our shamoon wanted to build a magic fence to keep humans out of our lands.*

"They thought the Gravewoods would protect the Ogrelands?" Ji asked.

A few ant lions nodded. *So they helped the Summer Queen.*

"Yeah, but—" Sally frowned. "Only because they were trying to protect their kids."

A wall is also a prison. It makes you smaller, weaker, brittle. Little cubs cannot grow into mighty ogres if they do not travel and learn.

"You mean cubs need to travel?" Sally asked. "Before they grow up they need to leave the Ogrelands?"

The Gravewoods stunts us. It chokes our land and starves our spirits.

The grief of Nin's mind-speak seemed to thicken the air. Sally dropped to all fours and trotted along an overgrown ramp to the lowest ridge. Ji followed, squeezing between trellises of snap peas tumbling over patches of flowers and herbs.

Sally bounded onto a leafy slab. "So there aren't enough ogres to fill the towns anymore?"

We'll be the last. The cubs my age. The last of the ogres.

"What does the Gravewoods have to do with that?"

We told you this! That's what keeps the ogres weak and withering. Our hillfoots turned to stone, our cubs trapped.

"The Gravewoods only traps cubs?" Ji asked. "Not grown-up ogres?"

We spoketold you this!

"You never said anything about ogres withering."

Roz shot Ji a quelling look. "Tell us again, please?"

We spoketold you. Cubs can't wanderstroll past the Gravewoods. Young ogres are trapped in the Ogrelands.

"That's not right," Ji said. "*You* crossed the Gravewoods when you went to Summer City. That's where we met you."

We got longlucky. Sorrow tinged Nin's mind-speak. *The other cubs who tried . . . didn't.*

"Oh," Ji said, swallowing. "I'm sorry."

Most cubs turn to stone faster even than humans—or half humans. And cubs cannot become ogres without leaving the hillfoots. Without finishing a cubwalk, we do not become adults.

"Cubs need to travel outside the Ogrelands before becoming adults?" Roz rumbled softly. "That's called a 'cubwalk'?"

A cubwalk, yes. A passagerite.

Roz frowned, her eyes shiny with tears. "But most cubs can't leave the Ogrelands now. Instead, they turn to stone."

The Gravewoods stops the cubwalk. The ant lions on her shoulder nodded sadly. *And we wither away. This evilmagic makes every generation smaller than the one before. Soon the last ogre will die.*

22

THE PATH MEANDERED from ramp to ramp, leading closer to Mount Atra. Honeybees buzzed on hillsides covered with bright flowers and fruit trees. Ji grabbed a papaya, while Chibo used his wings to find kumquats and plucked them by the handful. Roz pulled sweetbeets from vegetable patches, then ate them with loud crunching and rumbled apologies.

Juice dripped down Ji's chin as he followed Sally to the top of the ogre town, where a cobbled plaza spread between rock gardens.

"How come the snow doesn't melt?" Ji asked, gazing at the brilliant white peak of Mount Atra.

Dkeruckgctut, Nin explained.

"Oh, right."

The ogretowns are empty now. Tombstones. Marking the slowdeath of the ogres.

Lowering his gaze, Ji counted four empty hilltop plazas between them and Mount Atra. Each one beautiful, and each of them abandoned.

"We'll fix this," he heard himself promise.

"How?" Roz rumbled.

"The humans, they—" Sally stopped. "We. *We* won the war. Good for us. Victory is sweet, but this isn't honor. Choking the ogres to death over centuries isn't justice."

The evilqueen stole the humansparks, too, Nin said. *Your little magics of small things.*

"I'm not sure 'stole' is correct," Roz rumbled. "She needed to protect her people."

"That's what everyone says when they want power," Ji said over the thrum of anger in his mind.

How can we healfix this, Sneakyji? There is no way without defeating the evilqueen.

"Then we'll defeat her. I'm tired of running. I'm tired of losing. I'm tired of being hungry and afraid. The queen's hurt us enough. She's hurt everyone enough. The ogres, the goblins, the servants—even the blue-bats. We're going to stop her, whatever it takes."

Roz touched Ji's arm gently. "Perhaps not 'whatever' it takes."

"I'll do anything," he told her. "I'll do anything to set this right."

"If there's nothing you won't do, then what are you?" Roz asked, echoing a question he'd once posed to the Summer Queen.

"A monster," he said. "But that's what I *am*."

"That's not what you are."

"It's not what *you* are!" Ji snapped. "I don't care what you look like, Roz! You think a horn and hooves make you a monster? You think wings or fangs make you a monster? No. Only your heart makes you a monster." Ji thumped his chest. "I'm the only monster here, and I will not throw pinecones, Roz. I won't throw pinecones. I'll tear this realm apart if I can. I'll make them pay for what they've done."

When the air chilled, Ji grabbed carpets from a long-abandoned ogre home and fashioned them into ponchos. Wordless sadness trickled from Nin as they wandered through more empty villages and onto the snow-dusted slopes of Mount Atra.

Sally cocked her head. "Sounds like the human army's already at the first village. They're moving pretty fast."

With Brace gaining on them, Ji refused to stop even after the sun set and the night turned frosty. A biting wind rose, and weird shadows lengthened across the snowy landscape. Nin's ant lions clustered together inside the earth-filled pack, while Chibo's teeth started chattering.

Ji tucked Chibo's poncho tighter around his sprite-y shoulders. "There."

"Th-thanks." Chibo peered at the sky. "H-how many moons is that?"

"Two."

"At l-least we d-don't have to worry about k-kumiho."

"There's another moon rising behind the mountains," Sally growled, her fur ruffling in the wind. "I can see the sky lightening."

Sky lightning! A cluster of ant lions emerged from Roz's pack. *Where?*

"Not 'sky lightning,'" Sally told them. "Sky lightening."

Sky lightning?

"Sky lightennning! Getting less dark—" She paused. "I think I hear ogres."

"Ogres?" Roz rumbled. "Where?"

"Far away. Noise carries weirdly in the mountains."

Roz peered westward. "Is it the war party?"

"I don't know." Sally frowned.

We can't tell, Nin said.

"The goblins are closer too," Roz said. "Still tunneling."

Ji kicked a frost-covered weed. "I'm sick of all these frothing armies!"

"Maybe the goblins are attacking Brace," Chibo said.

The ant lions retreated into the pack as Roz frowned. "They aren't heading for him. They're heading for us."

"Great," Ji said. "We'll have to hike through the night."

"Chibo can't go on like this," Roz said.

"I'll carry him," Ji said.

"And what happens when *you* can't go on?"

248

"You'll carry me," Ji told her.

Mindless hours slogged past. The trees gave way to shrubs. The snow deepened until Ji's ankles disappeared at every step. He stayed warm, though, and a familiar tugging in his heart told him why: there were gems nearby, or precious metals. Not close enough for him to absorb fire, but a distant treasure hoard still warmed his blood.

Finally, Roz led them into a hollow beneath a shrub, which offered a little protection from the wind.

"Can you feel the Ice Witch?" Ji asked Roz. "With your troll-y awareness?"

She shook her head. "The mountain is mostly snow and ice. I can't feel much."

"Neither can my legs," Chibo said, his shoulders slumped. "If we cast one more spell, I'll have six wings and no feet."

"We're really beasts now," Sally growled. "Look at me. Look at Ji."

"Don't look at me!" he said.

"Antlers are kind of hard to ignore," Chibo said.

"Look who's talking, bug-eyes."

"Oh, yeah?" Chibo said. "Well, well . . . you have scales!"

"Between Ji's antlers and Roz's hooves," Sally said, "we've almost got a whole moose."

Chibo giggled and Sally stretched out, showing off the thick pelt beneath her tattered shirt. Ji skooched next to her yummy fuzziness. Then Chibo hugged her and Roz cuddled closer. Ant lions burrowed into her fur and Nin murmured *warmfurry toastycuddle* until sleep came.

Glimpses of treasure chased Ji's dreams. Gold coins turned to sand at his touch; rubies watched him through slitted pupils. Diamonds danced at the edge of his imagination, shimmering with the colors of the rainbow.

He woke before dawn, with Sally's tail in his face. He wriggled free, crawled from beneath the bush, and peered down the mountain.

They'd come a long way.

He peered up the mountain.

They had a long way to go.

"The humans are awake," Sally said, settling beside him. "They're breaking camp."

"How about the goblins?"

Her muzzle twitched. "Even *my* ears can't hear underground."

"They're still digging," Roz said, emerging from the hollow. "Straight toward us."

The day grew brighter as they climbed, and the snow deeper. Nin was right: even in the warm sunlight, the snow didn't melt. Sally prowled across the drifts, Chibo spread his wings and took some of Ji's weight, but Roz had to plow through snowbanks until she almost exhausted her troll strength. Finally, they reached a path. Well, an *ogre path*, which was a line of flat-topped boulders rising over the snow.

"We're at least a day's travel from the top," Roz said.

"I could fly there right now, no problem," Chibo fluted.

"I hope she's here," Ji said.

An ant lion crawled onto his cheek. *What if she is not?*

"Then we'll stay half beasts forever," Chibo said.

"Yeah," Ji said. But actually if the Ice Witch wasn't there, they wouldn't stay half beasts much longer—because the Summer Queen would catch them and sacrifice them on a water tree.

"The snow's not melting," Sally told Nin. "That means someone's using magic."

Chibo nodded. "It's got to be the Ice Witch."

A breeze brought the scent of evergreen, and Sally pricked up her ears. "We have to switch paths. The humans are on our trail, and they're moving faster than we are."

"What about the goblins?" Chibo asked.

"I can't tell," Roz said. "The mountain is crisscrossed with . . . burrows?" She frowned in concentration. "They're not goblin tunnels. What are they, Nin?"

Dkeruckgctut.

"Oh!" she said. "The old mines."

Stories say that mineshafts run from tailmountain to topmountain.

Roz brightened. "But that's perfect! We just need a mine entrance; then we can climb the mountain from the inside!"

We can head into a mining town, Nin said.

"What mining town?" Chibo asked.

The one for miners, Nin explained.

"For ogres?" Roz asked.

Of verycourse! The ant lions on Roz's shoulder pointed their antennae. *That way is the mining town.*

"You could've mentioned mine shafts earlier," Ji groused.

Maybe we did! Nin said.

"Except you didn't," Chibo told them.

Except you didn't, Nin said, and directed them onto a smaller path.

Having a plan lifted Ji's spirits. Maybe they'd actually do this. Maybe they'd actually succeed. He gave Chibo's skinny legs a squeeze as they followed a narrow, winding trail upward.

"So the ogres wanted to seize more foothills, right?" Sally asked Nin when she returned from scouting ahead. "I mean, in the first war."

Greedy ogres!

"So if the crown weakens, will the ogres attack again?"

Of course not, Sallynx!

Roz smiled faintly. "I'm sure they've learned their lesson."

At least not until there are plentymore ogres, Nin continued.

"What?" Roz rumbled in gravelly surprise.

If the towns are brimfilled with ogres, who knows? Maybe we'll get greedy again.

"Even after all this?" Roz gestured with a two-fingered

hand. "Even after the Gravewoods stopped the cubwalks and destroyed the ogre towns?"

"It's not freedom," Ji told her, "unless you're free to do the *wrong* thing too."

23

THE SUN WAS high and a warm breeze swirled with the distant bleating of goats. Sally and Nin followed a zigzag path toward the mining town, switching from one ogre path to another to confuse the pursuing goblins.

"I believe we've obscured our direction," Roz finally said.

"Huh?" Chibo asked.

"She thinks we lost the goblins." Ji looked at Sally. "What about the humans?"

"I can't tell." Her nostrils flared. "But I think I smell dead things."

"Magic," Chibo said.

Evilmagic, Nin said.

Sally grunted, then forged a winding course between

frozen cliffs. Slogging through the snow exhausted Roz, and the chill finally penetrated Ji's snaky skin. Still, they trudged onward until they reached a sharp bend in the mountainside path.

"C'mere," Sally said, peering around the turn.

When Ji crept up beside her, he almost fainted in relief. He'd been expecting some new horror in the gathering dusk, but there was just a massive quarry. Loads of stone had been removed from the side of Mount Atra, leaving a series of holes bigger than a manor house and deeper than a canyon. Ledges and bridges spanned sheer cliffs. Caves lined one wall of the quarry, and dozens of reindeer grazed in a snowy meadow that stretched between two ginormous pits.

"This is a mining town?" Roz rumbled.

"I can't see!" Chibo said.

"It's a huge quarry," Ji told him. "Except . . . bigger."

Extremely unsmall, Nin agreed. *And yes, Missroz, this sniffsmells like the place.*

Sally swiveled her ears. "There's nobody here but reindeer."

"Where are the miners?" Roz asked.

Long gone, Nin said, as Sally stalked farther along the path. *The mines have been mothquiet for generations.*

When the reindeer noticed them, the entire herd fell perfectly still for two heartbeats—then they loped away through the snow, as smooth and silent as daydreams.

The mine mouth is that way, Nin said, as two ant lions pointed deeper into the quarry. *Inside we'll find ladder-paths to the Ice Witch.*

Sally led the way down a series of snowy ramps and beneath a series of bridges. The sunset painted the clouds orange as she prowled into a field of crooked columns. Beyond that, the quarry widened into a valley. The clouds darkened and a tip of crescent moon glimmered behind a low ridge. Two round moons illuminated a wide road leading toward the mine entrance, which opened in the base of a sheer cliff a few hundred yards ahead.

"What I don't understand," Roz said, scratching her horn, "is how all these wars start in the first place. Nobody likes fighting."

Ji snorted. "Everyone likes fighting!"

"They do not, Jiyong. People do not enjoy fighting."

"Have you *met* people? Ask Sally! She likes fighting."

Sally curled her muzzle to show her fangs. "It's the only good thing about being a hobgoblin."

"Other than your fur," Chibo said.

"We fight when we must," Roz said. "Not because we enjoy it!"

"You punched an ogre off a cliff," Ji said.

Roz flushed. "I am not proud of that."

"I am! You were awesome."

Many aws, Nin agreed.

"It tossed me into a stone rosebush," Ji said. "My butt still aches."

"A pity you didn't land the other way," Roz said loftily. "Your head is hard enough to break stone."

Chibo giggled and Sally flashed a toothy grin before suddenly stopping in the center of the road. Her ears swiveled toward a massive arch that was carved into the cliffside fifty yards away. The mine entrance. Warm air swelled from the depths, making snow flurries swirl and whirl.

Ji peered into the darkness. "At least it will be warmer inside."

"Um, does anyone else think it looks like a dungeon?" Chibo mused.

Roz smiled at him. "It looks to me like the best way to reach the Ice Witch—"

"Another moon!" Sally barked, eyes narrowing. "Another moon is rising. That's four."

Ji scanned the quiet landscape. The snow suddenly looked like kumiho fur and the silence touched him with dread. "Do you hear anything?"

"Just some night birds. Frogs and crickets—"

An eerie shrieking tore through the night—the blood-chilling yowling of the kumiho. Roz clutched her backpack straps, and Ji's blood turned as cold as a petrified forest.

"I'm pretty sure *I* hear something," Chibo piped.

"Run for the mine!" Ji shouted, his voice thick with fear. "If they're far enough away, we can—"

All three kumiho prowled into sight on a high quarry ledge, bulky rodent-like faces glowing white in the moonslight.

"They're not far enough away," Sally said.

The kumiho leaped from the ledge. They landed on a sheer rock wall but didn't fall. Instead, they scrambled across the frozen cliff like spiders and vaulted down to the mine entrance. Guarding the arch. Pacing back and forth, but not attacking. Not yet, at least.

"Get back!" Ji shouted, pulling Chibo away. "Back, back!"

A feathery voice spoke from behind them: "Thou mayest not enter the mines, Winter Snake."

A woman's head—a hundred times life-size—appeared in the snow flurries that swirled in the mountain breeze. Ji recognized her wide mouth, square chin, short hair, and golden crown.

"The Summer Queen," he whispered, his heart pounding.

"Thou mayest not meet the Ice Witch," the queen thundered. "And my kumiho will prevent thee from leaving this place."

"Until Brace arrives?" Sally snarled.

"The prince will not arrive alone. I am here in the flesh."

"*You're* here?" Sally growled.

"Indeed. Your betrayal forced me to leave Summer City. I arrived hours ago, to aid in the pursuit—the capture."

Ji felt his fists clench. "Well, that's frothing fantastic."

"Remember your manners!" Roz hissed to Ji before curtsying to the queen. "Your Majesty, p-perhaps we can discuss this and c-come to a mutually satisfactory arrangement?"

"Thou art a young lady of superior understanding, Miss Songarza," the queen's huge, snowy head said. "So thou must see that *this* arrangement satisfies me perfectly. You cannot flee. And with the assistance of mine arcane arts, the Summer Army hath made rapid progress."

"They're right behind us," Sally gasped. "She must've cast a silence spell. I didn't hear them until just now."

"Thy bestial abilities are nothing beside the power of the Summer Crown," the queen said, her voice colder than the snow. "You are traitors to your people."

"You tried to kill us!"

"Filthy animals!" The snow swirled angrily. "You are a danger to the realm. You shall not escape—and your allies are too distant to help."

"Our allies?" Ji asked. "What are you talking about?"

"The nonhumans who seek to assist you."

"The goblins?" Sally interrupted. "They're our allies?"

The queen's mocking laugh sounded silvery in the mountain silence. "Wast thou attempting to evade them? Indeed, they sought to come to thine aid."

"I beg your pardon!" Roz rumbled. "The goblins are working for *you*. The White Worm brutalized his own people for *you*."

"The wisest of the goblins work for my realm. For my crown. For my peace. However, the rebels, the savage, uncivilized goblins, strive to end all that is good and proper."

"Oh, c'mon!" Sally grumbled. "We've been running away from the *rebels*? Can we catch a single break here?"

"Expect no rescue at nonhuman hands," the queen said. "Soon you shall contribute your souls to the Summer Realm instead of wasting your foolish, worthless lives on this childish resistance."

Ji took a breath. "Let us go."

"And leave my people unprotected whilst beasts ravage my lands? Why ever would I do such a thing?"

"Because you need Brace alive."

"And so he shall remain," the queen said.

"No, he won't. Not unless you leave us alone." Ji turned to Roz. "Do you know what they used to mine here? Gold. This whole mountain is veined with gold—"

Gold and silver! Nin said. *Mostly gold.*

"If I see a single knight," Ji told the queen, keeping his voice steady, "I'll set the world on fire. I'll burn your prince to ash."

"The friend of thine youth?" the queen asked. "Thou wouldst consign him to a fiery fate?"

"In a heartbeat."

"Thou art truly a dark-hearted creature, born of foul magic and evil urges."

"That's right," Ji said. "So you'd better let us talk to the witch. Then we'll turn back into humans and get out of your summery hair."

The queen's mocking laugh filled the quarry once more. "Thou art an expert deceiver, young boot boy! However, thou canst not lie to *me*. For five hundred years, the ogres mined every fleck of gold from this mountain—and sold it to the Summer Realm. My predecessors did not leave the Ice Witch a trace of treasure to aid her dragon-struck plan."

"Well, you missed some," Ji told her—lying desperately, because despite the hollow sense of power he'd felt since setting foot on Mount Atra, he couldn't raise a single spark.

"Mayhap thou canst sense an echo of long-departed treasure." The queen's snowy head started breaking apart. "Or mayhap thou merely liest. However, thou *shalt* serve my realm, thou wretched and ungrateful beast."

"Please, your majesty," Roz said. "Just listen to—"

"I shall impale you upon the water tree! I shall make something glorious from your worthless souls. Your lives will drain from the mongrel husks of your bodies and pour into the pure vessel of my prince, who shall rule for centuries after you are forgotten!"

Her swirling, snowy face collapsed, and nothing remained but the echo of her mocking laughter. Sally growled, Roz murmured a word that Ji had never heard her use before, and Chibo's wings drooped. Ji clenched his jaw. His bluff had failed and he didn't have any other ideas. Well, except one.

He swallowed and asked Sally, "How close is her army?"

"See for yourself," she told him, nodding across the enormous quarry.

A half dozen warhorses galloped down a ramp. Hooves kicked snow into the air and horse breath plumed in the moons-light. Two knights rode in the lead, just ahead of Posey and Nichol. Brace and Mr. Ioso followed closely behind, surrounded by sparks of white magic, and an entire battalion of knights gathered on the far rim of a deep excavation.

"Okay," Ji said, taking a shaky breath.

"Not really," Sally growled.

Ji turned toward the kumiho stalking in front of the mine entrance. Crooked teeth snapped. Black saliva splattered. A venomous aura of mindless violence oozed from the fox-demons, and fear clamped Ji's throat. Still, he knew what he had to do.

"Follow me into the mine," he said in a frayed voice. "The demons won't try to kill us with the queen so close."

"What are you talking about?" Sally asked. "They almost killed you once already."

"Yeah, but the queen wasn't there. Do they look well trained to you?"

"You're betting that they'll obey her if she's nearby,"

Roz rumbled. "But what if they don't?"

"If we stay here, we're dead," he told her, and started toward the mine.

Snake heads hissed and spat. Ropy kumiho muscles bunched beneath mottled-white pelts. Nightmarish fox muzzles raised into snarls, and Ji's heart curdled into yogurt.

Still, he took another step.

"You're not allowed to bite us," Ji said, his voice trembling. "The queen needs us alive, so you—"

A kumiho pounced at him, slashing with its razor claws.

24

"BAD DEMON!" CHIBO shouted, and his brilliant green glow lit up the archway.

The kumiho roared in fury, Ji cowered in fear—and Chibo flashed past, faster than a diving hawk, his sprite wings whirling like a dozen scythes.

"Chibo, no!" Sally barked, lunging forward.

Roz grabbed her tail in a fierce two-fingered grip. "Let him go!"

Emerald wings slashed and chopped while the kumiho dodged and pounced. A blur of mottled whiteness surged closer to Chibo. Teeth snapped, snakes hissed—and a wing tip sliced through the kumiho's shoulder. The demon shrieked and exploded into a cloud of what looked like white dust.

Ji's ears rang with the echo of the shriek. He blinked a few times, but nothing remained of the fox-demon except for a cloud of white dust swirling in the archway.

"Holy guacamole," Sally gasped. "You just destroyed a kumiho!"

"Sprites do that," Chibo said, a fierce note in his piping voice.

Roz released Sally's tail. "Sprites *are* the natural enemy of the kumiho! The demons cringed every time they saw Chibo's wings since the first—"

"Roz, look!" Ji said. "What's happening?"

The cloud of white dust was dividing into two streams, which swirled through the air toward the two surviving kumiho.

"Um," Sally said, "are the demons doing that?"

"I don't think so," Roz said. "I think—"

Her breath caught as the moon-glimmering dust flowed into the fox-demons . . . and made them stronger. Deadlier. Bigger. Mottled shoulders broadened, demonic legs stretched, and rattlesnake tails thickened.

"They were created by a single spell," Roz rumbled, lowering her horn warily. "When Chibo vanquished one of them, the magic sought Balance by pouring into the others."

"Brighter, Chibo, brighter!" Ji shouted, shaking off his fear. "Keep them away!"

Chibo's wings spread into a brilliant semicircle. His

265

green eyes shone like lanterns and the two still-expanding kumiho paced and growled and snapped—but kept away from the emerald glow.

"Brace is almost here," Sally growled, loping closer to Chibo.

"Get to the mine!" Ji tromped across the snow. "Through the arch! Stay close to Chibo!"

Sally loped ahead, the snow gleaming emerald around her. Ji and Roz followed as the two kumiho grew to the size of horses and prowled just beyond the reach of Chibo's wings.

Making the fox-demons biggergrow, Nin said, *is not the best cunningscheme we ever—*

"The spell seeks Balance," Roz repeated as the kumiho backed away from Chibo and blocked the mine entrance. "The magic from the defeated kumiho flows into the living ones."

"What happens if there are no living ones?" Ji asked, edging forward.

"We're about to find out," Chibo said, his piping voice hard.

Emerald wings whipped toward the two huge kumiho guarding the archway. Eighteen rattlesnake tails lashed in anger, eighteen rattlesnake heads hissed. Hateful demonic eyes glared at Chibo . . . but the beasts cringed away from his brilliant light.

A spark of hope ignited in Ji's heart. The kumiho were

going to run. They were going to flee from Chibo!

Then Brace's voice echoed across the quarry: "Stand your ground!" A throb of magical command sounded in his words. "OBEY!"

The kumiho stopped cringing and bared their jagged teeth, refusing to budge from the entrance—so Chibo launched himself at them in an emerald blur. Claws slashed and snakes snapped, but he corkscrewed untouched through the deadly gauntlet, slicing and chopping with his wings. And he pushed them away from the entrance, making an opening.

"Come on!" Ji yelled, sprinting toward the mine.

A kumiho slipped around Chibo and struck at him. Poison fangs flashed an inch from his neck—

"Bad fox!" Chibo snarled, and a green wing-blade chopped the kumiho's tail in half.

The injured kumiho wailed earsplittingly, and the other demon exploded into white dust from a blow Ji didn't see. The chalky cloud twisted into a tornado that fed the injured kumiho, which grew larger than a stagecoach, with bloated snake tails as thick around as Ji's thigh.

Chibo stayed the same size—scrawny—but he kept slashing at the enormous kumiho, driving it backward, backward, backward through the arch and into the abandoned ogre mine.

"Stay!" Brace's magically strengthened voice called from the quarry. "Fight!"

"Finish it!" Ji shouted to Chibo. "They're right behind us!"

"I'm trying!" Chibo clamored, more sharply than usual.

His emerald wings pushed the kumiho deeper into the mine. Ji, Roz, and Sally followed, wary of the sea-serpent-sized tails and raking claws. A massive cavern opened just past the entrance arch. In the green sprite-light, weird stone bowls and weirder stone tracks looped from the walls and ceiling. The kumiho swiped a boulder at Chibo, and when he dodged, the boulder smashed a wall and started a rock slide.

Ji stumbled across loose stones, and two knights rode warhorses through the arch behind him. A beam of white light swept into the mine from outside—from Brace or Ioso—and Ji shouted a warning to Chibo.

With a flash of his shimmering wings, Chibo swooped higher. The beam missed him by inches, smashing chunks from the rock wall. A crossbow bolt stabbed the empty fabric of Chibo's overlarge trousers, and Roz roared and flung a handful of dirt at the knights.

Except it wasn't dirt. It was a handful of ant lions.

Even with two fingers, Roz always hit what she aimed at. The knights screamed at the stings of ant lions. The warhorses slashed the air with panicked hooves. When Posey and Nichol galloped into the cavern, Roz threw more ant lions—but a shield of white light sprang up to protect the twins.

Brace and Ioso, crackling with magic, stalked through the mine entrance.

Ji clenched his fists and felt for gems in the mountain, for gold. For anything to kindle his dragonfire. But the Summer Queen had been right: hundreds of years of mining had removed every trace of treasure.

So he grabbed a rock instead. If you can't burn 'em, brain 'em.

The enormous kumiho yowled, and Posey fired her crossbow at Chibo again. Sally dodged a blast of mage-light and tackled Posey off her saddle, sending her crossbow hurtling across the cavern. When the two of them hit the ground, Sally snarled, "If you touch my brother I'll—"

Nichol jabbed his spear at her. "Get away from her!"

Sally ducked, and Mr. Ioso roared, "The ogre stung me!"

We buttstung him! Nin shouted gleefully. *In the butt!*

Ji ignored the chaos and slunk through the shadows, feeling the weight of the rock in his hand. Ioso furiously cast magic at Roz—his bald head gleaming, his eyes tight with effort—but Brace looked unruffled and calm. His diadem glittered golden, and sparks shot from his fingertips and blasted toward Chibo.

One spark cracked the wall behind Chibo, who spun and drove a glowing emerald wing into the enormous kumiho's chest.

For a moment, even the mountain held its breath.

Then the kumiho unleashed an otherworldly shriek and an explosion of energy roiled toward the mine entrance. Rubble blew past Ji, blasting through the archway and into the oncoming knights. Soldiers shouted and horses screamed. The shock wave scraped Ji across the floor and rammed him into a stone bowl.

A boulder bounced past. A sword flung past. A Sally hurtled past—

"SALLY!" Ji shouted, kicking desperately toward her.

She grabbed one of his scaly toes, swung in a circle, and flung herself higher, out of the blast zone, vanishing in a flash of fur and ears.

A moment later, the death throes of the kumiho ended.

Silence fell. Ji couldn't see much through the dust and couldn't hear much over the ringing in his ears, but he caught a glimpse of Chibo hunched inside the shield of his wings, his green eyes brighter than the sun. He saw Roz protecting Nin's backpack with her body—and, his mind doolally with fear, Ji thought, "I really need to mend that dress."

Then the mine caved in.

*Crack*s echoed through the cavern. At each *crack*, a cloud of dust puffed from the walls—until the entrance arch collapsed. Rubble avalanched toward Ji and jolted him into action. He scrambled deeper into the cavern, aiming for Chibo's dim green haze. The noise shook his bones; the dust coated his mouth. Sally bounded into sight, calling his name. A white glow cut through the gloom as Brace cast a protective globe around the twins and Mr. Ioso.

Pebbles pelted Ji's scaly back and whipped past his head. A furry paw grabbed his shirt. The lights vanished, and terror rose in Ji's chest. A mountain was falling on him. He was being buried alive. He'd never see the sun again, he'd never breathe, he'd never—

Sally yanked him into a protected nook between two boulders. He curled in a ball until the quaking stopped, then peered at the wreckage. Dust settled on mounds of stones in the front of the cavern. The arch was gone, and rubble completely blocked the mine entrance.

Roz and Chibo huddled together in a half-fallen tunnel, while Brace's globe of light shone from beneath the wreckage. Then the rocks rolled away, and Brace stepped into the cavern, his clothes impeccable. Posey, Nichol, and Mr. Ioso followed, covered in scrapes and dust.

"And now," Brace said, his voice echoing, "we wait for Her Majesty. It won't take long for her to shift this rubble."

"It'll take longer than you've got," Sally growled, stalking toward him.

Brace raised two glowing fingers. "You're more beast than human—"

"If you hurt her," Ji told him, "Roz will toss a boulder at your skinny a—"

"I won't," Roz rumbled firmly. "This has gone quite far

enough! Violence is not the answer."

"Depends on the question," Sally purred.

"We won't fight you, Prince Brace!" Roz said. "And if you cast magic, the cavern will collapse. See for yourself." She pointed toward the cracks in the ceiling. "You may save Mr. Ioso and the twins, but you cannot save all of us. And you need us alive."

The glow faded from Brace's fingers. "What I need is to protect the realm."

"Please, Brace. We used to be friends. Let's just . . . talk. I vow to you that I shall not resort to violence. None of us will. Sally, give the prince your vow."

Sally's ears flattened. "No way."

"On your honor!" Roz rumbled.

"Fine," Sally growled. "I vow on my honor that I won't use violence—unless they do first."

"Chibo?" Roz said.

"Me, too."

"Ji?"

He shrugged.

"Jiyong!" she said. "Vow on your soul that you will not use violence."

"Fine." He exhaled. "I vow on my soul that I won't use violence."

We didn't soulvow! Nin said. *We can still buttsting!*

"And I vow on behalf of Nin," Roz said.

Oh. Now we soulvowed.

"That's all very nice," Brace sneered, strolling across the rubble-covered cavern floor. "But surely you see the truth, Roz? You're a walking horror. Look at yourself. You're a monster."

Ji's fists clenched and his eyes narrowed.

"And you're a threat to the realm," Brace continued. "If we don't complete the Diadem Rite—and sacrifice you on the water tree—I won't be strong enough to control the beasts. They'll murder mothers, fathers, children. Entire villages. It will be the end of everything."

Another *crack* sounded, and dust wafted from above. Brace paused, and Ji stopped slinking through the shadows to glance at the ceiling.

"I understand that you're afraid," Brace continued when the mountain didn't fall on them. "I'd be afraid too. But in the end, I'd choose to protect thousands of innocent people. I'd choose to save the realm."

"The realm?" Chibo fluted, sounding newly confident. "The Summer Realm is beautiful and rich and peaceful— and just like your magic, it sucks the life out of everything it touches."

"Safety has a price, creature," Brace told him. "Would you rather live in a realm of ugliness and war?"

"I'd rather *live*," Chibo said.

"This is what I propose," Roz told Brace. "If we fight here, we'll all perish. Let us flee into the tunnels, and when Her Majesty arrives . . ."

"We'll follow?"

Roz nodded. "If you must."

"And if I refuse?"

"Then we'll bring this mountain down," Sally growled. "We've got nothing to lose."

"That's a good point for a rabid beast," Brace said. "But here's a better one: Mr. Ioso can keep me safe from falling rocks while I subdue you. Then we'll wait for the queen to arrive."

"What about Posey and me?" Lord Nichol asked.

"You will be remembered as heroes," Brace assured him.

"R-remembered? You mean you'll let us die?"

"To save humanity?" Brace nodded. "Of course. Yet nobody will ever forget the sacrifice that you made to protect the—"

THUNK.

Ji smashed Brace in the head with his rock, two inches from his stupid diadem. Brace collapsed, groaning, and Mr. Ioso's fists flared with light. He aimed a blast at Ji— but at an ominous *crack* from the ceiling, he extinguished his mage-light and cursed.

Posey aimed her crossbow at Ji. "You vowed on your soul!"

"I lied," he told her.

"Ji does that," Sally, crouching on a ledge above Posey, told her. "But I don't. If you pull that trigger, I'll make you eat your own braids."

Posey lowered her bow. "The queen will catch you."

"She'd kill you without blinking," Sally growled. "You and your brother both."

"Her Majesty will impale you on her sacred tree," Mr. Ioso snarled. "And I'll laugh to watch it."

"If you try to stop us," Ji told him, crossing the cavern, "we'll bury you."

25

A HUNDRED FEET from the cavern, the main tunnel branched into five passages.

"Which way to the mountaintop?" Ji asked Roz.

"There's too much magic," she said. "I can't feel the earth."

"Follow me," Sally said, her nostrils flaring. She cocked her head to the left, cocked her head to the right, then started toward a passage that headed downward.

"Isn't the mountaintop above us?" Chibo fluted.

"I know what I'm doing!" she snapped.

"Sheesh," he muttered, "all I did was ask."

"That's not all you did," Ji told him. "You also beat three kumiho. You know what you are? A demon slayer."

Chibo's eyes shone with glee, and he babbled about

the battle until the tunnel split into three levels. After a moment, Sally bounded to the middle level. She prowled through a forest of dangling ropes and onto a stone track that curved higher into the heart of the mountain.

And Roz kept looking at Ji. Not saying anything. Just . . . looking at him.

"Stop worrying about my soul!" he finally said.

"You broke a solemn vow."

"I don't believe in vows," he told her.

We know a vow that Sneakyji would never break, Nin announced.

"What's that?" Sally asked.

"You shut your ant hole," Ji told Nin, "and tell us how to find the Ice Witch."

We don't know! Ogres don't travel to the topmountain.

"Hobgoblins do," Sally said, and led them to a mine shaft that rose straight upward. "This is the place."

"Up there?" Chibo asked, stretching his wings into the shaft.

Hundreds of stepping stones jutted from the walls, like the inside of a rough-hewn chimney.

Sniffsmells like the topmountain, Nin said a little nervously.

"We're so close to finding the Ice Witch," Roz rumbled, gazing into the darkness. "So close to breaking the spell . . ."

"Last one there's a rotten eggplant!" Sally bounded

onto the lowest stepping stone, then sprang from step to step until she vanished overhead.

Chibo spread his wings and drifted upward, not even touching the sides of the mine shaft. Roz climbed steadily, her strength making the ascent easy. Only Ji struggled to pull himself higher, scrambling on every step in the warm air of the shaft.

The evilqueen cleared the rockslide, Nin said. *She's in the first cavern.*

"How do you know?" Chibo asked.

A few of us are still there, peekspying.

"At least," Ji panted, "they'll have a hard time . . . following us through this maze."

She is melting a straightpath through the rocks.

"Oh, great," Ji muttered, and kept climbing.

His lungs ached and his legs trembled. Then his lungs burned and his legs throbbed. Then he reached the top of the mine shaft and collapsed in a square room with marble walls and a marble floor and a marble ceiling. And no exits.

A dead end.

"What now?" Chibo fluted.

Ji peered at the cool stone walls. The marble was veined with pink and green, and marked with thousands of black flecks. The walls looked smooth and hard but mostly *solid*.

"Check the ceiling," he told Chibo after he caught his breath.

Chibo probed the rock with his wings. "I can't feel

anything." His green eyes widened. "Um, Roz? What're you doing?"

Roz was staring at one of the walls. "Yes."

"Huh?"

"Of course," she said, scratching her chin.

"Leave her alone," Ji said. "She's thinking." He squinted at an ant lion on the floor. "How far behind are the knights?"

We don't know—the evilqueen killed all our spylions.

"Are you okay?"

We're still here, there, and everywhere.

"Good." Ji turned to Sally. "Can you hear them?"

She shook her head. "The queen's casting her silence spell again."

"Oh." He exhaled. "Hey, Roz? This would be a good time to tell us what you're thinking."

"Me, too," Roz muttered, which didn't really help.

"I guess we'll wait," Ji told Sally.

He dangled his legs into the mine shaft, peered at the darkness, and tried not to panic. They'd come so far and survived so much. They just needed a little more time. Not much. He wasn't asking for much. Just a few hours, and they'd finally break this spell. But somewhere in the mountain, the queen drew closer every minute.

"What vow wouldn't Ji break?" Chibo asked Nin.

If he vowed on Missroz, Nin said. *He'd keep that promise.*

"Yeah," Sally said. "Roz is what Ji has instead of a soul."

"I have a soul!" Ji said.

"Maybe a teensy one."

"A regular-sized one."

"But worn and muddy," Sally said. "Like an old boot."

Ji snorted, still looking into the mine shaft. Then an ant lion crawled onto his chin and Nin said, *We wonder something.*

"What's that?"

If we backturn into an ogre—

"You mean *when* you turn back into an ogre."

When we backturn into an ogre, we won't be a cub for much longer.

"You'll get bigger, right?" Ji rubbed his aching eyes. "And you'll choose if you're a girl or—"

"Four lines, four lines, two lines!" Roz cried, brushing the wall with her troll fingers. "Interspersed with sonnets! The pink lines combine into couplets!"

Sally said, "Mraw?"

"It's writing!" Ji realized. "Those are words."

"They don't look like words," Sally said.

Ji shook his head in amazement. "She's reading the rock."

"This is an epic poem," Roz said, "composed in an ancient lyric verse, which—"

"*Rozario Songarza!*" Ji interrupted. "Does it say how to find the Ice Witch?"

"Oh! Yes, of course." She knocked on the wall. "There we go."

"Is that what all this says?" Ji asked. "Just 'knock'?"

"Of course not!" Roz told him. "There's also history and poetry and layers of meaning I cannot plumb."

We like plums, Nin said.

"Nothing's happening," Sally said.

"Knock again," Ji said, and footsteps echoed into the marble room.

A crack appeared in one marble wall, and a white-blue glow shone into the room. The crack widened, becoming an open door, and a beast shambled forward.

26

THE BEAST LOOKED like a six-eyed polar bear—hulking and white and furry—except for the turtle shell covering her back. She looked like a "she," too, though Ji couldn't tell exactly why.

"A bug!" Roz gasped. "A bear!"

"Whoa," Ji said. "Wow."

"Hoo," Sally added. "Boy."

"Hi!" Chibo fluted, spreading his wings happily. "I'm Chibo!"

We're Nin!

The bugbear gestured like a butler, inviting them to enter the white-blue glow beyond the door.

"A pleasure," Roz said with a slight curtsy. "May I ask if the Ice Witch—"

"And that's my sister, Sally," Chibo continued, swooping past the bugbear and through the open door.

He vanished into the glow. Sally growled and bounded after him, with Roz and Ji following. They darted past the bugbear into a hallway made of white-blue ice. The floor was ice, the ceiling was ice. Everything was ice. Warm ice.

"Okay," Ji said, "now *this* is happening."

Farther into the hallway, Sally grabbed Chibo's wrist. She snarled at him not to fly off alone, while Roz whispered, "This is where the Ice Witch lives."

When the bugbear touched her icicle necklace, the door sealed shut. She beckoned again, then headed down the hallway. Ji followed, staring through the translucent floors. The blurred shapes of bugbears moved on levels below him, like snapping turtles swimming in an icebound lake. Blue-white domes were lofted above semitransparent ceilings, and slabs of ice shifted and spun in caverns behind the glossy walls. Wonder and hope chimed with each of Ji's footsteps. They'd survived demons and goblins, armies and mountains and magic. They'd reached the Ice Witch's palace.

The hallway ended in a great hall that stretched wider than a dozen ballrooms and rose higher than a castle tower.

Chibo gasped.

Nin mind-spoke in Ogrish.

Roz rumbled, "Beautiful."

Sally eyed the bugbear suspiciously.

And Ji stared in awe, stepping onto a balcony decorated with sculptures of snow and carpets of frost. Ice columns lined the ground floor, and a dozen more balconies clung to the walls. A white-blue chimney, big enough for an entire river of smoke, opened in the ceiling. In the center of the hall stood an enormous onyx platform holding a boulder-sized crystal.

"Do you think that crystal is the Ice Witch's throne?" Sally asked.

"It doesn't look like a throne," Ji said.

"What does it look like?" Chibo asked.

A *cloudyboulder,* Nin told him. *On a tablestone in the middle of an emptyfloor.*

"Oh," Chibo said. "Thanks."

The bugbear gestured toward a curving stairway that swept down to the ground floor. Except there were no stairs. It was a slide—a wide, curving *slide*way—and the bugbear shuffled onto it and glided away. Her white fur ruffled and her six eyes glittered. She didn't even hold the banister; she merely slid off when she reached the lower floor.

Sally bounded onto the slide, keeping her balance like a miniature version of the bugbear. "Wa-hoo!"

Ji stepped onto the slide and whizzed downward. Too fast! He heard Roz rumble in alarm behind him while Chibo hooted in pleasure. The world whipped past; then

Ji landed on the softest rug in the world. Well, not a rug exactly. More like a bugbear belly. Still really soft, though.

The bugbear set him aside and caught Roz's arm when she stumbled off the slide.

"Th-thank you," Roz said.

The bugbear led them across the white-blue floor to the onyx platform. The cloudy crystal atop the platform reminded Ji of uncut diamonds, and he felt the throb of treasure *somewhere*, but not close enough to touch. He followed Sally up the platform stairs to the crystal, his heart pounding in his chest.

"Are we supposed to knock again?" Chibo asked, flitting beside him.

"I have slept for six huNdred years," said a voice like hail on a frozen lake. "Waking only for each diadem riTe."

Ji jerked away from the crystal. "You're the Ice Witch?"

"The crystal?" Sally growled. "The crystal is the witch?"

Crystalwitch! Nin said, as ant lions dropped from the backpack and spread across the platform.

"We—" Roz curtsied. "We are pleased to meet you, ma'am. We've come a long way to beg for your help."

Blue-white light gleamed along the facets of the crystal. "I've waiTed for centuries, Winter Snake. I watched you travel to my mouNtain."

The words "Winter Snake" dug a pit in Ji's stomach, but he managed to say, "Then you know why we're here."

"You're the Winter Snake!" Chibo stared at Ji. "You

really are the Winter Snake."

"He is not *the* Winter Snake," the crystal said. "He is *a* Winter Snake."

Roz touched Ji's arm. "He is Jiyong, ma'am. Nothing more and nothing less."

"Any human bespelled iNto a dragon is a Winter Snake." The crystal gleamed. "I knew this day woulD come! I knew the day would come when a winter snAke ventured to my mountain to end this tyranNy."

"There's something in there," Sally growled with an edge of fear. "Something's moving inside the crystal."

The bugbear tapped the crystal again, and the cloudy quartz cleared.

Ji's breath caught. Because a tiny figure stood in the center of the hollow crystal—a woman the size of Ji's forearm. She looked like a glass sculpture: delicate and beautiful. Sapphire and garnet gleamed on her skin, emerald and ruby and opal swirled in her gown.

"You're inside the—" Roz gasped, caught between shock and wonder. "I . . . We didn't know, we thought—"

"I've slepT in this crystal bed for centuries," the tiny glass-woman said. "The summer queeNs imprisoned me, yet I turned my prison into my palace. Now my tiMe comes to an end. Today my dreams will succeeD or fail."

"Ours, too," Ji told her, his throat tight. "Will you break the spell?"

"I shall." The Ice Witch stepped toward him inside the

crystal shell. "But first you must grant me a faVor."

"Sure," Ji said.

"Wait a second," Sally said, her eyes narrowing. "What do you want from him?"

"Slept for centuries?" Roz rumbled, pressing her hand to her chest. "So you're the *original* Ice Witch? You witnessed the final battle and met the first Summer Queen and—"

"I didn't meeT the first Summer Queen," the Ice Witch interrupted. "I *was* the first Summer Queen."

27

"I DON'T—" ROZ swallowed. "I'm afraid I don't understand."

"I defenDed my people," the tiny Ice Witch told her, "but I brutaliZed the other nations. I gave the White Worms power and trapped ogres in their mounTains."

"We . . . all make mistakes," Roz said.

"And we must fix them," the Ice Witch told her. "I have planned for ceNturies to repair the damage I did. Do you wonder why snow does noT melt in these mountains?"

"Yes, ma'am."

"Because I do not let it. Six hundred years of snowfall is collected on these mouNtain peaks."

"That's a lot of snowflakes," Chibo fluted.

"And this is my tasK for the Winter Snake." The Ice

Witch turned her gemlike face to Ji. "You must melT all of that snow."

"Then you'll turn us human again?" Ji asked, trying to stick to the main point.

"You want him to melt the snow?" Roz furrowed her granite-flecked brow. "Won't that unleash a flood? A six-hundred-year flood?"

"Yes," the Ice Witch said.

"That much water . . ." Roz shuddered. "An ocean would pour down from the mountains! It would drown entire villages and sweep away everything from Mirror Lake to Summer City—"

"Thus destroying the humaN realm," the Ice Witch said, her tiny eyes glittering. "And fixing my mistaKe."

"It would kill thousands of people," Roz rumbled in horror. "Tens of thousands."

The dread in her voice sent a shiver down Ji's spine. Destroying villages? Drowning kitchen maids and foot-men? Killing boot boys and goblins? He'd vowed to pay any price to stop the Summer Queen, but what if he couldn't? What if he shouldn't?

"It will free the ogres from the Gravewoods," the Ice Witch told Roz. "It will bReak the power of the White Worms and return magic to the huMans."

"If any survive," Sally growled.

"You'd let the oGres die?" the Ice Witch demanded. "You'd let the goblins live in slavery?"

"I'm not saying that!" Sally's ruff rose. "I don't know!"

We cannot let the ogres forever die, Nin said. *We cannot.*

Ji nodded slowly. Nin was right.

"We also can't drown thousands of innocent people!" Sally snarled.

Ji frowned slowly. Sally was right too.

"Nobody is inNocent," the Ice Witch told Sally. "The humans flourished using the laNd and power I stole."

"They never asked!" Chibo fluted angrily. "They never asked for any of it!"

"You are correct," the Ice Witch told him with a regal nod. "They neVer asked where their victory came from. They never cared."

Ji tapped his claws on the cool crystal shell. Forget about humans and goblins and ogres, forget about realms and floods. What about Roz and Sally, Chibo and Nin? Forget everything else; he needed to take care of *them*.

He needed to lie.

"You want me to melt the snow?" he asked the Ice Witch. "You want me to flood the valley?"

"That is the only way to defeaT the Summer Queen."

"Then you'll turn us human again?"

"Yes."

"Turn us human first," he told her.

The crystal shell gleamed. "And afterward, you will refuse to meLt the snow."

"And afterward, I'll do whatever you want," he promised.

She gave him a knowing look. "If you do not flood the reaLm, the Summer Queen will simply caSt a new Diadem Rite and raise a new water tree."

"Well, yeah, but—" He frowned. "Melting the snow won't stop her from casting a spell."

"It will," the Ice Witch said. "The queen will exhauSt her power trying to protect her people from the fLood. She'll have no strength to transform you again."

"Okay." Ji paused. "That actually makes sense. If I flood the realm, she'll have other things to worry about."

Chibo's wings flared. "Like all those farmers dying . . ."

"All those servants," Roz rumbled. "All those families."

"And horses," Sally added. "Trapped in stables . . ."

"And the weaver kids," Chibo whispered. "Tied to their looms."

What about cubs trapped by the Gravewoods? Nin asked. *And goblins trapped in hatecollars?*

"So if I flood the realm, the queen will be too weak to kill us," Ji told the Ice Witch. "But I can't. There's no treasure here."

"There is a single gem," the Ice Witch told him. "One jewel, crafted for centuRies. This crystal is my cell but also my shield. Not even you can feel a geM through its walls."

"What are you talking abo—" he started.

The Ice Witch sang a throbbing note, and panes were shed from the crystal to shatter on the floor. As the translucent shell collapsed, the roar of treasure filled Ji's ears. The thunder of a priceless gemstone struck him like a battering ram. His skin tingled and his eyes burned. Hunger seized his heart and fire climbed his spine.

"What's happening?" Roz asked him, stepping closer. "What is it?"

"She—" Ji pointed a shaking finger at the Ice Witch, who now stood exposed on a crystal podium. "She turned herself into a living gemstone. If I touch her, I can melt every flake of snow in this mountain range."

"What if she still won't turn us human?" Sally growled.

"With this much power," the Ice Witch said, "the Winter Snake can do it himself."

Despite the dragonmagic roaring through him, Ji managed to stammer, "I c-can?"

"Dragons can do more than transforM gems into fire." Shards of crystal gleamed on the onyx platform. "Your magic is the same as that of the Diadem Rite."

"It's the s-same?" Ji asked, his body trembling.

"Identical."

He shook his head in disbelief. "It's the same magic? Stealing fire from treasure and stealing souls from people?"

"Yes. You can draw humanity from your eneMies, just as you draw fire from gems."

"I can use their souls," he whispered, "to fix ours."

"*After* you melt the snow, or the queen will simply

transfoRm you again." The Ice Witch pointed to the hole in the ceiling. "Shoot your flaMes into the chimney and spread them across the mouNtains until—"

"You'll die," Roz told her. "If Ji draws on your power, you'll die."

"I have lived too long," the Ice Witch said, her jeweled face serene. "I must repair the damaGe I caused."

"You cannot repair damage by doing more damage," Roz said.

"You cannot repair damage by doiNg *nothing*."

Roz looked near tears. "There must be another way!"

"Unless you can defeaT the Summer Queen, there is not."

"We can't beat her," Sally growled. "Nobody can."

"I know that!" Roz rumbled. "But this is horrible and wrong and—"

"HumaNs have reigned for too long." The Ice Witch lifted her miniature hand toward Ji. "It is time to balanCe the scales."

There was no other way to break the spell. No other way to survive. If Ji melted the snow, he'd hurt the humans but save his friends. If he didn't, he'd hurt the ogres and goblins—but lose his friends. He didn't want to make this choice. He didn't want to hurt anyone. But did that matter? Kitchen maids didn't want to pluck chickens, boot boys didn't want to shine shoes. The world didn't care what you wanted, it only cared what you did.

"Okay," he said.

The Ice Witch smiled and rested her palm on his finger. Dragonpower thrummed in his chest and—

"Stop!" Brace shouted, and ice shattered across the great hall.

28

WHITE LIGHT GLEAMED around falling chunks of the shattered wall. Armored in magic, Brace and Mr. Ioso strode into the hall. Posey and Nichol followed closely, while farther back the queen melted through icy walls for her army of knights.

Fear spiked in Ji's chest. He needed to stop them. With a grunt, he reached for the Ice Witch's arm to draw on her power.

She jerked away. "Don't waste your dragoNfire on this fight! Melt the sNow!"

"For the Summer Queen!" Brace called, his eyes glowing. "For her realm!"

Mr. Ioso blasted magic at Ji. "And for her prince!"

The Ice Witch sang a crystalline phrase, and a snowy shield blocked the attack.

"Bugbears!" Ji told the Ice Witch. "Make your bugbears stop them!"

"They're not mine," she said, uttering another chant. "And they don't fight."

She was right: the bugbears didn't fight. Instead, they turtled, curling beneath their shells, while shimmering white snakes formed around Brace.

"Well, I do," Ji told the witch, reaching for her again.

A sheet of ice blocked his hand. "I can handle the pRince."

"The queen's right behind him."

"I shall holD her off." A massive block of ice rose to repair the shattered wall and delay the queen. "While you do what muSt be done."

"Ji!" Brace yelled, sending white snakes slithering between the ice columns. "You'll kill thousands of people!"

Ji scowled. "Like you've been trying to kill *us*?"

"Please listen, Prince Brace," Roz said, as Chibo's wings struck at the white snakes. "You're asking us to sacrifice the ogres and goblins. We must—"

"Of course I'm asking you to sacrifice the beasts! They're *beasts*."

"And so are you," Mr. Ioso said, bringing his glowing fists together.

Magic crackled around him, but an even brighter glow glimmered deeper in the ice palace: the glow of the queen burrowing through the final wall at the head of her army. The Ice Witch's chants thickened the ice almost as quickly, her glimmering white-blue snow swirling from the air.

"They're people," Roz told Ioso. "As are we. Not humans, but peop—"

Mr. Ioso's blast smashed her shoulder, spinning her around. "Die!"

Roz grunted, Sally bounded forward, and one of Brace's snakes smacked Chibo against an ice column.

"Roz is right!" Posey said. "They're people. We need to—"

With a flick of his hand, Brace swept two bugbears into the air and whipped them together, crushing Sally between their shells. She fell gasping to the ground, a spray of blood at her muzzle.

Rage reddened Ji's vision. Without even touching the Ice Witch, he drew on the power of her gemstone form. His heart turned to fire. Flames roared in his eyes, then erupted at Brace. A white shield sprang from Brace and Ioso and blocked Ji's attack, while the Ice Witch chanted faster, keeping the queen from breaking through the wall.

"All this," Brace said, through gritted teeth, "to save filthy animals."

With a snarl, Ji unleashed more flames. "Why should humans rule?"

"Because we're human," Brace said.

"That doesn't mean—"

"Remember the games we used to play?" Brace's voice shook with the effort of maintaining his shield. "We were always the heroes, Ji. But you're the villain of this story."

"I'm not," Ji snarled.

"You're the Winter Snake," Brace spat. "Now, Ioso!"

Pouring all their power into the white shield, Brace and Ioso forced the dragonfire backward. Sweat beaded on Ji's face. His eyes stung, his fists clenched—and he remembered what the Ice Witch had told him: stealing fire from gems and stealing souls from people was the same magic. Dragonmagic. His magic. *You can draw humanity from your enemies. . . .*

Ji clenched his fists. *Fine. You want a villain? I'll show you a villain.* He snuffed his flames and lashed out with his hunger instead. Not his hunger for treasure—his hunger for souls. And dragons didn't need a water tree. Tendrils of pure magic erupted across the hall and grabbed Brace's soul like a pebble in a goblin's hand. When Ji seized Ioso and the twins, he felt their souls flowing and shifting like fire, like opal and amethyst and lapis lazuli.

Power and revenge beat in Ji's chest. He understood everything now: how to drain Brace and Ioso and the twins, how to break the Diadem Rite. He felt the Summer Queen coming through the wall, a hundred times more powerful than Brace or the Ice Witch—but she was too late. He would drain Brace's soul, killing the queen's heir, breaking the diadem spell, and healing his friends. Souls fluttered in Ji's mind like blue-bats in a bottle. He touched

298

Roz, Sally, Chibo, and Nin with his magic, gently preparing them to receive the humanity that he'd steal from the others.

And he felt their souls, too: honorable, strong, goofy. Dignified, curious, hopeful, stubborn. Brighter than any diamond, purer than any gold. Sweeter than any revenge.

For an endless heartbeat, Ji balanced on a knife-edge. He wanted to return his friends to their true forms. He wanted to hurt Brace and Ioso and the queen. But Roz and Sally and Chibo and Nin deserved better than stolen souls. They *were* better than stolen souls. Maybe Ji wasn't, but they were. He felt their goodness shining in his mind, and knew that they wouldn't want him to do this. They wouldn't let him.

So he muttered, "Stupid goodness," and released his dragonmagic.

Brace and Ioso fell gasping to the ice-covered floor. The twins groaned and the Ice Witch chanted. Roz helped a limping Sally toward the onyx platform, while Chibo's wings gathered stunned ant lions around the shattered crystal.

"What just happened?" Roz asked Ji.

"You ruined my plan," he snarled at her. "You and your dumb souls."

"We're running out of time," Sally growled, wiping blood from her muzzle. "The queen's almost through the wall."

The Ice Witch spoke to Ji while still chanting, like she

had two voices: "Melt the snow, Winter Snake. Or you will perish and the humaNs will reign for another thouSand years and the ogres will die and the goBlins will weep."

She was right. If he did nothing, nothing would change. He lifted his gaze to the chimney and called fire into his eyes.

"No," Sally told at him. "You can't do this."

"Then all the ogres shaLl die," the Ice Witch said, "and the goBlins suffer."

"How come keeping the same people suffering feels easier than making new people suffer?" Chibo asked. "I think that's bad."

You must burn, Nin told Ji. *You must snowmelt.*

"Enough!" Roz rumbled. "What do *you* think is right, Ji?"

"Nothing's right!" he cried, and grabbed the Ice Witch's hand.

The awful power of a dragon roared through him. He looked at the chimney and imagined snow melting and floods crashing across the realm. He saw raging currents pounding fishing villages into mud, smashing Primstone Manor into kindling. He heard the Ice Witch chant *now, now, now,* and flames burned his cheeks . . . except they weren't flames, they were tears.

Ji wept for the ogres, he wept for the goblins—and he didn't unleash his flames. *I'm sorry, Nin. I can't destroy the realm.* Chibo was right: watching the same people suffer didn't feel as bad as hurting new people. The ogres and goblins were used to hardship. They were tough; they could take it. They didn't expect any better.

Except no. No. Hardship shouldn't strike the same people every time. The fact that the ogres and goblins were used to hardship didn't mean they needed less help, it meant they needed more. And what if Ji controlled his fire? What if he kept a grip on his power and—

Flames blazed from his eyes.

A column of fire shot into the chimney. Ji's head snapped backward, his spine locked. His eyes opened impossibly wide, sending flames roaring across the mountain to unleash a murderous flood.

29

THE ICE WITCH'S grip tightened on Ji's finger and her gemlike hand blackened and flaked. Cracks spread across her arm as Ji transformed her life into dragonfire, but her voice chimed with exultation: "Let my sins be fixed but never forGotten. Cast aside the yoKe of—"

A wall of the great hall exploded inward to reveal the Summer Queen. Shards of ice slashed Ji's clothes and sliced his skin. Sally growled and Roz spun to protect Chibo. Nin jabbered about "shamoons" and "Mer-Lin-Su" while ice columns melted and became serpents of living water that flanked the Summer Queen as she strode ahead of her army.

"Thou shalt bow to the might of Summer!" the queen cried.

"More!" the Ice Witch—raising slabs of ice to block the queen's approach—shouted at Ji. "All your poWer, now, now!"

Ji jerked his hand away from her. "No."

Even after he broke contact, a conflagration flowed through him. Somewhere far above, flames vented from Mount Atra, melting snow into torrents every second, sending rivers crashing toward the human realm. He needed to control himself. He needed to rein in the fire. He clenched his fists and gritted his teeth. *Last chance. Last chance to stop this. Last chance to make your own choice instead of serving the witch or the queen like a boot boy on his knees—*

With a howl of effort, he crammed the dragonfire back into his heart and slammed the lid shut. His fingernails dug into his palms and his pulse pounded in his ears.

"You didn't melt enough to desTroy them," the Ice Witch chimed. "You stopped too soon, Winter Snake! You—"

"I'll start again!" Ji shouted at the Summer Queen, over the roar of flames in his mind. "Come any closer and I'll start again."

The queen paused, her golden crown reflected in the watery snakes flanking her. Brace stepped to her side while Mr. Ioso and the twins fell in behind them. Nin chattered, *Almost here, Missroz! Snowbiting fast as snowbiters snowbite!* while dozens of knights scrambled across the ice-covered floor and two bald women, mages with fierce eyes, crackled with magic behind Mr. Ioso.

"I'll melt the snow," Ji yelled at the queen. "I'll destroy your realm."

"Don't wait, you fooLish boy!" the Ice Witch chimed. "Finish what you staRted!"

"Roz, please," Ji begged. "Tell them."

Flames flickered in Ji's vision. He didn't know what he wanted Roz to say. Something kind, something wise, something trollish. He knew this wasn't his best plan ever: melt the snow a little, then hold the Summer Realm hostage and pray that Roz saved everything. Still, it was the only plan he had.

"If Ji continues, Your Majesty," Roz told the queen in her gruff voice, "he will destroy your realm."

"He muSt," the Ice Witch said. "There is nothing more imPortant than—"

At a gesture from the Summer Queen, a fist of water rose from the crystal pedestal and grabbed the Ice Witch, silencing her. Despite her blackened arm, she glittered brilliantly in the magnified water, her mouth open in fear and surprise.

Ji drew on the fire still in his chest to blast the queen and—

"Ji, wait!" Roz bellowed at him. "Everyone, wait! Your Majesty, Ji will not flood the realm if you free the goblins and allow the ogres to roam the foothills."

"Thus permitting them to attack the humans?" the queen asked Roz.

"They won't!" Roz said. "Well, hopefully not. But if you don't agree, Ji will wash your realm into the sea."

"And if they attack, defend yourselves," Sally snarled at the Summer Queen. "You can't keep them in chains just because you're afraid of what *might* happen."

"Chains are bad," Chibo said.

"If they had emerged victorious," the Summer Queen asked, resting her hand on Brace's arm, "would they have shown humans such mercies?"

"We act with honor because *we* have honor," Sally said, "not because they do or do not."

The snowbiters snowbroke through! Nin jabbered to Roz.

"You've forgotten one thing," Brace said, his voice ringing across the shattered hall. "Her Majesty is the *Summer Queen*. None can stand against her. Not a hundred mages, not a thousand knights. Even if you had an army—"

"We do," Roz said, and gestured toward a half-collapsed balcony.

Ji's breath caught when he followed her gaze. So that's what Nin had been nattering about! "Snowbiters" meant that goblins were chewing through the ice. Between threatening the queen and shooting flames, Ji hadn't noticed goblins and ogres pouring from a frozen tunnel. Ji recognized the goblin in front—Chiptooth—and most of the ogre war party stalking across the balcony. The gorilla-ogre roared, the bull-ogre bowed her head to Roz, and smaller ogres gathered in the center, each with crimson, glowing tusks.

Shamoon! Nin said. *Shamoon are here! And burrow-fighters!*

"Look there," Sally breathed. "In the walls . . ."

Faces appeared in the cracked blue-white ice of the balcony wall: Ti-Lin-Su and three other mermaids, white hair flowing gently in a distant current.

"You will require the aid of a mightier army than that," the Summer Queen scoffed.

Nichol stepped forward. "We're not mighty, Your Majesty—"

"—but they've got our aid," Posey finished.

"No way," Ji breathed.

"You're *joining* us?" Sally asked, peering in shock at Posey.

"You're *betraying* us?" Brace asked, glaring in fury at Posey.

"I'm sorry, Prince Brace," Posey said. "The hobgoblin is right. There's no honor in this."

"You're traitors to the Summer Realm," Brace snarled, as glimmers of light traced the edge of his diadem. "Traitors to your race and your family!"

While he ranted, the twins crossed the hall to stand beside Sally, who flattened her tufted ears warily. Chibo waggled his fingers in greeting and Ji stared in shock. Posey and Nichol were the last people he'd expect to do the right thing. He almost resented them: if you couldn't enjoy hating a couple of highborn bullies, who could you enjoy hating?

"You're still a filthy beast," Posey muttered to Sally.

"You're still a spoiled brat," Sally replied.

Then they stood side by side, facing the queen.

"And in the end, you're nothing," Brace finished. "All together you don't have a shadow of Her Majesty's power."

"Perhaps not," Roz told him. "But she cannot defeat us before Ji melts the snow."

"Not while the Ice Witch lives," the queen said, her crown gleaming.

Crackles of golden light arced into Mr. Ioso and the other mages. They shriveled like leaves in a fire as the Summer Queen absorbed their magic and their lives. Her eyes glowed golden; then a fourth spark burst in the fist of water around the Ice Witch, and her tiny gemstone body started to crack and blacken.

"Oh, no," Ji breathed. "No, no."

"I only wanTed to . . . ," the Ice Witch whispered before she crumbled into ash.

Ji felt his dragonpower fade—and his anger grow. He'd barely known the Ice Witch, and he hadn't liked her much, but he hated the queen for taking her life as if stepping on a bug.

He unleashed a fireball across the hall. "No more!"

The queen smiled, and a shimmer of white magic absorbed the flames. "You've lost."

"We must work together," Roz rumbled. "We must act as one to—"

"Attack!" Sally shouted.

A black glow shone from the tusks of the shamoon and the crash of waves sounded from the mermaids. The ogre war party surged forward and goblins opened tunnels beneath the knights. Chibo's wings deflected Brace's magical onslaught while ant lions dropped from the ceiling. Roz pounded toward the queen, her ragged dress flapping. Nichol fired his crossbow, and Sally and Posey waded into battle together.

Ji gathered his anger and fear and hope and hate into a single burning spear and shouted, "NOW!"

The shamoon and mermaid magic roared at the queen while Ji's blast ripped through the air. All three blows struck the Summer Queen at once. The impact shook the mountain. The queen staggered, and bolts of lightning, brighter than the sun, flashed across the hall. The roof trembled and cracked, filling the air with white-blue shards. Bugbears curled beneath their shells, and soldiers—human, ogre, and goblin alike—cowered from the hail of falling ice.

The Summer Queen's brilliant white glow dimmed beneath the rubble, then faded away.

30

SHARDS OF CRYSTAL littered the onyx platform around Ji. He stared at the massive mound of wreckage that covered the Summer Queen, her army—and his friends. Goblins chuffed and knights moaned and Ji breathed his friends' names. Then Ti-Lin-Su's voice sounded above a faint rumble of waves. Roz, Chibo, and Sally—and hundreds of tiny ant lions—sifted from the rubble. Scraped and slashed and bleeding, but alive.

Relief, warmer than any dragonfire, burst in Ji's chest. He trotted toward his friends, crunching over shattered ice while the tusks of the shamoon glowed feebly. A black tint touched the blue-white shards, and the twins slid from the wreckage, along with a few dozen humans, ogres, and goblins.

Ji hugged Chibo tight. "You're okay!"

"Did we win?" Chibo moaned. "I think we won. Did we win?"

"Of course we won," Sally purred, brushing debris from her fur.

Ji hugged Chibo even tighter. He didn't know exactly how they'd won, but he didn't *care* exactly how! They'd done the impossible: they'd beaten the queen.

"Even her voice is adorable," Posey told Nichol as she limped toward Sally. "And look at her ears!"

"At least I can walk," Sally growled.

"On your furry little pawses," Nichol said.

Furrylittle footpaws! Nin agreed as ant lions hopped from a toppled ice column onto Chibo's bald head. *Now the evilqueen's terrorgrip will loosen! The Gravewoods will soften, the goblins will freewalk! She is defeated and we—*

"She's not defeated," Roz rumbled, frowning at the mountain of wreckage.

The warm glow of relief in Ji's chest turned to cold sludge. He didn't want to look; he didn't want to know. He didn't want to fight anymore.

"She has to be," he said. "We've got nothing left."

No Ice Witch, no gems. No dragonfire. The shamoon and mermaids were exhausted and the ogres and goblins were battered and limping.

Except, of course, Roz was right.

White magic gleamed beneath the rubble. The ice shards melted, flowing into the center of the hall. A blue pool deepened around the onyx platform and the Summer Queen and Brace stepped from the white glow.

Unhurt, unscathed, unruffled. Undefeated.

"The reign of Summer shall never end," the queen said, her crown glowing golden. "Thou art defeated, Winter Snake. The paltry magic of thine allies is spent."

When the light of the Summer Queen's crown seeped into the floor, the blue-white ice rippled with the color of dried blood. The ogres roared in anger—then bellowed in alarm as red-brown stripes of clay branched through the ice.

One streak touched the bull-ogre and transformed her huge ogre paw into a human-sized boot.

A terra-cotta boot.

A wave of clay rose on the ogre's body, coating her legs and chest, shrinking her into the shape and size of a terra-cotta warrior. Clay stripes marbled the floor, striking every goblin and human, every ogre and shamoon, warping them into clay statues. Posey and Nichol transformed in an eyeblink, and the clay even struck through the ice wall, twisting Ti-Lin-Su and the mermaids into blank-faced terra-cotta soldiers.

Then the spell ended and silence fell.

Silence and dread.

Roz covered her mouth with her two-fingered hand,

her eyes shining with grief. Sally's tufted ears drooped and Chibo whimpered, while Nin's mind-speak echoed with an ogre lament. Ji trembled, trapped in a nightmare. Everywhere he looked, another horror appeared: the magnificent ogres were lifeless clay; the weird goblins were identical statues. The wise mermaids and mysterious shamoon—and even spoiled, brave Posey and Nichol—were nothing but unthinking mud.

"Turn them back." Sally prowled toward the queen. "Turn them back."

"Even I cannot reverse that spell," the queen told her, stepping toward the rippling blue pool. "So long as the Summer Crown reigns, they will remain our most loyal subjects."

"Our most loyal objects," Brace said.

"You've turned people into things," Roz rumbled, a blaze of contempt in her voice. "And you don't even know why that's wrong."

White ribbons sprang from Brace's hands. "I know we won, Roz. Good always triumphs over evil."

Sally leaped at Brace, her claws slashing—and a ribbon of white magic lassoed her in midair. Three more ribbons snared Chibo and Roz and Ji, while a fifth tore Nin's pack from Roz's back and wrapped it in a glowing net. The ribbons lofted them high and left them dangling like sides of beef in a butcher's shop.

The Summer Queen turned to Brace at the edge of the

blue pool. "Art thou ready, my prince?"

"I am, my queen," Brace said.

"Dost thou pledge thyself to the realm?" she asked him. "To hold the welfare of humanity even above thine own?"

"I do, my queen," Brace said.

"I don't!" Ji snarled, and the ribbons tightened around him, stifling his words.

"After unseemly delay, we bring the Diadem Rite to completion," the Summer Queen intoned, raising her arms.

A geyser burst from the pond. Streams of water branched until a tree loomed overhead. The water tree. The end of the road. The end of Ji's hopes and dreams, his plans and schemes. The end of freedom for goblins and of life for ogres. The end of his future, the end of his friends. Chibo's huge emerald eyes filled with tears, his wings trapped by the ribbons of light. Sally struggled in her bonds, her ruff raised and her ears back. A few ant lions tried to sting the ribbons, while the rest of Nin clustered inside the net. Thick ribbons wrapped Roz, but despite her ragged dress and her trollish horn, she looked dignified.

"I'm sorry," Ji said, in a choked voice. "I'm sorry for everything."

"I'm not," Roz said.

"You know we're about to die, right?" Sally growled at her.

We're too cub to die! Nin cried.

Chibo sniffled. "We're too sprite to die."

"I'm scared of dying," Roz rumbled, her voice strong. "I'm scared, and I'm sad that I'll never see Sally become the knight she already is, or watch Chibo light up the sky without even using his sprite wings. I've dreamed of meeting the glorious ogre Nin would've become." She fell silent for a heartbeat. "But no, I'm not sorry. These last weeks have meant everything to me. They've been so difficult, and such a precious gift."

Tears sprang to Ji's eyes. "I'm still sorry."

"So am I," Brace said from beneath them. "But you lost, Ji, and now you pay the price."

"There's a price to winning, too," Ji told him.

Brace frowned in confusion—then his diadem glowed and the water tree heaved.

The trunk uncoiled like a scorpion's tail. Smooth limbs whipped across the hall and pierced Roz, Sally, Chibo, and the entire ant-lion colony. The final branch stabbed Ji's chest, and a terrible wave swept him away.

31

WHEN JI OPENED his mouth to scream, water filled his lungs. Lights shone above him: a sun and a moon. Despite his terror, he couldn't swim toward the air, he couldn't move. He couldn't breathe. The wave suffocated him and a current surged from inside his chest toward the lights.

No, not a current. His *self*. His *self* flowed toward the lights—toward the Summer Queen and Prince Brace. To join them, to feed them, to strengthen them. And he wasn't the only one: he felt Roz and the others nearby, fading like ripples in a pond.

When his mind touched them, he understood two things:

First, they'd shrivel into corpses in a few seconds.

And second, he knew how this worked. After using his

dragonpower to pierce Brace, he understood this magic.

His vision cleared. The ruined hall blurred into sight around the water tree, which shuddered as its glossy branches stole their souls. Ji felt himself weaken. His spirit flowed from his chest . . . and he resisted. He threw every ounce of his strength into reversing the flow, into reclaiming his self.

A surge of power answered from the Summer Queen and Brace, and for a moment they played tug-of-war with Ji's soul. He didn't have power on his side, only terror. Yet for two beats of his dying heart, it was enough.

Then the queen and Brace drew upon the full might of the crown. The current tugged at Ji's chest, powerful enough to uproot his deepest self. Too strong, too strong. Ji couldn't stop them. They were too powerful to resist . . . so he stopped resisting.

He stopped pulling at his soul and instead he *pushed*. And as in a game of tug-of-war, the other team stumbled backward. The queen and Brace faltered—yet Ji kept pushing, forcing his innermost self from his chest.

Not toward the queen and Brace, though.

Instead, he poured his humanity into Roz and Chibo and Sally—and even Nin. Because "humanity" was the wrong word: Ji flooded his *self* into them.

Roz's horn flattened and her skin smoothed. Sally's tufted ears vanished into her mop of curly hair. Chibo's hunchback shrank, and the ant-lion queen swelled into a red-skinned ogre cub. Currents rippled across the water tree, and Ji felt the magic seek Balance. *Balance.* As the others regained their original forms, Ji lost his completely. The ceiling lowered over his head. The water tree seemed to dwindle into a shrub and the Summer Queen into a doll—

Ji grew into a full-blooded dragon.

Shifting scales of opalescent armor covered his serpentine body; golden antlers branched from his forehead. His crimson eyes grew larger than cartwheels and his white teeth stretched longer than elephant tusks. A spiked ridge ran along his jagged spine and his scaled legs ended in four-toed paws with golden eagle talons.

His roar shattered the water tree.

32

THE SUMMER QUEEN slammed to the floor, her eyes
wide with terror. The boy prince collapsed in a tangle of
limbs and scrambled across the wreckage.

The dragon roared again and curled his snakelike
spine. The sun and all four moons spun in his eyes. His
plated chest heaved, and flames issued from his nostrils.
He swiped with a paw the size of a horse to kill the queen
and prince, his claws gleaming like scimitars, and—

A tiny girl in a ragged dress stood between him and his
prey.

He paused midswipe.

The girl said a word he didn't understand. She touched
his razor claws with her soft, five-fingered hand and—

"Jiyong," she repeated, and diamonds glittered on her
cheeks.

"Rozario," he said, his voice an earthquake. "You're crying."

"I thought we'd lost you. I *felt* us lose you."

"You preciousgifted yourself to us." Nin wrapped a red arm around Chibo's trembling shoulders. "To heal us."

Chibo peered at Ji. "And you broke the spell!"

When Sally marched toward Ji, her curly hair trembled in his breath. "Not for everyone. Not for himself."

Ji's crimson gaze considered Sally. So small and so fierce. "Sally," he roared.

She gulped. "Yeah?"

He liked how her name echoed in the ruined hall. "Sally," he rumbled again.

"We'll fix this," she told him, only trembling a little. "We'll find a way to—"

A blast of white magic struck Ji's chin, like the sting of a wasp. He swung his head toward the Summer Queen and Brace, who stood defiantly against a shattered column.

"Thou shalt never—" the Summer Queen started.

Ji closed his paw around her head to crush her skull and— No!

No, to take her crown with the razor tips of his foreclaws. To take the Summer Crown and feel a million lives, a million sparks of human magic, buzzing in the tiny golden circle. Light beamed from Ji's antlers as he pulled the crown from the queen's head. Ten thousand chains broke, ten thousand cell doors slammed open, and ten thousand collars crumbled into rust.

A swarm of golden sparks flew like lightning bugs in a summer field. One struck Roz, one struck Sally, one struck every human in the hall before the rest streamed through the mountain toward the realm.

"It's our magic," Roz breathed, her voice soft with awe. "The human magic of little things is retur—"

"My queen!" Brace cried, weeping over the fallen Summer Queen. "Don't go, don't leave us, we need you."

Behind him, sheets of clay flaked from terra-cotta warrior statues. Humans and goblins, ogres and mermaids returned to their original forms. Ogres hugged, goblins chuffed, and humans shifted nervously.

"Ji's still a dragon," Sally said. "Roz! Why isn't he turning back?"

"I'm sorry, Sally." Roz lifted her smiling, tear-streaked face toward Ji. "He always had a dragon's heart."

"I'm not sorry," Ji thundered, and he opened his mind to show them the truth: he'd never change back. He'd given away too much of his humanity. That had been the price he'd needed to pay.

"It's not fair!" Sally clenched her fists. "It's not *fair.*"

"Ji never believed in fairness," Roz said. "He only believed in us."

"I'm going to turn you back," Sally told Ji. "I'm going to get rid of all—all this." She showed him a brave, watery smile. "You know I always wanted to slay a dragon."

When Ji laughed, the explosion of his breath sent Sally

tumbling across the floor. She flipped onto her hands and leaped away, somersaulting in the air and landing on a cracked balcony.

"You still move like a hobgoblin!" Chibo said, a green glint shining in his brown eyes.

"Maybe I can still buttsting!" Nin said with a waggle of ogre bottom. *No, my butt is stingless. Oh! Oh, oh! Do you hear that, Snakyji? I still mind-speak! Into your mind! Speaking without noise into your mind like—*

"My queen!" Brace sobbed as the Summer Queen crumbled into ash in his arms. "My queen!"

"She's returning to her true form," Ti-Lin-Su said. "After living for hundreds of years."

Brace's diadem turned to water that mixed with his tears as injured goblins marched past him, then knelt on wobbling knees.

"We bow to our new monar-ka!" Chiptooth said. "Wear the ka-rown and rule the realm."

The ogres bowed low, horns and tusks dipping. The bullish ones knelt on front legs, touching their horns to the ground. Even the mermaids in the ice wall ducked their heads.

"A new monarch?" Chibo asked.

"Someone's got to wear the crown," Sally told him.

"Don't you dare bow to Ji!" Roz said. "All he's ever wanted is freedom! He won't serve you as boot boy and he won't serve you as king. Nobody loves Ji more than I do, nobody owes him more, but—"

"They're not bowing to *him*, Missroz," Nin said.

"What on earth are you—" She stopped when she realized what Nin meant. "Oh!"

"They're bowing to you," Nin continued.

"Goodness!" Roz said.

Ji unsheathed a claw and offered her the Summer Crown. "I wouldn't trust this to anyone but you."

"And me," Sally said, wiping tears from her cheek. "He'd trust it to me."

"You will rule wisely," Ji told Roz. "You will rule well. We will bow our heads to wisdom and kindness for a change."

Roz didn't answer. She didn't even look at the crown. She gazed into Ji's crimson eyes, and he felt her looking beyond the dragon, looking at *him*. He remembered her saying, *He is Jiyong. Nothing more and nothing less.* He saw her the same way: Rozario Songarza. Nothing more and nothing less.

"Perhaps the problem isn't power," she said. "And perhaps the solution isn't wisdom. Perhaps the problem is in the bowing of heads."

"Perhaps," Ji thundered.

"We don't need a queen," Roz said. "We simply need to start talking to one another—"

"Oh, boy," Sally muttered.

"—and to keep talking even when we'd rather not."

"You won't wear the ka-rown?" Chiptooth asked.

"No." Roz smiled gently, then looked at Ji. "In general I am against breaking things, but in this case, would you do me the favor . . . ?"

Ji closed his paw around the Summer Crown. So much fear and pain and loss swirled in that tiny circle of gold. And why? Because people were so afraid of pain and loss. When he opened his paw again, a swarm of blue-bats swirled from his palm—but the crown was gone.

"What have you done?" Brace demanded, his cheeks streaked with tears. "With nobody in charge, you've doomed the world to war."

"Maybe war is the price of freedom," Jiyong thundered. "Or maybe we can choose what price we pay."

"With the crown gone," Roz told Brace, "all the nations are free. Even ours."

33

FROM THE AIR, Isalida Forest was a rich tapestry of autumn reds and yellows veined with ridges and roads. Jiyong swirled through the clouds toward the treetops, the wind whistling between his antlers.

"Faster!" Chibo cried from his back. "Faster, Jiyong!"

Missroz looks a little green, Nin warned.

"I'm quite fine," Roz murmured.

"She looks pink to me," Sally said. "What kind of person wears a dress on a dragon?"

"A special occasion requires my favorite dress," Roz told her.

"It's pretty, I guess," Sally said dubiously. "Posey says it brings out your eyes."

"Brings her eyes out *where*?" Nin asked in alarm.

Chibo wrinkled his nose at Sally. "I still can't believe you and Posey are friends."

"Yeah, that's the unbelievable part," Sally snorted. "We're riding a dragon, Chibo."

"At least Posey is good at leading the humans," Chibo said.

"You really must stop saying 'the humans,'" Roz told him, a hint of laughter in her voice. "It alarms the humans."

"You're all humans and huwomans!" Nin announced. *Except Snakyji.*

"He's draconic," Sally said, and Jiyong felt her soft hand stroke his armored spine.

He didn't say anything. He rarely spoke these days. Sometimes Roz asked him to talk, just to check that he still could. He liked listening to her read stories as much as ever, though. He liked the music in her voice and the wonder in her eyes.

"He's a symbol," Roz said. "He represents something to the Council."

The Council had been Roz's idea, and because she was extremely clever and often escorted by a dragon, people tended to listen to her. The Council met in the Forbidden Palace, which only Chibo now called "the Welcome Palace." Representatives of the human, goblin, and ogre realms—and Ti-Lin-Su and Roz—bickered about borders and trade and treaties. They didn't agree about much, but everyone seemed happy with the arguing. Ji didn't really understand why. He just opened one eye and peered at anyone who made Roz angry.

I peeksee the perfect spot! Nin said, dangling from one of Jiyong's antlers. "Land there, that hilltop clearing!"

Jiyong slithered downward to hover above the grass, his mind echoing with silent laughter. Nobody else recognized the rocky hilltop clearing, but he knew that elegant lacebark tree and those prickly wasp pepper bushes: this was where they'd waited to rob the library coach after fleeing Summer City.

"Delicious," he thundered.

Roz inhaled deeply. "The forest does smell lovely this time of year."

"So what now?" Sally asked Nin.

"Now I kisshug you!" Nin lifted her into a bear hug. *And we all happycry.*

Sally squirmed. "Then what, you doolally ogre?"

"Then I wander for a moon or seven," Nin said, setting her aside. "On my cubwalk. When I return, I will be an ogre."

"Are you going to be a boy or a girl?" Chibo asked as Nin hefted him into the air.

The cubwalk will help me decide, Nin said. *Now kisshug!*

Chibo gave Nin a kiss on the cheek. "I'll miss you."

"Or you'll 'mister' me. Depending."

Roz laughed and cried and told Nin, "Come here, my sweetest cub."

Finally a little happycrying, Nin said, spinning Roz in circles.

A breeze rustled through the forest, bringing the scent of tiny yellow flowers blossoming a mile away, and the sound of a goose scolding her goslings. Somewhere in the distance a goblin dug and an ogre climbed, and a human added a drop of magic to a fresh-baked pie.

Nin bounded onto Ji's snout and said, *Stonefriend.*

Stonefriend, Ji answered.

When I return, Nin said, "I will be different."

"Good," Ji rumbled.

Because things changed. You couldn't stop the unfolding of new days. You couldn't lock the future in chains. You couldn't freeze an ogre cub in time—or a realm, or even a boot boy. Ji would stay with his friends as long as they needed, he'd return whenever they called . . . but one day soon he'd fly past the horizon to dance with the moons.

Maybe he wasn't a hero, but he wasn't a villain, either. A true story never ended. That's what the Summer Queen hadn't understood. No heroes were forever triumphant and no villains were forever defeated. True stories rose and fell like ocean waves, always flowing, always changing, always more.

Chapters ended, but the story never did.

Acknowledgments

Many thanks to Caitlin Blasdell, Alyson Day, Manuel Blasco, Renée Cafiero, Megan Barlog, Laura Kaplan, Brian Thompson, and Joel Tippie.

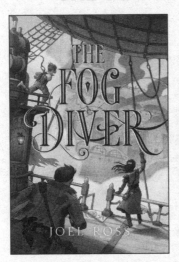